THE PHOENIX

S. Alden Reilly

HILLIARD & HARRIS PUBLISHERS

Published by

HILLIARD & HARRIS PUBLISHERS
P.O. Box 3358
Frederick, Maryland 21705-3358

ISBN 0-9704304-0-X

Book Design by HILLIARD & HARRIS

Illustration of Phoenix by S. Alden Reilly

Manufactured in the United States of America

September 2000

For Shawn, and Erin, and Vic. Thank you for all your support and encouragement and for helping me keep the dream alive all these years. You are much loved.

THE PHOENIX

" Most beings spring from other individuals: but there is a certain kind which reproduces itself. The Assyrians call it the Phoenix. It does not live on fruit or flowers, but on frankincense and odoriferous gums. When it has lived five hundred years, it builds itself a nest in the branches of an oak, or on the top of a palm tree. In this it collects cinnamon, and spikenard, and myrrh, and of these 'materials builds a pile on which it deposits itself, and dying, breathes out its last breath amidst odours. From the body of the parent bird, a young Phoenix issues forth, destined to live as long a life as its predecessor. When this has grown up and gained sufficient strength, it lifts its nest from the tree (its own cradle and its parent's sepulcher), and carries it to the city of Heliopolis in Egypt, and deposits it in the temple of the Sun."

Ovid's Metamorphoses, Book XV-beginning line 579

THE PHOENIX

PROLOGUE

I don't know what made me hesitate. When the light turned green, I accelerated into the intersection and signaled for a left turn onto Interstate 70 in Western Maryland. I had a green arrow, but I hesitated.

Without warning, a huge dump truck, a rusted red giant, came barreling down the hill toward me. The driver blasted his horn and slammed on his brakes spewing clouds of bluish, acrid smelling smoke, but the truck careened right for me. I closed my eyes. I could already hear the impact, the groaning wrenching of metal, the explosive cracking of glass. I had heard it almost every night in my dreams since my husband was killed. I'd wake up; my heart pounding like it was now, my body clammy with the sweat of dread.

I was going to die the same way Michael died. Suddenly I heard a pinging sound like ten thousand marbles pouring onto a sheet of glass. I opened my eyes. The truck had swerved just in time to avoid me. The noise came from a shower of gravel bouncing over my Trooper.

I sat there for a moment with both hands on the steering wheel. My knuckles white unfamiliar knots. I couldn't let go, and then I realized I was still in the middle of the intersection. No one was coming so I completed my turn and pulled to the shoulder of the on-ramp. My knees were shaking so badly I could barely drive.

S. Alden Reilly

I turned the car off and sat for a minute with my hands, still curled like claws, in my lap, my head against the headrest. The only damage I could see was a chip in the windshield. It was about the size of a pea just below eye level on the passenger side.

I sensed rather than heard the knock on my window. A man wearing a faded blue baseball cap asked me if I was all right. I nodded yes. The truck driver, I guessed. He said he was sorry. The concern in his eyes was genuine. He hadn't seen the signal until he crested the hill. He was so glad I was okay. I nodded again and started my car so he could see I was fine. I even managed a wave as I merged onto Interstate 70.

I wasn't fine, though. I drove the fifteen miles to my house with tears pouring down my face and a tremor in my legs. I was oblivious to the clear air of the summer day, oblivious to the Van Gogh greens and yellows in the fields along the way. I noticed nothing
on the drive home. The next day I went to work and asked for a leave of absence then I went home to figure things out.

That was in June. Three months later I still hadn't come to terms with my husband's death.

CHAPTER ONE

My name is S. Ann Strayer, nee' Jones. The S. stands for
Stella, my father's idea. My mother always called me Ann. I
think she associated Stella with commonness or vulgarity.
Maybe she just didn't like *A Streetcar Named Desire*. Anyway,
she called me Ann and raised me to be socially correct,
elegantly groomed, and well educated. I said these were her
goals for me, whether I actually achieved them is another
matter.

When Michael was killed I was the Dean of Academic
Affairs at Harding College, a small private institution just
north and west of Washington, D.C. I started there as an
English professor, but found I had a talent for counseling
kids. My job was to sell them on an education, enroll them,
then keep them on track until they graduated. I was pretty
good at it.

My own brush with death made me realize that I had
been completely derailed. My life had been on a predictable
track, career, marriage, and children. I had two beautiful
daughters who were away at college. Now one of the
supports had been kicked away. I was confused.

The day I came home from Harding College, I
retreated. I didn't go out and overate until I couldn't fit into
my clothes. I began to dislike the company of other people
so I spent most of my time at home. My latest thing was to

think up projects for myself to keep busy. I don't know when I decided to paint most of the rooms in my house white, but I was just about done.

It was September 7, a cool brisk day that hinted at the fall to come. I was restless. This condition may have been caused by the overcast day, the gusts of wind that tugged and blew at me, or the fact that I was still recovering from the shock of my fortieth birthday a few days ago.

Maybe that edginess and the fact that I'd always considered seven my lucky number was behind the fact that I had allowed Layne Brody to convince me to go out that night. Or maybe it was the desperation in her voice when she called.

Layne was a friend from Michael's and my brief social period. When Michael was a crime analyst at Quantico, we had lived closer to DC and had partied with the best of them, but we'd outgrown it. Layne and her husband, Franklin Brody, never did.

Even though Michael and I dropped out of the group, Layne and I remained friends. We got together for lunch. Went shopping. Stayed in touch.

I pulled into my driveway and headed for the garage. I live in a small town in Western Maryland about an hour equidistant from Washington D.C. or Baltimore. Circe is a town of only twenty-two hundred people just eleven miles west of Frederick. We have a school, two traffic lights, a state trooper post, and various small stores including a grocery and hardware store. Most of the houses were pre-Revolutionary War, built right up against the street. Once log or red brick, they were now covered in various shades of vinyl siding. If I had been content with a quart can of Chinese red or Appliance white enamel, my trip to Frederick would have been unnecessary. Primary colors, that's all the hardware store in Circe carries. It's kind of a comment on the townspeople who generally see most things simply, very black and white. I've been a resident for ten years and I'm still considered a newcomer.

My house is built into the side of a hill with a view of South Mountain. Made of old river rock, it looks like a cross between an English cottage and a Victorian castle designed by Edward Gorey. The garage is a separate stone building in the back of the house. The yard that joins them is the only open area because the rest of the grounds are wooded. I like the privacy.

I got out with all my paint paraphernalia and walked around the truck heading for the house. I drive a dark green Isuzu Trooper. It's a big boxy station wagon on steroids with four-wheel drive. I'm a real bad ass in the snow. I noticed that little cracks were beginning to radiate from the chip in the windshield to form a star pattern.

"Great, just great." I mumbled as I stomped to the back door. I let myself in and went back to my painting. I guess I lost all track of time because when the doorbell chimed, I almost dumped my paint pan. "Damn," I cursed at the mess. I'd slopped some paint, but most of it fell on the drop cloth. I wiped the rest off the floor with a rag and ran for the front door.

CHAPTER TWO

Layne Brody was standing on my doorstep. She was a pretty woman with dark brown hair and eyes. She had a slim figure, about 5'6", with a sensual face and those full lips that are all the rage today. She had the best wardrobe of any woman I'd ever met. But in spite of being beautifully dressed, there would always be a flaw somewhere. A streak of mascara on the end of her nose, a smear of ink on a finger, or maybe a blob of jelly donut on her skirt. It was a condition that was often contagious if you got too close.

Today she was the picture of a little preppie in her designer blue jeans and white Calvin Klein tee shirt. Her white tennis shoes were new and unsmudged. Her hair was pulled back into a ponytail. She carried a small, blue canvas tote bag and matching jacket. She looked perfect, adorable, with the exception of one stray piece of hair that straggled straight up from her forehead.

"And what are we dressed for?" I said. It was obvious that this was a costume. Layne never wore jeans.

"Ann! What have you done to yourself?"

The note of shock and dismay were hard to take. I looked down at myself. She wasn't seeing the Annie she was used to. Short, petite (size six), shiny blonde frosted hair in a career cut bob. Nice face, blue eyes, small hands, Manicured nails. I looked at the white paint caked in my cuticles. No, she was seeing a pudgy woman with no makeup and faded blond hair wearing a paint-stained mismatched sweat outfit that was a little snug.

"Don't depress me. Just tell me what you're up to." I ushered her inside.

"Where is everything?" She was looking into the living room, which was populated by three rickety ladders, soiled drop clothes, and two rush bottomed chairs splattered with white paint.

"In storage."

"Oh, I'm sorry. It just looks kind of strange."

"Well, after the break-in I decided to make some changes."

My house had been burgled, or, I guess, just vandalized since I couldn't find anything missing, right after Michael's funeral. The whole downstairs had been trashed. It sparked something in me. I wanted to change everything.

"Picasso had his blue period," I indicated the room with a sweep of my arm. "This is my white period."

Layne laughed. She had recovered herself. "I've really missed you Annie. Of course . . ." The little piece of hair bobbed as she talked. "I didn't know you'd gone off the deep end. Why didn't you call me?"

"I'm fine. I'm coping," I said rather hotly. She flashed me a sure-you-are look. "What is the big mystery you couldn't talk about on the phone?"

"I need your help tonight. Say you'll go with me." She was pleading.

I didn't want to go out, but she was sincere, the emotion in her voice real. I looked down at my sweat outfit. "I'll have to change my clothes."

"No don't. It will make a good disguise."

"What?" I never thought an evening with Layne Brody would take this turn. A woman who was most at home in the shoe department at Nordstrom's was hardly a candidate for intrigue. "Disguised as what?"

"Not what. We want to look normal, just different. That's why I brought these." She pulled two frumpy wigs out of her bag.

"We're going to look normal in these? What have you been smoking?" I said laughing.

Layne shrugged. "Well, I guess no one would recognize you anyway." A direct shot. Did I mention that Layne could be very thoughtless at times? "I'm sorry." She gave me a sheepish look. "I'm just upset. I know Franklin is seeing someone. Tonight I'm going to prove it."

Franklin Brody was Layne's estranged husband. They had been battling each other for a year over the settlement in their divorce. They weren't even legally separated yet.

"I gather a lady friend would help your side?"

"Yes." She handed me a wig. It was red. At the look on my face she began to plead again. "Please, Ann. I need you to come." She seemed on the verge of tears.

"Okay." I looked down at the wig in my hand. "I'm going to look like a fat Lucy Ricardo in this."

"Come on, you know you've always wanted to be a redhead." The tears were gone. Now there was just excitement in Layne's voice.

"Not this way, I didn't." I slapped the thing on my head. I started to stuff the rest of my hair up inside the cap.

Layne pulled a honey blond number on over her own hair. "Why is it pouffing up on top?" She asked pushing down on my wig with her free hand.

"I don't know. Maybe my head's too big."

"Your head's not too big." She pulled down on my wig with both hands. "But something is definitely wrong."

"Wait, I've got an idea." I went into the kitchen and dug around in the pantry. I pulled an old red baseball cap out of the closet. It had 'I got the crabs at Ernie's' embroidered in yellow across the front. I pulled it on over my wig. It felt snug.

When I walked back into the living room, Layne's reaction was mild shock followed by derisive laughter.

"Hey. It was a gift from one of my students. Let's go."

At the front door Layne turned to me. "Don't you want to turn off a few lights?"

"No. I always leave them on. My electric bills are high, but I can't help it. The light makes me feel more secure." I locked the door and followed Layne down the walk to where a car was parked at the bottom of the drive. "This isn't your car. Where's the Mercedes?"

"At home in the garage. We're in disguise. This is a rent-a-wreck."

"I'll say." It was an old Ford station wagon. The kind with the wide, dumpy rear-end. It looked like it had once been metallic gold, but now it had the dull luster of primer.

"Watch this." Layne made a show of opening the door. She looked at me expectantly.

"Okay." So it's a door, I thought, and not a very attractive one either.

"No. Listen," she said at the blank look on my face. "There's no sound."

"Oh, right." I climbed in on the passenger side.

"I sprayed both doors with lubricant so they wouldn't creak."

"Good idea." I wondered what I'd gotten myself into. "Since when do you follow your soon to be ex-husband around? I thought you had detectives for that."

Layne started the car and pulled away from the curb. "Since

I've almost run out of money. Besides, they haven't turned up shit." She grimaced like someone who's gotten a whiff of something nasty. "I know how he thinks. They don't." She was dead serious and she'd used the 'S' word. Layne never swore.

"Okay. I'm ready for anything." It did beat a blob of paint in the eye. I felt strangely exhilarated. "Do you know where he's going tonight?"

"Pretty much," she said matter of factly.

I looked at her profile in the dark car. I never expected her to have this much gumption. She'd always been the attractive wife of a successful man. She had a loopy kind of charm, that kind of dithery quality that seems to work so well with men. I had always suspected it was partly real and partly an act. With a man like Franklin, though, it would probably be best to hide any intelligence or an independent streak because he would crush it. "How do you know?" I asked with new respect.

Layne flashed me a sideways smile as she maneuvered through lanes of traffic. We were heading down Interstate 270 toward DC. "I stole his American Express bill out of the mailbox."

"What? That's mail fraud!"

"Tampering with the mail. A federal offense," she corrected. I couldn't believe my ears. "Franklin is a creature of habit. I knew he was seeing someone, probably on a regular basis. So I just lifted his bill to see what restaurant he was using for his rendezvous."

"Ingenious. Isn't he smart enough to move around?"

"Smart enough but too arrogant to think I'd catch on." She tapped the steering wheel with one pointed pink nail. "In the last four weeks he's eaten at Chez Louis exactly six times. Four of those on a Wednesday. So we're going to see if I'm right."

I leaned back in my seat.

"What if you're right, what then?"

"We follow them."

"Them?" Visions of the old horror film where the little girl keeps saying 'Them' flashed into my head. "Who are them?"

"Franklin and whatever woman he's seeing."

"God, this is going to be some evening."

Layne exited and headed down Wisconsin Avenue into Chevy Chase. Within a few minutes we were driving slowly past Chez Louis, a particularly popular and elegant little French restaurant.

"Is that his car?" I tried to keep the excitement down in my voice. I pointed to a black Cadillac at the end of the driveway.

"Could be. She checked the license plate as we drove by. Yep, it's him." Layne kept on going up the street then turned around and came back, parking on the same side of the street about a half block from the restaurant. We had a good view of the front, the parking lot, and the Cadillac from where we sat.

Layne reached into the back seat and pulled out two brown paper bags. She handed me one. I opened it. Raisins, shredded wheat squares, plus a bottle of orange juice.

"How did you know I'd gained weight?"

"Marlena said you hadn't been in the shop for months." Marlena's was a favorite dress shop of mine. I'd met Layne in there years ago. "I figured you'd gained a little."

She pulled a ham and cheese sandwich out of her bag. I was about to protest when she took a bite. The rye bread smelled heavenly, but I looked down at my baggy sweats that weren't baggy anymore and reached for mini wheat. I bit into the tiny biscuit dispiritedly. "You're right. I need to get a grip on myself." I was on the verge of telling her about my dump truck revelation but thought better of it. If I was confused, Layne didn't have a clue.

"You'll be a size six again in a month."

"Thanks for the vote of confidence," I said eyeing the ham and cheese.

"Look, he's coming out!" Layne came to attention.

Franklin Brody appeared at the door of Chez Louis. Alone? No. He was with someone, but not a woman. It was another man. They shook hands and the man walked away. Franklin handed a ticket to the parking attendant. A slight breeze ruffled his silvery hair. Franklin was tall with distinguished features. He looked like a senator from Texas and had the ego to match.

"Maybe Franklin is gay," I whispered.

"Very funny." Layne hissed emphasizing each syllable. Out of the corner of my eye I saw Layne fishing around for something in her duffle bag. God, I thought, she's going to shoot him!

She pulled out a small black object that looked like a cordless phone and hissed into it.

"Phil? Phil?"

"Okay Lila, what have you got?"

"Subject leaving Chez Louis. Black Cadillac. Stand by."

My mouth hung open. "Lila?"

Layne shrugged her shoulders. "It's my handle, short for little lady." She looked at me and laughed. "The agency hired a helicopter to follow him tonight. He's always managed to give them the slip before."

"You sound like Dick Tracy."

"Laugh if you want, but it's the best idea I've ever had."

The best idea Layne ever had was to divorce Franklin, but I played along.

"The walkie-talkies?"

She gave me a patient look. "No. Following Franklin myself. I'm getting pretty good at it. He hasn't been able to lose me for two weeks now."

Although we had been friends for years, it was a friendship based on an artificial level. You know, the social niceties that we get ourselves into. The polite little parties where everyone talked about their hair, but no one let it down. This was different. I was seeing the real Layne, or at least a real part of her, for the first time.

She pulled out, maneuvering the old wreck into traffic. She allowed two cars to merge in between our car and the Cadillac. She kept him in sight, but held back.

I have to admit I was fascinated. We were following a suspect or at least a suspected errant husband. At any minute we could be in a high-speed chase through the streets of Chevy Chase. I looked at Layne. I wasn't sure I was ready for that experience. Ahead, the black Cadillac suddenly accelerated.

"Okay, you bastard. You're not going to trick me again." Layne put her foot to the floor, and for the next fifteen minutes we chased the Cadillac through a maze of streets zigging, zagging, and doubling back until I wasn't sure where we were anymore. Just somewhere north. The only thing I was sure of was that Layne had been watching too much TV. The Cadillac disappeared around a corner. Layne stepped on the gas and we flew down a quiet residential street somewhere off Connecticut Avenue.

"Damn!" We'd come to an intersection where two streets forked to the left. She flipped the walkie-talkie button. "Phil, I've lost him."

"He took the hard left. It's not easy to see him through the tree cover, but I got a good make on him just now," Phil answered back through a blur of static. Layne swung to the left.

"Is that him up there?" I pointed as we turned on to Olive Avenue. We crept down the street of small fifties type bungalows.

"Where?"

"He just turned up there."

We drove past several houses until we came to the second one from the corner. Layne cut the headlights and coasted to the curb. The house was cream colored with a wider yard than the other houses on the street. A narrow driveway started at the right of the front porch and curved diagonally across the yard to a small garage.

"I thought he turned in here," I said.

"Well he's not here now." Layne said despairingly. "Damn it."

"Come on. Let's take a look." I was out of the car before I finished speaking.

Layne brightened. "Yeah. Maybe he pulled into that garage behind the house." She joined me in front of car.

We set off across the lawn with the stealthy nonchalance of a couple of professional thieves. The grass was damp and crunchy under our feet. The air smelled sharp, smoky. I felt like a kid trick or treating the neighborhood. The only light came from a window near the front of the bungalow. It threw a rectangle of light across the yard that we skirted on our way to the house.

We ducked behind some evergreen hedges that surrounded the house and found ourselves under the lighted window. I eased myself up on my toes until I could see inside.

It was, evidently, the living room. A light, airy, little space with plump off white couches, lots of plants, and Matisse posters framed on the wall. The only occupant was a slim young woman with golden red hair that curled around her face and down her back. She was watching TV. It looked like one of those nature shows on PBS. Layne eased up beside me.

"Do you know her?" I whispered to Layne.

"No." Poor Layne, the girl had the classically beautiful face of a Botticelli nymph, delicate, fragile, infinitely feminine and not more than twenty. Women like that always made me feel like an oafish clod. Layne's expression was indescribable.

I poked Layne in the ribs. "I don't see Franklin. Let's check the other windows." We crept around the house like a couple of overactive peeping Toms. No sign of Franklin.

"The garage," I whispered. We turned away from the house. I was glad. The evergreens were prickly and probably full of spiders. I was sure something was crawling on me and brushed my hands down each arm as we crunched our way across the frosty lawn to the garage.

It was an old building with heavy double doors that opened out. Age had made them sag toward each other so that they didn't close properly. Someone had remedied this lack of security by attaching a large hasp and a padlock as big as my fist.

"Is his car in there?" Layne whispered.

All the windows and the glass partitions of the double doors had newspaper taped over them on the inside. I was on my knees straining to see through the gap in the double doors. "No. It's empty. Dirty, but empty," I said getting to my feet. I started walking around the garage to see if there were any other doors when I noticed tire tracks. Right there in the light from the street lamp in the sandy soil running around the garage and out the back of the yard into an alley. "Look at this. He could have pulled right out here and kept going. I think he's given us the slip."

"Shit."

"You know Layne, you've really got to do something about your swearing." She stuck her tongue out at me.

We hurried back to the car. The walkie-talkie sputtered on the front seat. "I've got him. He's moving south on 355," Phil, the copter pilot, reported.

Layne looked at me. At that exact moment something large and dark hurled itself against the car. "Oh my God!" I croaked with my heart in my throat. Layne screamed. A huge Rottweiler with fangs the size of smoky link sausages and about the same color was trying to eat my face through the windshield.

"Get us out of here!"

"Hold on!" Layne said recovering herself. She peeled the wreck away from the curb in Indy flat time. The dog jumped off and contented himself with chasing us down the street for a block.

We headed south on Route 355 in Maryland. Greatly exceeding the speed limit, I might add. I was just grateful my underwear was dry. I looked at the road ahead.

"Do you suppose he's heading for your house? Your old house?" I quickly corrected. Layne had rented a small apartment after filing.

Layne nodded. "Well, at least I have the satisfaction that I probably ruined his plans for the evening.

"You still got him, Phil?" she said into the walkie-talkie.

"Yeah. He's heading down 355 toward Bethesda."

"Well, let's call it an evening then. I can't afford any more time tonight," Layne said.

"You're the boss," his voice crackled back.

"Jeeze," Layne sighed, "I probably racked up at least four hundred dollars tonight. Practically my last four hundred dollars and for what?" Her confidence leaked out of her like air from a punctured swim mattress.

"Come on," I said, "you found out who he's been seeing."

"I did?"

"Sure you did. How else would he have known about that driveway back to the alley?"

"I guess you're right," she said her voice pumping up a little. "Are you hungry? I'm starved."

I looked down at myself. "You want to be seen like this?"

"We're in disguise. Remember?"

"I laughed. "Sure. Why not? Just call me Lucy."

CHAPTER THREE

Layne drove south on 355 into Rockville. We pulled into the parking lot of the Retro Diner. An authentic stainless steel, bullet shaped diner with a menu of great burgers and fountain drinks from the fifties.

I played nervously with my red hair as we entered. I wanted to keep my hand up by my face in case I needed to cover up, but no one gave us a second look. Perhaps that said something about the type of patrons they got late at night.

We slid into a booth in the corner with a view of the kitchen. I watched a gray-haired, heavy-set man expertly shove a pile of hash browns around on the grill, flipping them until they were evenly brown. Why did food suddenly mesmerize me?

"Frustration," Layne said dejectedly. I looked at her. Had I said the thought out loud? Food mesmerized me because I was frustrated? "That's why I can't let go." She sunk down a little in her seat. Her body sagged a little. "Men suck."

Oh, we were talking about her. I reached for a menu and handed one to Layne while I thought about what to say. She roused herself and sat forward opening the menu. "I'm sorry. I guess they're not all bad. You got a good one."

I got a good one? Again, I was trying to think of a response when a young man with blonde hair hi-lighted with purple streaks came and asked us for our order.

Adrenaline must excite the appetite. Layne looked up at the kid. "The triple-decker cheeseburger platter and a large coke."

I only hesitated a second. "The same." I ignored Layne's cautionary look. I felt like I was in high school again. Stuffing French fries in my face at the Huddle in Indy after the ball games was something I hadn't thought of in years. I hate to admit this but I was excited about getting a hamburger. My life had really deteriorated.

"Life sucks and then you die," Layne sighed after our waiter brought our giant cokes.

"I thought men sucked, now all life sucks? Are we a little depressed?"

Layne grinned. "I'm sorry, Ann. I have been bitter and depressed lately." She took a sip of her coke. "In fact it seems to consume my life. The divorce, I mean."

"Believe it or not it will be over soon. At least you look fabulous, even as a blonde." I teased trying to cheer her up. She looked like she was about to utter another pithy observation about suction when our waiter returned with two heaping platters. The French fries had that delicious smell of hot oil combined with potato scent that made my mouth water. "Could we have some Catsup please?" I can't eat French-fries without Catsup.

"Well, so much for body beautiful." Layne wiped greasy bits of burger from her fingers. A small crumb clung stubbornly to the corner of her mouth. We'd developed a non-verbal communication concerning hygiene over the years. I pointed discreetly to my own mouth and she quickly wiped hers with her napkin.

"This was the best food I've eaten in years." I leaned back in the booth. I was glad my sweat pants still had a little room in them.

Layne was flipping through the songs in our little tabletop jukebox selector. "I wonder if Franklin is at home?" She met my eyes. Tammy Wynette was singing 'Stand by your Man.' She made a face and flipped to the next list. "I wonder if they have 'D.I.V.O.R.C.E.' on here?"

I looked at the pattern of the baby blue tile on the floor, at the pink Formica countertops, and the aluminum trim. I remembered when I'd been obsessed with a boy named Billy Thompson in the eleventh grade. I would drive by his house every night to see if he was home. I started to feel foolish. "You should just let him go. Settle with him and get on with your life. This is killing you."

I'm never going to let him go until I get what is mine." Her voice was so fierce, so intense that I decided not to bring up my Billy Thompson example.

But I also knew from my Billy Thompson days that nothing would deter her from driving by his house. "Okay, I'm game. Let's go see if roving boy had returned to his lair."

We left the restaurant and headed south into Bethesda. We wound back toward Old Georgetown Road into Layne's former neighborhood. It was an area of older homes with ivy covered brick fronts and mature trees that said 'old money'.

The Brody house was an oddity in the general colonial theme that prevailed. Michael and I had always referred to it as the bunker. It was a series of low flat buildings strung together like a series of huts. The central hut was anchored with enormous carved mahogany double doors. There also a twisted piece of metal that was supposedly a sculpture in the oval center of the circular driveway. The effect was eccentric. A Mayan temple redecorated by Claes Oldenburg.

Layne killed the headlights as we pulled up in front of the house. Through the trees you could see the driveway slope down to the three-car garage. The doors were open. Franklin's black Caddy was in one bay. A blue pickup truck was parked in the bay next to it.

It wasn't any ordinary pickup. This was a shiny monster with oversized tires, spotlights mounted on the roof, and those chrome mud flaps with the silhouettes of the big-breasted women facing each other.

"Franklin's got company," Layne said.

"Well, I'd like to meet the woman that drives that rig." I was just joking, but Layne coasted past the driveway, parking on the shoulder under the trees.

"I'm going to see what he's up to."

Before I could protest, she was out of the car and headed down the driveway. "Great, just great," I mumbled to myself stumbling after her.

The moon was almost full so we had plenty of light once our eyes adjusted. The property was ringed by trees, which gave way, close to the house, to a meticulously clipped lawn. Not much cover. Boxy hedges outlined the perimeter of the building. We slipped through them to the side of the house. At least these hedges were soft, probably full of spiders, too.

Layne pointed her finger at the window, a strange look on her face. We could see into the hall from our vantage point at the dining room window. Something dark was huddled there on the floor. It gave me a bad feeling.

I was straining to see better when I heard a roar. I leaned back out of the hedge in time to see the blue pickup truck tearing down the driveway. "Come on, Layne. Let's get out of here."

S. Alden Reilly

"Do you think something's wrong?" She spoke slowly, worrying as I dragged her away. Honestly, men can be total bastards, treat women like hell, and we still get emotional when we think something's happened to them. I tugged on her arm. She came with me reluctantly.

"We'll call the police. They can check it out." I kept us moving away. We were halfway across the lawn, just about even with the twisted paper clip sculpture when I heard it. A muffled sound that got louder and louder. "Run!" I screamed. But it was too late. A wave of fire and explosive wind engulfed us, rolling us up onto its crest until it flung us against the ground.

I heard several more explosions, then nothing. I was lying face down in the grass. It cushioned my face. My ears were ringing. My whole body tingled. I couldn't sort out if I was hurt or not. I decided to just stay still for a while, but a fierce crackling sound brought my head up slowly. The opening where the front doors had been was the burning maw of a furnace with ferocious flames, reddish yellow with hot blue centers. I lay back down on the grass. Then I heard Layne moan.

I started to turn my head but something was wrong with my face. It felt numb. I pushed myself up off the ground on to my knees. My hands were scraped, sore. I felt my face gingerly, moving my fingers in a parody of Braille across my own features. My nose seemed to be out of place. It had always been somewhat centered on my face. Now it had a definite east-west orientation. It shocked me, but I remembered that I never liked it anyway. Too long, too crooked.

I stood up, tottering as if I'd just gotten up from a three Martini lunch. I glanced down at my sweatshirt. There was blood and an incredible amount of dust and grit. My legs worked although my knees seemed to be newly double-jointed. I still had my fingers and toes. I staggered off in the direction of Layne's voice.

The scene was unreal. Rubble littered the yard. Little fires consumed the larger chunks scattered over the lawn. The finer pieces ranged down to dust size. The metal sculpture was on its side. The blast had partially straightened it. It looked better. Both the entry doors had been blown out. One door lay flat on the driveway. The other door was wedged against the concrete lamppost. I found Layne behind it.

"Ann?" Her voice was dazed, weak. At least she was conscious.

"Hey, I'm right here. Are you okay?" I knelt beside her and smoothed the hair back from her forehead. She was covered with dust and one of her new sneakers was gone, but the door seemed to have sheltered her from the worst of the blast. It was a miracle it hadn't crushed her instead. She did have a big lump on the side of her head.

"Yeah," she said, "how about you?"

"I think something's wrong with my nose. If I look like Frankenstein, don't tell me. There's plenty of time to face it later."

"Let me see." She seemed to have difficulty focusing her eyes. "You're right. You've got two noses now.

"Great." I said sinking down beside her. "Isn't this where I yell 'medic'?"

"Don't make me laugh. I'm afraid I'll throw up." She closed her eyes.

"I know this is an exclusive neighborhood, but someone will respond to that blast. Their curiosity will get the better of them." A siren sounded in the distance.

"See, what did I tell you?" I thought I could see people moving toward us. I felt my eyes close, too. The next part is hazy. I remember being lifted up, brief snatches of an ambulance ride during which someone seemed to hold my head so I couldn't turn it, and arriving at the hospital.

CHAPTER FOUR

"You've got a broken nose, some cuts, some scrapes, but no concussion. We'd like to keep you overnight." I was staring into a pair of gentle brown eyes. Dr. Gonzalez was the name on his badge.

"Is my nose going to be all right? Do I look like Frankenstein?"

"Trust me, you're not going to look like Frankenstein," he said smiling. I looked at his eyes again, kind eyes in a kind face. I trusted him. I was about to say so, but somehow I went back to sleep before I could tell him.

I woke up several hours later in a quiet cocoon of white: white room, white curtains, white sound. I floated there for awhile. Safe. Comfortable. Then I realized I was in a hospital bed. The curtain was pulled around me. I couldn't hear anyone else in the room, but the TV set up on the wall was between stations, buzzing with a static noise.

I reached my hand up to my nose. It was bandaged with strips of tape down the length with more pieces running across. The finishing touch a plaster cast type thing, which ran the length of my nose and stuck out at the end in a point. I probably looked like a cross between Jason, the hockey-masked monster and the Tin Man from the <u>Wizard of Oz.</u> I wondered if my nose would end up looking like Grace Kelly's. Right now it felt like I had a stuffed manicotti on my face. I also came to realize that I could only breathe through my mouth, a fact that panicked me if I dwelt on it. I was scanning for TV stations with my remote when a man peered around my curtains.

"Mrs. Strayer?" He was tall, slim, and black, his skin the color of coffee with two creamers. Although deeply lined, his face was handsome. His wavy black hair was slightly graying at the temples, but the mustache that shielded his top lip, drooped on each side of his mouth, and included a little tuft of hair under his bottom lip was pristine. No gray there. Dark brown eyes with little hints of amber in the depths searched mine.

"Mrs. Strayer?" He extended his hand. "I'm with the police department. Detective Sergeant Harrison. Vin Harrison. Your doctor said you might be awake."

I stared at his hand for a minute. Strong lean fingers with short clipped nails. I extended mine, scratched, rough, bruised. "Awake, but not very presentable. Nice to meet you." I wished I could have a screen pulled around my head. I hoped my hospital gown wasn't revealing too much. Of course it had to look better than the sweat outfit I was wearing what seemed like a year ago.

He gave my hand a gentle shake while he eyed my nose and the cuts on my face. "I'd say you look pretty good for a blast victim." He turned and pulled a chair closer to my bed. "I'd like to ask you a few questions, if you're up to it." He had a deep voice. It was pleasant to listen to, reassuring and firm.

"I'm fine."

"Good," he said with a small, slightly ironic smile. "What were you and Mrs. Brody doing at Mr. Brody's house?" Great. It was time to confess to being a loony toon. I could feel my face turn beet red. He must have noticed because he said, "Are you sure you feel well enough to answer?"

"Yes. I'm well enough. It's just very embarrassing." Harrison cocked his head expectantly. "We were following Franklin. Mr. Brody. Mrs. Brody was…" I thought about my next words for a moment. "She was convinced that Mr. Brody was violating the terms of their separation."

"She thought he was seeing another woman." He said it as a statement of fact.

"Was he? We never caught up with him all night," I said innocently.

"Until you went to his house."

"Yes."

"Why did you go to the house?" He fixed me with his penetrating brown eyes.

I could feel the heat in my face go up another degree. Good question. 'You kind of had to be there', I thought to myself. He looked at me patiently. "Well, I think we just wanted to confirm that he was at home." I tried to swallow and ended up choking over the next few words. "And that he was alone. It was a stupid, inappropriate thing to do, but we acted like high school kids and went there anyway."

"Is that what you're so embarrassed about?" Harrison smiled kindly. "Would you like some water?"

I knew he was handling me, being understanding so I'd let down my defenses. I'd used the same psychology with my students. Knowing the method didn't make it any less effective. I was ready to tell him everything. Maybe it was the drugs.

"Thanks," I said, taking the glass he poured for me. "I knew better," I said taking a sip. "But we got caught up in the whole thing." I wasn't going to tell him that I'd been a recluse so long, I'd OD'd on adventure.

"Yes." He looked at his notes. "Mrs. Brody had a helicopter, a rental car…"

"Wigs," I added, immediately regretting it.

"Yes, we did find shreds of synthetic hair. Were you the blonde or the red head?"

"The red head." I wanted to sink through the bed. Was this important evidence?

"Good thing. It seems to have saved your scalp." He started a new page in his notebook.

"Tell me what happened. Just the way you remember it."

I went through the whole story, well, not the whole story. I left out the fries at the diner and the red-haired girl. I just mentioned the house. I wasn't going to admit to being a peeper, too.

Harrison flipped back through his notes. "You said you thought Mr. Brody might have used the alley behind the house to evade you?"

"Well, it's only a theory, but it did look like he turned in there."

"Maybe it was the house next door."

"No this house was the only one that had a clear driveway that led away from the house. The houses on either side had short driveways that were blocked with parked cars."

Harrison looked at me for a moment and smiled. "Most people are not as observant as you, Mrs. Strayer." He made a couple of notations in his book then flipped to another page. "Had you ever seen the blue pickup truck you described at Mr. Brody's house before?"

"Well, I haven't been to Mr. Brody's house in over a year, but, no. I don't think I would forget it."

"And you couldn't see the driver?"

"No. The windows were tinted very dark."

Harrison flipped his book shut. "What does the S. stand for?"

"What?"

"It says S. Ann Strayer on your hospital chart."

"Stella. Stella Ann."

"Very nice. It suits you, you know." He got up from the chair by my bed. "Thanks for talking with me. It's been very helpful."

"You're welcome," I said not very wholeheartedly. This man probably thought I was the biggest fool he had ever met.

He reached for my now empty glass and returned it to the little bedside table. Then he stood for a moment. He was so tall he hunched his shoulders a little as he looked down at me. "If I have any more questions, I'll get in touch." He stopped. "Or if anything comes to you over the next few days, please call me."

He handed me his card and then just for a moment, he squeezed my hand. Suddenly he looked as if he was carrying the weight of the world on his shoulders. His expression was inscrutable. I must have looked really bad.

"I will." I spoke weakly just for the effect although it really was hard to talk and breathe at the same time. I was worn out, but I wanted him to think the charm was working. When he was gone, I started worrying.

CHAPTER FIVE

I woke from what must have been an hours long non-stop nap to the clanking of dinner trays in the hallway. Someone was pushing a pillow into my face. I was suffocating. My head was pounding. My nose ached. Little throbbing pains tingled along the nerve endings in my face. I realized that I had been dreaming. I was still in the white cocoon. I sat up and swung my legs over the side of my bed. I balanced there for a few minutes trying to get my strength then pushed back the curtain around my bed. That was a big mistake. I got dizzy and ended up hanging on to the curtain for a few minutes until I got my balance again. Luckily, I didn't rip it out of the ceiling. That's when I noticed I had company. A woman lay in the next bed. An IV was running to her left arm. The right was in a sling. Her head was wrapped in a bandage with the gauze wound over her forehead. It was Layne.

Her eyes were closed, but I stood up and walked shakily over to her bed. "Layne?"

Her eyes fluttered open then focused on me. "God, you look like a raccoon."

"Nose job. I got a multiple injury discount."

"Oh," she grimaced, "don't make me laugh. My head feels like it's got a big hole in it."

"Well, you look pretty good for a blast victim," I said, "at least that'll be the softener."

Layne looked at me like I was speaking Greek. "Never mind. I've got to see my face."

"Are you sure you should be up like that?" she said in a concerned voice.

"That bad, eh?" I inched my way into the bathroom. I hurt and I was chicken to look, but I steeled myself. It was bad. My face was peppered with little bruises, cuts, and scrapes. My nose did look like a stuffed manicotti. Bloody bandages and the plaster nose cast obscured most of my features. Another bandage criss-crossed my face horizontally under my nose so that my upper lip was hidden. My eyes were circled in dark blood-red bruises and swollen almost shut.

"Not bad for a blast victim," I murmured to myself.

"Ann? Are you all right? Should I ring for the nurse?" Layne called.

"I'm fine," I said, taking one last look. I made my way back to my bed, grateful to be able to collapse into it. I hoped I might achieve presentability again someday. It didn't look good. "This is unreal." I pulled my blankets up to my chin. "I feel like all this is happening to someone else or I'm watching a movie with me as the star."

Layne sighed, a hint of tears about to be shed in her voice. "I can't believe that Franklin's dead."

I wanted to head off any emotional scenes. I couldn't handle one at that moment. "Did you talk to Detective Harrison yet?"

"Not really, he came by to see me, but I was really out of it so he didn't stay."

"He asked me a few questions," I said, "I told him pretty much everything I could remember."

"Everything?"

"Everything except," I turned on my side so I could keep my voice low, "the redheaded girl in the house."

"Oh." Layne thought about that for a minute. "I won't mention her either." She sounded a little confused.

I laid back and looked at the ceiling. "It doesn't really matter. I just felt that we'd violated enough people's privacy for one night."

Layne didn't answer. I supposed I'd hurt her feelings and stole a cautious look in her direction. She was asleep. Good. We both needed the rest. I closed my eyes and fell into welcome oblivion.

I was allowed to check out of the hospital the next morning after promising not to drive home and having about twenty feet of gauze pulled from my nose. They also ripped a few bandages off for good measure. It had hurt like Hell, but at least I could breathe again. Layne had to stay because her neurologist wanted to keep her under observation for at least another twenty-four hours. She had a concussion.

I was released at about ten o'clock, a time that coincided with the beginning of visiting hours. I had just finished dressing when I heard a low murmur of voices.

Elliott Segal was standing by Layne's bed with a half-crushed bunch of red roses clutched to his chest. "Ann, you're awake."

He always made a habit of stating the obvious. Elliott was a tall, stoop shouldered, professor of music at Harding College. He'd met Layne at a party at my house last Christmas and fallen hopelessly in love with her.

He was sweet, considerate, attentive. All traits that a woman dreamed of in a man, but with Elliott it was in excess. It was even irritating. He was a man begging to be abused, and Layne was happy to accommodate him. It didn't take a psych degree to figure out the pay back for Franklin. I didn't feel like watching it today.

Elliott looked at my face then his eyes traveled down to my soiled sweat clothes. Horror was the best way to describe the expression in his eyes. I'm sure he'd brought a complete wardrobe with him for Layne to consider. "Are you sure you're well enough to leave, Ann?" Elliott said. It was just for show. He couldn't wait for me to leave.

"Fine. I'm fine."

"Sorry about your nose," he said in an effort to be human.

Layne squeezed my arm with her good hand. I knew she'd been pretending to be asleep. I also knew I should have felt, 'poor Elliott', but I didn't. Layne had tried to end the relationship shortly after meeting him, but he persisted in seeing her. His seeming affability was a blind. He was passively aggressive about getting what he wanted, and he would be like a burr on Layne's saddle blanket until she pulled him off. Even then I suspected that he would continue to harass her. I'd dealt with students over the years that had been subjected to the affections of young men of his type. It sometimes became ugly.

"Maybe it'll be an improvement."

I headed for the door. Elliott turned back to Layne cutting her off from view before I got it open.

CHAPTER SIX

I took a taxi home. The driver gave me one surprised look, probably partly for my appearance and partly for the distance, than minded his own business all the way to my house. What a professional. I knew I looked like the wrath of God with my smashed nose, black eyes and collection of bruises. He was a skinny little guy with greasy hair and a black tee shirt that must have been turned inside out because I could read the Hanes label on the back of his neck. I didn't say anything and neither did he. When he pulled in my driveway, I gave him a big tip.

It was good to be home. I went upstairs and threw myself down on my bed. Not such a good idea, my whole body ached. I called Zara and Arianne, my daughters. I let them know I'd had a little accident. My kids get so angry if I don't keep them posted on every little detail of my life, like getting blown up. They're sweet.

Ari was worried. Zara thought I was acting out because I'd never come to terms with my grief for their father. Arianne is the emotional, artistic daughter. Zara is my shrink in training who prides herself on processing every experience logically and reasonably. However, she is just as emotional and creative as her younger sister, Arianne. I know. I'm her mother.

THE PHOENIX

After I hung up the phone, I just lay for a while with my eyes closed. Zara was right. I hadn't come to terms with my feelings about Michael's death.

I opened my eyes and looked around my bedroom. I had repainted this room first. But not white, it was a pale shade of purple, my favorite color. All the pictures were down, put away. I hadn't put any curtains up and the hardwood floor still had drips of dried paint to be cleaned up. But the walls were great.

What were my feelings about Michael? A man I'd married when I was just nineteen. A man who was brilliant, quirky, aloof, and controlling. Sometimes grief for what might have been, sometimes relief that I was free from the day-to-day pain of our relationship, and guilt for any feeling that didn't seem normal. What I'd finally begun to realize, dimly at first, then more powerfully every day, was that I didn't understand what my feelings were. I missed him, but part of me almost dreaded that he'd come back. It was easier not to think about him at all.

I'd taken all his personal things, his tools, his files, his books, and locked them up in the trunk of his car right after he was killed. Maybe my own brush with death was behind it because I decided to get them out; to face them and the memories of him once and for all.

I got up and went downstairs. The key to his workshop was still on the shelf by the back door. Michael's workshop, or lab, because that was what it really was, was in a small building that kind of grew out of the side of the garage. I looked into it through the window in the door. Steel shelves, a big Formica worktable with a sink set into one end. Completely bare, it still had the power to move me. I could see him in there tinkering with his test tubes and chemicals. I had cleaned everything out, but his energy lingered.

I moved to the garage and unlocked the door. I grabbed the bottom and thrust upward. With a rattle the door rolled up. Michael's black 1958 Buick Roadmaster shone in the sunlight. If he'd been driving the Buick the day of the accident, he might have survived. Instead he was driving the department's car. A small American made station wagon that the local counties had bought for Michael when he consented to be their medical examiner. He'd been broadsided on the driver's side by a pickup truck. The driver had escaped the scene on foot and the truck had turned out to be stolen. It was a hit and run, they never caught the driver.

I opened the trunk. It swung open noiselessly. Michael had kept the car in mint condition. It probably looked better now than it did in 1958.

Everything was there: his tools, his notes and files, books, some of his clothes that I wouldn't give away. I glanced at some of the books. Laser technology and fingerprint identification, DNA sequencing, subjects that were way over my head.

I picked up the box of his notes. He kept a journal and files on all his cases. The essence of him was so overwhelming that I just took the box and slammed the trunk lid down again. I closed the garage door and headed back to the house.

I went into my study, opened the box, and pulled out a bundle of files. I stacked them on one side of the desk and reached back into the box. I pulled out journals, loose notes, more files and stacked them neatly until the box was empty. Then I began to sort through it. I picked up the journal, opening it to the first page. His precise printing with long strokes like manual EKG patterns filled the page in neat paragraphs pertaining to each case he'd handled.

THE PHOENIX

At first I felt a little ashamed that I hadn't turned these over to the new M.E. But as I read a few of the entries, I realized that the new M.E. was never meant to see them. These notes seemed to be his oddity or hunch notebook where he put comments, questions, gripes, that for various reasons he didn't want to commit to the official case file. Michael was very impatient with other people's shortcomings or incompetence. Usually, he made no secret of it, but perhaps he had learned to channel his frustrations into his notebook. All were cross-referenced to the actual case files by his own code.

I matched up a few. His journal entry on one case that concerned an elderly woman's death cross referenced Michael's journal notes that indicated that the death may not have been by 'Natural causes' but possibly suffocation. Evidently there was not enough clean evidence because of a botched police investigation to pursue a 'suspicious' outcome. He'd had a hunch, though, and made himself a note. I looked at the file again. All the documents were copies. He had made a duplicate file for himself, probably for every case where there was a question in his mind.

It was fascinating reading. I'd never known that Michael's work had been so interesting. I sat for a minute, sadness flowing over me, as I wondered why he'd never shared any of this stuff with me. Confidentiality aside, it would have been possible to use me as a sounding board or shared a hunch with me that paid off. There were several that evidently had done just that because he'd put little doodled stars after them and even occasionally an exclamation mark.

I looked around my study, my room, my retreat for years from Michael and the girls. The room where I worked on my great American novel from time to time in bursts of creative energy. I had just refinished it to make it my version of a Victorian era writer's study. As if Dr. Watson had recorded Sherlock Holmes' adventures at my desk. Rich woodwork, small violets on the wallpaper, Tiffany lamps, a romantic armchair upholstered in dark green velvet in front of the fireplace. I didn't keep tobacco in an old Persian slipper, but you get the idea. No wonder Michael and I had grown apart. I was in 1890 and he was in the year 2090.

It was sad, very sad, but part of me felt a little better. Michael had created his own little world so I no longer had to feel guilty about so frequently retreating to mine. We'd married so young I guess we needed these private parts of our lives.

I picked up his journal again and kept reading. I was about three-quarters to the end of the journal when I saw it. An entry, a name, jumped out at me: Franklin Brody. There were three others. I looked for the cross-reference codes and found the file. Evidently, Michael had done a favor for Franklin about a year ago. He'd fingerprinted Franklin's office after a robbery.

It was odd. Michael taught criminology courses at Harding, and he also was a trainer for the FBI Academy in Quantico, Virginia, but I'd never known him to do all the forensics on an investigation before. He usually called in his regular team. Franklin must have wanted to keep this robbery quiet, and Michael, because they were friends, had helped him.

I reread Michael's entries again. Apparently some case files had been stolen from Franklin's office. Michael had dusted for prints and come up with five sets, which included Franklin's own prints.

Michael had written a name out in the margin: Nicholas Fortuna and a phone number. He'd also doodled Franklin's name with several question marks around it.

I reached for my phone and dialed. Yes, dialed, it was one of those gold Victorian type phones. Not easy to cradle to the ear, but suitable to my décor.

"Fortuna Investigations," a woman's voice answered. She had a slight twang, not southern but countryish.

"Hello. May I speak to Nicholas Fortuna please?"

There was a slight hesitation then the voice said, "Mr. Fortuna is deceased. I'm Cheverly Fortuna, may I help you with something?"

Just for a second, a millisecond, my head took a trip to a far out galaxy. When it returned, a thread of an idea came to me, focusing my brain like nothing had in the last forty years.

"May I come and see you, Ms. Fortuna?"

"Sure. Anytime is fine. I'm here all day."

I hung up and sat in stunned silence for a few minutes. My mind raced along again. I got up, went upstairs and took a shower. I was back down in fifteen minutes. This time I had on a clean sweat outfit and my hair pulled back in a ponytail. I looked like Hell, but I was clean. I whipped the Trooper into gear. Ordinarily Davidson was a good thirty-minute drive on the two-lane highway I usually used. I made it there in fifteen.

CHAPTER SEVEN

The Fortuna Agency was housed in a small gray building that had once been a two-bedroom bungalow but now had a modern front with plate glass windows. 'Nicholas P. Fortuna, Investigations' and 'PUSH' were painted in four-inch high gilt letters on the heavy glass door.

I pushed through to the reception area. The former living room was now a waiting room. Black naugahyde couches were shoved at right angles into the right corner. A small table with a black lamp in the shape of a rooster held them at bay. The aggressive stance of the fowl and the slightly cocked lampshade gave the room an edge. On the left was a desk painted flat black with a matching black naugahyde swivel chair. In the chair was a very pretty little blonde woman in a neat black suit that emphasized her rounded curves. She was surrounded by computer equipment with one monitor on her desk and another on a black credenza behind her. She hung up her phone and looked up at me.

"Gawd! What happened to you?" Her voice held a mixture of concern and friendliness. She came around the desk and put an arm around me. She led me to a chair that faced her desk. "Sit down, honey. Are you sure you shouldn't be in a hospital somewhere?"

"No. Actually, I just got out of one."

I watched her as she walked back around to the other side of the desk. She was about my age with long frosted hair halfway down her back. Her features were pretty; big, round brown eyes, small upturned nose, and a full mouth with impossibly perfect cupid bow lips. She was a wholesome combination of Jean Harlow and Tammy Wynette.

"I got blown up."

She looked at me with as much reaction as if she saw four or five blown up people a day. "Did you call earlier?" She asked.

"Yes, I did." I paused a moment. "I wanted to ask you if Mr. Fortuna had ever worked for Franklin Brody."

"Ahh," She said considering for a moment, "you didn't happen to get blown up at Brody's house night before last?"

"Yes, as a matter of fact, I was."

I let her digest this piece of news. She looked at me for a moment. "Nikki did work for Brody. What do you need to know?"

Her manner was more guarded now, but still friendly. I liked her. I thought I could trust her. "My name is Ann Strayer." I reached across the desk to shake her hand.

"Cheverly Fortuna." She clasped my hand firmly. "After the town," she added grinning. "My dad was a long distance trucker out of West Virginia. My brothers and my sister are named after cities my Dad carried loads to. Nikki was my husband."

"I wish I had a name with some romance to it." I leaned back in the chair.

"Well I could say my sister's name is Minnie, short for Minneapolis and it might discourage you," she laughed, "but she's really named Bethany." She folded her arms on the desk. "What have you got to do with that weasel, Brody?"

41

I gave her a brief version of my adventures with Layne that night. Cheverly took it all in without interrupting me.

"It was this morning that I found Brody's name in my husband's journal. Michael had worked for Brody on an investigation before his death. Your husband's name was in his notes on the same case reference so I called you." I looked down at my hands then back up at her face. "I just wanted to know when your husband died and how he died."

"My God," Cheverly's voice was low, "Nikki was shot about six months ago. He was shot in the chest. They called it a drive-by shooting. I'm still trying to find out who did it."

"The police don't have any suspects?"

"Not unless you count me and everyone he's ever worked for."

"Why you?" I asked surprised.

"Honey, the spouse is always the main suspect. Nikki always said check the relatives and follow the money." She nodded her head at me like a first grade teacher trying to stress a particularly important point to one of her naïve students. "Don't you know that most people are murdered by someone they know? Besides, I had plenty of good reasons to kill Nikki and most of the police force knew them."

"What?" It was inane, but words failed me.

"Don't worry, I didn't kill him," she laughed. Her laughter was warm and infectious. "Come on, let me fix you a cup of coffee. Your look like you could use one."

She got up and locked the front door, propping a little sign with a clock on it that said 'we'll back at...' She set the hands to three o'clock. "It's Friday. I don't feel like working today anyway," she said as she led me down the little center hall into the kitchen.

A tiny round dinette table with a white Formica top and blue spindle legs was set up as if to serve lunch for two. I glanced at my watch. It was well after lunchtime.

"Am I going to be in your way?" I glanced at the two blue checked place mats with china and silver all arranged.

"Hell no," she motioned to one of the blue chairs, "sit down. I just set two places because Nikki and I always ate lunch together. You'll be my company today and it won't look like I'm nuts for a change." I sat down and she poured me a blue china mug full of coffee. "Chicken salad all right?"

"Great."

I thought of the wheat squares and oranges I was supposed to be eating and shuddered. Cheverly busied herself for a few minutes then she sat down and put a plate full of sandwiches between us.

I took a bite of one and practically swooned. It hurt to chew. I would be a size six in no time. I contented myself with nibbling my sandwich around the edges. It was delicious.

"Why would the police think you killed your husband even if they suspect the family?" I realized I was being rude. "If you don't mind me asking."

"Hey, no harm. Nikki was a pistol. He was a talker. He lied as easily as someone else tells the truth. He cheated on me with other women." Cheverly paused, sandwich in hand, "but I loved him. I loved the lying son-of–a-bitch right to the end." She took a bite out of her sandwich with the ferocity of a snapping turtle.

"I can't figure out what I feel about Michael."

I did think I was closing in on it a little better, though.

She stopped chewing then began again. It had a ruminating quality, like Elsie the cow, deep in thought. "I don't know that I've figured it out, either," she sighed, "Nikki was bigger than life. Death seems too small for him. Do you know what I mean? I guess he really still lives for me."

I thought about what she had just said. Michael seemed just the opposite to me. He was larger in death than he had been in life. What did that mean? "Cheverly?"

"Call me Chev. Everybody does."

"Okay, Chev, do you have your own theory about who killed Nikki?"

She played with the spoon in her coffee then folded her hands on the table. "Yes, I do. Nothing concrete, but I have a few ideas. Nikki was smart, too smart sometimes. He'd think he was so slippery he could get away with anything," she smiled, "then I'd bring him back down to the real world. He was working on something that he was worried about. I could tell it involved a woman." She sighed. "I thought he'd found his next love interest, but now I think it was more. I think he was working on a case for a woman and she killed him."

"Why do you think a woman killed him?" I was intrigued.

"Because the only time Nikki got hurt was when he got stupid. Women made him stupid."

"Interesting theory." I stirred my coffee again. "I have a small idea myself." She waited, watching me. "You see, Michael was killed, too, about six months ago. Hit and run driver. They never caught the guy."

Chev just waited. Like most women she was good at it, listening, that is.

"One thing always bothered me. No skid marks." I looked at her. "I went to the accident scene. I needed to see it for myself," I said as way of explanation. Her brown eyes were stern. "Even if it had been a drunken driver I think there would have been skid marks. If they were too drunk to brake, then how did they get away so cleanly?" I paused for emphasis. "I think there's a connection to all three men. Why are all of them dead now in a matter of months?"

Chev picked at the polish on one of her nails. "So Nikki wasn't killed by a client?"

"No, I didn't say that. I just think that whoever killed Nikki may have had a reason to kill Michael and Franklin, too." I pulled Michael's journal from my shoulder bag. "Look at this. It's an entry dated January 25 of this year. Michael made notes about fingerprints he'd lifted from Franklin's file cabinet. Your husband's name and phone number are in the margin. You said Nikki worked for Franklin Brody. Was it around the first of this year?"

"Yes, he did. I was thinking about it when the news came on last night." She rubbed the back of her hand across her forehead. She had pretty hands, short slender fingers with rings on almost every finger. She looked up and caught my glance. "Like my rings?" She continued before I could answer, waving her fingers in front of her face. "You've heard of mood rings, class rings, friendship rings? Well, these are guilt rings."

"From Nikki?"

"Yep. Each one of these babies was an affair, and just the ones I caught him in."

"God." I didn't know what to say.

"Don't worry, honey. I knew he was sick. He did, too. He loved me, though."

"I'm sure he did," I said in what I hoped was a sincere tone.

She snapped her fingers. "Sorry. I got off track. Nikki was hired by Brody's law firm to investigate a robbery. Someone broke into Brody's office and stole the files on one of his cases. They finally had to settle it out of court because original evidence was missing."

"And Nikki found out who did it?"

"Found the perp," she said instructionally, "it was an inside job." It was fascinating, her combination of tough talk and total femininity. "It was thin, but everything pointed to a girl on Brody's staff. She resigned, end of story."

"What happened to the girl?"

"Probably still lives around here somewhere. Want me to look it up?"

"Great, it'll give me somewhere to start."

CHAPTER EIGHT

We went back out to her desk. Chev was digging in the file cabinet when the phone rang. "Hello, Mrs. Connor. You're always right on the money." She shuffled a file open on her desk. "The title was originally issued to Clarence Jones." She read off an address and phone number. "I talked to him this morning. The car was totaled in '96. No way it can be safe. Probably one of those welded jobs to make the car look like new. Looks like they've tried to pull a fast one." She smiled. "I'll fax you the accident report... hey, don't mention it."

She hung up and continued her search through the file cabinet. She shrugged a shoulder at the phone. "That's how I make my living now."

"How?" I was curious about the phone call.

"Researching. Troubleshooting, I call it. I always did all the legwork for Nikki." She pulled a file from the drawer. "You know, the paperwork stuff. Call the MVA for some guy's registration, check the courthouse for wills or deeds. Get copies of the microfiche at the library for the case history." She ducked her head a little. "I used to be a police aide. I thought I wanted to be a cop so I decided to try it out slowly. I helped with paper work and research."

"Did you become a policewoman?" I was fascinated.

She smiled rubbing her hand across the file folder. "No, being a cop wasn't for me, but I have a lot of contacts, and that's how I met Nikki. He was a cop, then he started this agency and I worked for him." She placed the file on the desk and sat down. "How many evenings did I spend in dark car drinking coffee on surveillance? You don't want to know," she laughed. It was infectious. "Now I get paid to look up things for people. I check out things they want to buy, people they want to marry, potential business partners. And I don't use my legs much anymore."

She pointed proudly at her computer. "I used Nikki's insurance money to buy all this. I can access information from across the country or around the world. Kind of tame investigating, but still useful and profitable."

"What a great idea." I sat back down in my chair. "I bet you keep pretty busy."

Chev smiled proudly. "Yeah, I do. I've got all my contacts from over the years and I feel good when I help somebody." She opened the file and handed me a detailed outline of the notes inside. Very organized. "Here, see if anything here helps you."

It was pretty standard stuff. A break-in of the most amateurish kind, which only made it more likely that it was an inside job. Michael had dusted for prints and turned his findings over to Nikki. Several sets were on the file cabinet. All accounted for by the office staff. Michael had also used laser technology to enhance some prints from the files themselves. He'd come up with one set that shouldn't have been there. They belonged to an intern who had no business handling the files in Franklin's office.

The girl, a certain Cynthia Reeves, had an explanation. She said someone left a stack of files on her desk that she recognized as ones from Mr. Brody's current caseload. She'd gone into his office to return them to his secretary because she knew of their sensitive nature. She claimed she placed the files on Brody's desk and left. Important documents were missing. Brody pressured her over the incident and she quit.

I pulled out Michael's notebook, remembering something I'd read there. He'd found her prints on only two files, which, although potentially damning, could have supported her story.

"Well, what do you think?" Chev watched me with interest.

"What was the case about, or maybe I should say, who was the client?"

Chev leaned toward me. "It was all very hush hush, but remember the name Anthony Deseeca?"

"Deseeca . . . Deseeca. Wait, I remember." It came to me in a flash. "He's the big developer who sued the Parnelli Brothers Construction Company for supplying him with shoddy material for that new office building off L Street in D.C. Franklin Brody was his attorney."

"Right." Chev leaned back in her chair her softly rounded arms hugging themselves across her chest. "Supposedly Deseeca had documents showing that the Parnelli Brothers Construction Company, who have been rumored to have mob ties, deliberately falsified the specifications for most of the materials. The concrete, the steel mesh to strengthen the walls. All of it was substandard. But the evidence got swiped. So Tony had to settle for a lot less than he'd hoped for and the Parnelli Brothers are still in business scamming the public making buildings that will pancake someday."

"Franklin must have been between a rock and a hard place on that one. I wouldn't want to have either side mad at me."

"Yeah," Chev gave herself one last little hug and leaned toward me again, "He was on the phone to Nikki three or four times a day."

"Did Nikki find any of the evidence that was stolen?"

"Nope, he never did. As a matter of fact Franklin dropped the investigation. Just told Nikki to forget it, but then Nikki got a retainer to continue. It was anonymous. We don't usually accept any arrangement like that, but Nikki was obsessed about the case. So even though I didn't like it, he put the money in our escrow account and kept working on it. When Franklin found out that we were still active he wasn't too happy."

I mulled that over for a few minutes. "So he was still pursuing the case when he died?"

"Yes. And it was worrying him. I know because he wouldn't tell me everything. Actually, the night he was killed, he was on a lead about the case. He was supposed to meet a woman who had some information about the robbery and the missing evidence." She looked down at her rings unconsciously rubbing the knuckle of the ring finger on her left hand. "I guess that's why I thought he may have been tempted again. The woman never turned up. Nikki called me from the meeting place. Said she was a no show, said he was going to wait another fifteen minutes and then be would head home. But he never came. He was shot sitting in his car." She sat for a moment staring at her hands then shrugged it off and looked at me.

I knew the pain she was experiencing. I was living it myself. I picked up the rest of Nikki's files she'd stacked in front of me. "You don't mind if I go through these?"

Chev looked at me, her round brown eyes crinkling in the corners. "Honey, we both know that you're going to get to the bottom of this with my help."

"You don't even know me," I laughed. I don't even know me, I could have added. "How can you be that confident?"

"Well," she leaned back in her molded naugahyde chair and played with a small sapphire ring on the pinky of her left hand, "You had the stuff to pull yourself together and come out to see me. I know you feel lousy." She paused and moved to the next finger. A ruby twinkled on this one. "You think like Nikki. I can see the wheels turning right now. And," she moved to a small Navaho styled turquoise ring, "I bet at least ten people stop you every day to ask you directions."

"What?"

"You've got that kind of face, you know, approachable, friendly."

"How can you tell?" I said lifting my hands to my bandaged nose.

"I can tell. It's your eyes. You've got honest eyes. Pretty blue eyes that are kind, that someone can trust. That's why I'm going to work with you."

"It might turn out to be dangerous. Look what's already happened."

"Hell! I want revenge, too!"

I picked up the Brody, Borman, and Tate file and started reading. Revenge? Was that what I wanted? I honestly didn't know.

CHAPTER NINE

Cynthia Reeves was a good, quiet kid with top grades at Georgetown University. She had come to Franklin's firm as a summer intern. She was doing a good job. Then the file disappeared and ten thousand dollars was deposited to a savings account in her name. She claimed to know nothing about it. The fingerprints, the money, everything seemed to point her way. But it was too pat. I didn't like it. Evidently Nikki didn't, either. He'd spent more time on investigating the two parties to the lawsuit. Neither Deeseca nor the Parnellis had been upright citizens.

From Nikki's notes he'd believed that the Parnellis had paid someone off in Franklin's office to steal the evidence. He had noted a list of possible suspects. Franklin Brody's name was at the top with a big question mark beside it.

"Have you read this?" I asked Chev.

"Yeah, keep reading, though, I want to see what you think. I'll get us some more coffee."

I read on, going through every note. Chev had typed and cross-referenced all Nikki's entries so it wasn't hard to follow the line of the investigation. It definitely looked like Cynthia Reeves had been the scapegoat.

The other people in the office who had access to the file had all been checked out. One name other than

Franklin's had been underlined, Mona Freeman, Franklin's secretary. It seemed as if they'd been having an affair off and on for years. Nikki had receipts, deeds, and well- researched documentation to substantiate their relationship.

I could feel the heat flushing up my neck into my face. That bastard. How could he treat Layne that way? Only the fact that he was in little pieces all over the driveway at 229 Park Glen Drive helped to cool my skin again. Maybe I was more vengeful than I realized.

Chev returned with fresh coffee. Just in time. I was feeling very tired. I opened the next file. It only had a few pages. It was the start of the investigation for the anonymous client, building on what Nikki had already discovered. There was one interesting item, a note to meet the woman Chev had mentioned. She called and claimed to know something valuable. Nikki had gone to meet her the night he died. No name.

I closed the file and stacked it on top of the others. "Okay, who starts?"

"You," Chev said. She held her coffee cup with both hands breathing in the steam that rose from it like it was a vital source of oxygen or she was thinking of giving a commercial endorsement.

"Did Nikki really confront Franklin about his suspicions? He seemed to think Franklin had something to do with it."

"He never got a chance to. Franklin fired the girl before Nikki was done. Asked him for an invoice and his report to date. Paid it, and it was over."

"So he went ahead on his own time and then he got the new client," I said, mulling that one over. "I think Franklin's robbery might have been manufactured. It seems that Nikki was suspicious."

"A set up."

"Yeah, a set up for someone's benefit. Someone got paid off well for that, I bet. Did Nikki follow the money on it?"

"He tried. At least, I tried. That was my job. I didn't find any. Just the ten thousand that turned up in the kid's account. She claimed to know nothing about it. Nikki believed her."

I took a long drink of coffee, letting the hot liquid burn down my throat. "What if Franklin did it himself? Tony Deseeca would be a dangerous man to cross. Maybe Deseeca sent the retainer to hire Nikki. Trying to keep up the pressure on Franklin Brody."

"Hell, Franklin was in big trouble if he stole the evidence for the Parnellis, too. Do you think they'd let him hold that over them?"

She had a point. I could see that the list of Franklin Brody's enemies would be a long one. "You said that the woman from the phone booth never came forward. Did you try to find her?"

"Yes, Nothing. I tried and I came up empty. The police worked on it too, but it was like she never existed."

"How did she contact Nikki?"

"A phone call, turned out to be from a public phone at Union Station. We traced it back from here."

"Nobody saw the caller?"

"No and tons of prints on the phone."

I could see that Chev blamed herself for the lack of success. I decided to change the subject. "What do you think about the explosion?"

Chev twirled a long strand of hair around her finger. "Could have been a timer. The explosion set to go off by remote control."

"I guess the police will figure it out."

"Don't count on it. Word is that Brody had the Gas Company out several times complaining of a gas smell in his house. They couldn't find one, but he'd called in at least four times in the past month. If it looks like an accident, they won't go looking for trouble. They may just want to question the driver."

"How do you know all this?" I asked amazed.

"I still have several friends in the police department. They keep me in the loop." She smiled. "Actually, I called in about something else. I got this info as a bonus. It's the big news today. The crime scene guys are having a rough time scraping up enough of Franklin to make an ID."

"I can't believe they'd let this pass as an accident."

"If it closes the case, they will."

"That's a cynical way to look at things." I ran my hand up through my hair in frustration. Bad move. Little jolts of pain from the bruises reminded me how lousy I felt.

"Not cynical," Chev said, taking no offense, "just practical like the police are. Closing cases is the business they're in. They've got too many and not enough cops to go around." She reached over and put her hand on my arm. "You know, I think you've just about had it. Come on." She got up and helped me to my feet. Every joint in my body was stiffening up.

"I'll be okay." I reached for my shoulder bag. It must have weighed two hundred pounds. "You're right, I think I'll go home and take it easy the rest of the day."

"You want me to drive you home?"

"No thanks, I'll be fine." I said as I walked to the door. I felt like a two thousand-year-old mummy and was about as agile.

"Here, I'll let you take these files." She grinned. "But I'll carry them to the car for you."

S. Alden Reilly

Once I was in the car, Chev leaned in the window. "Why don't I come by tomorrow around lunch time and we can get ourselves organized." She said.

"Great." It was embarrassing to be such a weakling all of a sudden. "I'll make lunch. How about twelve thirty?"

"Okay," She took my hand and gave it a little squeeze, "get some rest now."

I gave her my address and drove off. I could see her in my rear view mirror. She watched me until I turned the corner.

CHAPTER TEN

On the way home I pulled myself together. My car is comfortable and I actually like driving. Good thing, too, since everything is about an hour commute from my place.

When I pulled in the driveway a car was already parked in front of the garage, a gray '71 Buick LeSabre, Bertie's car.

She opened her door when I pulled in beside her. A small, spry woman in her late sixties dressed in powder blue polyester pants with a red I.U. sweatshirt. Indiana University was my alma mater. Wearing Reeboks, she was, as usual, ready for anything.

"Stella, where have you been?" The girls called me and said you'd gotten yourself hurt." She put her arm around me and practically carried me to the door.

"Bertie, I was going to call you, but I got side tracked." I protested as she took the keys from my purse and unlocked the door. Actually, I thought about it at the hospital but lacked the courage to tell my aunt about my misadventures while lying in a hospital bed. I was supposed to be more responsible than that.

My aunt's name is really Bertha Amelia, but everyone calls her Bertie. She was the oldest of seven children, my father the youngest. She has called me Stella since the day I was born. My mother claimed it was just hatefulness because she, my mother, insisted on Ann. Bertie, when confronted, would insist that I was the spitting image of her own Grandmother Stella Selene and persisted. My poor mother, with grandma and Betie around it was like having two mothers-in-law.

"Good lord, child!" Bertie got a good look at me once we were inside. She took my coat and purse away. Then she started to stick the files on a shelf in the kitchen, but I took them back.

"I'll take these upstairs."

"Good," she said. "Then you're going to get in bed with them because that's where you're going."

Did I mention that Bertie is often very bossy as well as obstinate about family names? Actually, I was glad to let her lead me upstairs and put me to bed. Bertie has been my unofficial parent for years. My own parents died in a plane crash while I was away at my first year of college. Bertie took charge of me then. Making sure I finished my education, later helping me with my own babies. I loved her dearly. I climbed the stairs with the stiff-legged gait of a cowboy who's ridden his last bronco.

"Ouch, ouch, ouch!" Bertie was helping me out of my clothes. She tends to get rough when she's worried about you. She comes from the old school where most emotional communication is non-verbal. "Bertie, take it easy. I know you're mad at me for getting myself hurt, but it wasn't my fault."

"I'm not mad at you, I'm just mad, period," she said skimming my flannel nightgown over my head and shoving my arms into the sleeves. "Now get settled and I'll bring you up something to eat."

I lay down. The files were on the floor by my bed. I turned and shoved them underneath. The covers felt luxurious. I'm a bed person. I love to lie in bed, sleep late in the morning, feel snug, soft, and warm.

THE PHOENIX

I was half dozing when Bertie came back upstairs with a tray of food. Her face was flushed pink, her soft gray hair fluffed around her head. She had remarkable blue eyes that were barely visible behind the steamed up lenses of her glasses. She pushed the ottoman over near my bed with her foot and set the tray down. Soup, little crackers, hot tea, toast, all the kind of comforting sick-kid food I used to get as a child.

"Here Hon, sit up a little." Bertie only called me 'Hon' when she was really worried about me.

"I'm okay, honestly, Bertie," I said as I pushed myself up against the pillows. "Why don't you sit down and keep me company?"

Bertie placed the tray across my lap. "Eat, then you can tell me about it and I'll decide if I think you're okay." I said she was bossy. I smiled in response. I had always admired her. Strong, independent, and smart, she'd always gone after what she wanted in life. I dutifully ate my soup and all the other invalid goodies on my tray. It tasted good. I was comforted. Bertie took the tray away and came back to sit beside me. "Now, tell me what's going on."

I gave her a reader's digest version of my adventures of the previous night. I mentioned my visit to Chev, too. I left out my theories, but I could tell she could read between the lines.

"Layne is a lovely woman, dear, but she hasn't got the sense God gave a..." she struggled to find something sufficiently dim, "...turnip."

I grinned. "I know, I used to think that, too, but she's different. She surprised me."

Betie gave me a skeptical look. "Well, you almost got yourself killed, and it sounds like you're looking for more trouble. Now, don't get that stubborn look, Stella. I know you."

"Don't worry. I won't do anything stupid." I yawned. I felt myself slipping away. Down into a cozy warm cocoon. Sleep killed all arguments.

THE PHOENIX

CHAPTER ELEVEN

I awoke to the smell of food. Bertie must have stayed over. I got up and followed the scent downstairs. My kitchen runs along the back of the house. It's a big room, light and airy with long windows that look straight into the woods. Today a mist lay over the ground like some giant had stuffed cotton in and around each tree.

"Well good morning, sleepyhead." Bertie was pouring coffee for someone already seated at the table, a small blonde in neat jeans and a blue turtleneck sweater.

"Chev?" I looked up at the kitchen clock. "God, I'm sorry. I was going to fix your lunch."

"Hey, your aunt is making us crepes. Don't worry."

"You needed to sleep, Stella. Now come and sit."

"Stella? I thought you said you didn't have an interesting name." She grinned mischievously.

"You think Stella is an interesting name?" I said as I eased myself onto the wooden seat of one of my kitchen chairs. God, why didn't I get some comfortable furniture in this lifetime?

"Bertie just calls me..." I looked again at her smile, "Oh, I see you've already heard the story about Stella Selene."

Bertie turned around, two plates of her famous strawberry crepes in her hands. "Yes, and she thinks I'm right." She thunked my plate down in front of me. "Stella means star and that's just what your great grandmother was. You could be, too." She snagged the coffeepot to refill Chev's cup.

"Oh please, I can't dance or carry a tune."

"There're other ways to shine," Bertie said mysteriously.

I looked at Chev. I wasn't sure if Bertie's little speech had impressed her or the coffee fumes were taking effect because she said, "I'm going to call you Stella, too. I like it." Great. Now I would be out of synch with two people in the vast configuration of the world. I wanted to go back to bed.

"Stella, drink some coffee. You'll feel better," Bertie said as she sat down beside me. I took a long drag on my coffee. She was right. I dug into the strawberries. "Delicious. I didn't know I had strawberries in the refrigerator."

"You didn't," Bertie said with that tone that signaled a lecture to come. "I had to go to the store because you didn't have any food in the house."

"I know. I like carry-out," I said defiantly.

Bertie looked at Chev with a now-you-see-what-I-have-to-put-up-with look on her face. Chev ducked her head. I could see a smile on her lips. Bertie fixed a deadly blue stare on me, and then happily changed the subject.

"I can't stay much longer because Pauline has arranged for the girls and I to go to the craft show at the fairgrounds."

Pauline and the girls, Vivian and Mildred, were women my aunt's age. All widows, they went everywhere together. They even took a trip to Ireland on an ocean liner last year. My daughters and I referred to them as the 'Gang of Four'. There were times when they were just as dangerous as the originals.

When we finished eating and cleaned up, Bertie came up and put her arms around me. "Stella, you know I love you. Please take care of yourself." She hugged me mindful of my bruises. "And I'm not mad at you for not calling me from the hospital. I know you didn't want to worry me, but you don't always have to be so independent."

"Look who's talking, Ms. Independent." I held her face for a moment and kissed her cheek. "I love you, too." I hugged her back. It always surprised me to feel how delicate she was. She was indomitable, feisty, adventurous and ninety pounds dripping wet. Then she was off. The gray Buick fairly spun out of the driveway. The rest of the gang was waiting for their leader.

CHAPTER TWELVE

"Your aunt is a real interesting lady," Chev said pouring us both more coffee.

"You can say that again." I looked down at my robe. "I'll get dressed then we can get going. I started toward the hallway. "God, what is wrong with me. I forgot to call about Layne." I went to the wall phone by the refrigerator. The phone rang and rang, then the call transferred to the information desk. A nurse told me that Mrs. Brody had been released. Into Elliot's custody, I guessed. "She's out so I guess we'll be hearing from her soon."

I asked Chev to bring her coffee upstairs. We talked while I showered and dressed. Then I dragged Nikki's files from under the bed and we took them downstairs to my study. Chev seemed to be impressed with my Sherlock Holmes redecoration.

"This is great. The only thing that's missing is the V of bullet holes in the wall."

"I know, I draw the line on actual structural damage." I dragged a chair over to my desk.

"Maybe faux bullet holes." Chev teased.

I grinned. "Here," I handed her Michael's journal and files. "You read the journal and I'll read these again. Then we'll talk."

It was a long silence, but comfortable. For a change I didn't mind having company. Maybe I'd turned some kind of corner.

Chev broke the silence. "Okay, do you want to know what I think?"

"Of course."

She made a face. "First of all, I think your husband was a bit of a prick." I just looked at her. "Yeah, well we can talk about that later." She hurried on, "he did keep good records. And with what's in here I can get some information from one of my contacts in DC that could help us. The only other thing that strikes me is this…" She pointed a hot pink nail at another entry Michael had entered a short time after the break in at Brody's. It said 'Damon Edwards' with a question mark. Michael had doodled a huge DNA type doodle with a Baroque frame around it. Little question marks flew off the edge of the page.

"Michael always doodled when he worked at a problem. This must have been a big one." I looked at the marks in the book. "He was a prick sometimes."

Chev looked up. "I'm sorry. I always shoot my mouth off before my brain takes aim."

"Look. I like honesty. I need it, especially now."

Chev looked at me for a minute, understanding in her eyes. She pointed at the name in the book again. "Damon Edwards is a name from a missing persons inquiry we had late last year."

I looked at the note again. Evidently Nikki had brought in some print specimens for Michael to enhance. They were old file prints from twenty years ago. Most old inked fingerprints are practically useless unless the personnel who took them were properly trained. Michael was a whiz at that kind of stuff. He had laser enhanced the prints. His notes described the points of identification as he did with all fingerprint work, but several were underlined as if for emphasis.

"God, Michael, what were you getting at?" I said puzzled.

"When was Michael killed?"

"The last day of February."

Chev was still for a moment. "I remember how upset Nikki was when he heard about your husband. Of course, we thought it was an accident at the time." She paused. "Nikki was killed on March 15, the ides of March. He loved the play *Julius Caesar*. He was superstitious about that day."

"Something about this Damon Edwards thing had Michael really wound up. What was that story?"

"Got a call from another detective agency, Palmer down in Rockville. They needed some old prints enhanced from a missing persons case. Nikki took the print sample to your husband when they were working on the Brody case together. And I sent them over to Palmer when they came back."

"Could you see how it ended up? I'd like to know what Michael was trying to get at."

"No problem, it's on the list." She said making a note. "I found out what happened to Cynthia Reeves. I called her mother after you left yesterday."

"Bad?"

"No. Just a waste."

"What?"

Chev twirled a long strand of frosted hair around her finger. "She dropped out of law school. Her mother says she's working as a waitress in some little bar in Georgetown."

"Great. I bet her mother's heartsick."

"Yeah, if you mean pissed, you've got it." Chev flipped the strand of hair back over her shoulder.

"Well, how are we going to do this?" Chev just looked at me. "You know, question these people and everything?"

"You're the boss."

"Me?" I started to object. "But Chev, you've actually got an agency," I protested.

"Not really, not since Nikki died. Look, I can follow a fact to the ground. I can tail suspects, sit on surveillance, and keep the records straight, but I'm not an out-on-the-street detective. It's okay to know your limitations," she said softly. "I'll do all the follow up but you're going to have to handle the people."

"You think I can do this?"

"Yeah, I think you can do this."

"Okay, I guess I'd better see Cynthia first."

"I got the name of the bar she works at from her mother." She held up one of her hands and ticked off each painted nail as she elaborated. "And I set up an appointment for you with Mrs. Reeves. Then I checked with Brody, Borman and Tate, from now on to be referred to as B.B.& T. because it's too hard to say." She grinned, "Just try saying it fast three times in a row." She turned serious again. "I found out that Mona Freeman, Franklin's secretary is off for a few days, but I got her home address for you. I think that's enough for one day," she ended with a smile.

'Wow!' was all I could think to say.

Chev slipped her hand inside a black purse, which could have doubled as an overnight bag and pulled out a pad of paper. She peeled the top sheet off and handed it to me. The names and addresses of the women were on it.

"I guess you do think I can do this." It was nice to have someone have confidence in me again. If only I could.

CHAPTER THIRTEEN

We had just started another pot of coffee when the doorbell rang. "It's Layne," I said, going to the door to peer out, "and she's got Elliott with her."

I opened the door to them. Layne looked pale and drawn in a pink jogging outfit. Elliott, well, he was just Elliott. Layne turned once inside the door to stand beside me. "I'm okay now, really, Elliott." She linked her arm through mine. "Ann will take care of me now."

I took a mortal wound from the daggers in Elliott's eyes before he leaned to give Layne a little peck on the cheek. "Okay, dear. Just call me when you're ready for me to pick you up."

"Thanks," I hissed as he retreated down the walk. I shut the door.

She sighed, "I just didn't know how to get rid of him."

"Well, casting me in the role of a rival is not exactly fair to either of us," I scolded as we walked into my kitchen.

Chev looked up. "Who's a rival?" She asked curiously.

"Cheverly Fortuna, meet Layne Brody, battered and a little worse for the wear, but still able to twist men around her little finger."

I hoped Layne behaved. She could be a little standoffish at times. Layne gave me a dirty look then extended her hand. "It's nice to meet you."

"Same here," Chev said, smiling.

"Are you from West Virginia?" Layne asked before she let go of Chev's hand.

"Yeah. My accent, huh? I guess I've still got it."

"Just a little. But I would recognize it, anyway. I'm from West Virginia, too." She gave Chev a warm smile.

It was my turn to be surprised. "What? I thought Franklin said you were from Philadelphia, upper crusty and all that."

Layne flopped down in one of my kitchen chairs. There was no time to warn her. She grimaced slightly. "Franklin told everybody that stuff. He was really from Tennessee. Did you know that?"

"No. But, I've begun to realize that I've been mistaken about a lot of things lately." I took out another cup for Layne. "Why did he lie about that?"

"I guess he didn't think I was classy enough with a West Virginia background." She turned to Chev. "No offense, Cheverly."

"None taken."

Layne turned to me as I dug in my cabinets for a cookie or cracker to offer her. I came up with some stale cereal. "That detective came to see me again."

"Harrison?" I bit into a square of frosted wheat. I poured the rest in a bowl. Maybe I had some raisins. I could make a half-assed trail mix.

Layne looked over at me. "Ann, just come and sit down. I don't need anything to eat."

"Thank god," I said. "I need to make a trip to the grocery store. So what did Harrison have to say?"

Layne clasped her hands together and cupped them over her knee. "He said that the Gas Company had been to the house four times in the past few weeks. Franklin was worried about a gas leak."

"Did they find anything on any of those visits?" I asked, looking at Chev.

"No. There was an odor but they couldn't find a leak. Detective Harrison said it looked like an accident."

"You were right," I said to Chev, who gave me a big grin. "Well, at least he doesn't suspect you." Layne gave me a dark look.

"The spouse is always a suspect," I said winking at Chev.

"Well, I guess I should feel lucky. There's something else." Layne said in a lower tone. I sensed impending doom.

"What?"

"No money. All Franklin's money is gone. All my money, I should say." She enunciated every word clearly. The deliberation was obviously a way to control her own anger and panic.

I was shocked. Franklin Brody had been a successful attorney in Washington D.C. for years. Certainly he and Layne had maintained an affluent lifestyle, but Franklin had never struck me as the frivolous type, nor as the type to suddenly go broke.

"Maybe he was trying to pull a fast one on you before he got killed. Or maybe he tried to pay someone off and it didn't work."

Chev piped up. "Have you got access to all his bank accounts, you know, his credit lines?"

"I've looked through everything," Layne said dejectedly. She rubbed her left eye with the back of her hand. A smear of mascara trailed across her eyelid.

"His sock drawer, under the mattress…" Chev continued.

Layne laughed at that. "There's not much left of his sock drawer, I'm afraid." She looked at us guiltily. "I know this will sound cold, but I called the bank and our broker when I got home from the hospital. My lawyer had all his financial information for the settlement agreement, which he wouldn't agree to. I checked my copy and called them. Everything's gone."

I looked at Chev. "I think we need to talk here." I outlined for Layne some of the conclusions Chev and I had come to. "We're going to pursue these deaths. They were related somehow. We were just getting a list of people together when you came in." I told her what we planned.

"Well, there's a few more from Franklin's past you'll need to see."

"You're right. We've got a lot to cover."

Chev ticked off, "The Parnellis, Desecca…" She looked at Layne.

"His partner, John Borman, and a few dozen disgruntled clients," Layne added.

I groaned aloud. "We'll keep the list small at first. We can expand it if nothing turns up. Maybe Chev could look into this money thing for you, Layne." I looked at Layne. "How do you feel? Do you think you can help out on some of these?"

She gave me a look of pure bafflement. "Oh, I couldn't, Ann, really, not the way I look."

I put a hand up to my face and fingered the bandages over my nose. "You know, I'd forgotten. I know I look rotten, but I can't afford to lie around waiting to become more socially presentable." I probably sounded a little testy.

Chev looked at me then at Layne and laughed. "Hey, it's the weekend. Why don't we wait and get started on Monday?"

"I thought detectives never rested. That they just kept going until they dropped," I said.

"Well, I hate to disillusion you, but most of it is pretty dull stuff. You just keep asking questions until you find the right answers. Sometimes you don't find them, but that's the breaks." Chev stretched and stood up. "Besides most detectives at least start their investigations in one piece whether they end up that way or not." She shouldered the overnight bag-purse. "Take my advice and rest tomorrow. Once we start rolling you'll need it. I'll get you the rest of the addresses you'll need and drop them by tomorrow afternoon."

The doorbell rang just then. It made us all jump. I went to the door. It was Elliott. He had the expectant face of a six-year-old. I waited for him to ask if Layne could some out to play. "Layne! Elliott's here to take you home." I know it was uncouth to yell it out, but I was too tired to fool with social graces. Chev had come up behind me. She ducked her head to hide a smile.

Layne came from the kitchen. She looked out of sorts. "Elliott, I said I would call you if I needed you." I expected Elliott was in for a rough ride home. She turned to Chev. "I'll call you on Monday about the matter we discussed." It was a nice rebuke to Elliott. Layne air kissed the side of my cheek. "I guess I might as well go. I'll call you tomorrow." She shrugged away from Elliott's arm and walked down to his car. He followed like an eager puppy.

"What does she see in that guy?" Chev asked. She was looking at my painting project in the living room.

"A chance to be on top for a change. She was definitely in Elliott's role with Franklin."

Chev watched them drive away. "Maybe I can find a guy to cheat on." She began, "Nah, way too much aggravation just to get even with the male sex."

"My sentiments, exactly." I said as she left. I closed the door and slid the dead bolt home. All I wanted was my bed. I didn't intend to get out of it for the rest of the day.

It was dark when I woke up. I stumbled downstairs driven purely by hunger. I opened the refrigerator. I remembered an apple with a big brown spot on it, but Bertie had thrown it away. In its place was a quart of fresh milk, bread, and lunchmeat. God, I loved her meddling ways. I made myself a triple-decker club sandwich. My Miracle Whip was still good, thank God.

I took my snack over to the table. I was oblivious to everything but food, so it was only when I began to wash up that I noticed the light was on in Michael's workshop. I was sure I never turned it on yesterday, but I had no intention of crossing the yard in the dark to investigate. I went into the pantry and opened the electrical box. I flipped the circuit breaker for the garage to the off position. I could do it properly in the morning. At least the utility company wouldn't get any more money. I checked all the doors and windows again and went back upstairs.

I lay down, but I couldn't sleep. My long nap had fixed that. I ended up getting a spatula and some soapy water from the kitchen. I spent the next three hours prying the paint drippings from the wood floor in my bedroom. By the time I finally went to bed, the floor was clean.

CHAPTER FOURTEEN

I felt almost human when I woke the next day. The light from the window played on the walls of my bedroom. I lay still for a little while luxuriating in the soft lavender glow, then I got moving. I went to the store. I wanted to get groceries in before any more people came by. Yesterday had been humiliating enough. They say that you should never shop when you're hungry. Two carts later I can definitely say they are right.

By the time I got everything put away and straightened up the kitchen, it was well into the afternoon. I got out a package of chicken breasts and started cutting them into chunks. I was chopping the vegetables when I remembered Michael's workshop.

I put my knife down and went out the back door grabbing the keys from the shelf on my way. When I got to the workshop door, it was slightly ajar. I went inside and flipped the light switch off. Nothing was disturbed. I reasoned with myself that sometimes the door had to be pulled shut with some force or it wouldn't catch. It had been windy yesterday. Still, it didn't feel right.

I went around and peered in the front of the garage at Michael's car. Fine. Nothing wrong. Something touched my shoulder and I jumped. I guess I screamed, too, because Chev started laughing.

"Sorry. I didn't mean to startle you. Really. I called you from the front of the house. When you didn't answer, I walked around here." She was wearing white leggings with an oversized fuchsia colored sweater. Her long hair was in a ponytail.

"I guess I'm a little jumpy. This place still gives me the creeps." I pulled the door shut locked it. We walked up to the house. "You look like you're going out."

"I've been out. I had a few errands to run." She said as we went into the house.

"Oh," I said, "want some coffee?" I already knew better than to ask. We walked into the kitchen where I started the pot.

"I have the rest of the addresses as promised." She extracted a file folder and a small box from the giant purse. She lay the folder on the counter but handed me the box.

"What's this?" I opened it. Inside were small, neat rectangles with 'Stella Jones, Investigator, Fortuna Agency' printed on them and the address and phone number. "Business cards!"

Chev smiled. "You might want to go back to Harding College someday. I don't think they'd like to hear that Professor Strayer was out beating the streets for perps on a possible murder investigation."

"You're right about the college. Very conservative." I said fascinated by the cards. "How did you get these so fast? And how did you know my maiden name? Did I tell you?"

"No, I did a computer check on your MVA record. Used your license plate number." Chev pulled one out to admire it. "I've got a friend. A printer. Sometimes you need things fast. That's his specialty."

"Thank you. You know, you're so efficient. I don't think you really need me." I was very prone to self-doubt lately. I sounded like a whiner even to my own ears.

"Hey, we've been through all that. I'm the support team, the pit crew, the helper. I like it that way." She grasped my arm. "You can do this, and I want you to do this." She shook her finger at me. "Now don't ask me again," she laughed.

"Okay, I believe you." I took out some cards and filled the little imitation leather case the printer had provided. I stuck them in my purse. I put the box on the counter. I poured two cups of coffee and handed one to Chev. "Would you like something to eat?" At the doubtful look on her face I said, "I went for groceries. Honestly."

"Okay." Chev sat at the table while I put flour tortillas on a cookie sheet. I sliced chicken and arranged the pieces on the tortillas. She watched me as I worked. "How's your nose?"

"It feels better. I get the bandages off in a few days." I had checked my face in the mirror when I got up. Bruises circled my eyes in lovely shades of bluish purple fading to green and yellow, like an eye shadow palette from hell. At least they were open. My nose suspension bridge was still in place too.

I added vegetables to the chicken and some shredded jack cheese then topped it with another tortilla. After 20 minutes in a hot oven, I was ready to serve. I took two plates of chicken quesadilla and salad to the table. Chev set everything up while I poured us each a glass of seltzer water with a slice of lemon.

"Sorry, I'm on a health kick right now." I grinned. "Well, this is the first day."

Chev looked at me. "Do you mind if I ask you something?"

"What? Go ahead." I ate a fork full of chicken. It tasted good.

"Are you trying to loose weight?" Chev asked delicately.

I laughed. "You don't have to be so polite. I've gained about 15 pounds. I want to get back to a good weight and feel healthy, too." I paused. "This is probably the worst I've looked in my life."   Chev grinned. "Well, the nose scaffolding aside, I don't think you look that bad. You've just lost your identity as a woman. You thought of yourself just as a Mom and a Wife. Now you're back in the game and you don't know how to cope. So you fattened up. It's a good defense."

I was surprised. It was so honest and straightforward it caught me off guard. "You're right. I just want to get *me* back except I'm not sure what 'me' is."

Chev touched my arm. "You're not alone." She leaned back in her chair and resumed eating. "This is like the protein diet. You eat lean meat and you can have cheese and fruit and vegetables, just no starch. You know, white potatoes, rice, bread, and pasta. It gets the weight off fast and you have plenty of energy." She smiled. "It worked for me."

"You were heavier?" I couldn't imagine Chev dumpy and fat.

"Honey, I've gone through everything you're going through. I just did it a few years earlier." She looked down. "Right when I found out about the first affair." She sighed. "We'll talk about it one day. Let's just enjoy our dinner." She picked up her glass. "By the way, you can drink wine on the protein diet."

"Well that's the first good news I've had today." I said laughing. I felt warm and comforted somehow.

We were just finishing up, when there was a knock on the back door. It was Bertie and she had brought a friend.

Chadwick. A big white, seventy-pound, English Bulldog. He was her pride and joy.

"Chaddy." I welcomed him with a Ritz cracker or 'cookie' in dogese. He rolled it up into his mouth with a backward curl of his tongue and slid into home under the kitchen table after a small side detour to slobber a greeting on Chev's slacks. Once under the table, he spit out the cookie on the floor to snuffle at it. It passed his inspection because his tongue came back out and tagged the gooey cracker like a frog eating a fly. It was a fascinating process. He lay contentedly with his massive head flat on the floor. He'd be snoring in a few minutes.

Bertie beamed like a parent whose child has just done something adorable. "You look much better, dear." She said, diverting her attention to me. I got a pat on the shoulder and a kiss on the cheek, too. Bertie declined a helping of quesadilla. She'd already eaten. I did get compliments on my efforts to restock the larder. Bertie looked knowingly at Chev. "She's needed something to focus on."

"We all do," Chev said gallantly.

"Don't worry, Chev. I'm used to Bertie talking about me as if I'm not present."

"I just do it when I'm trying to make a point," Bertie said good-naturedly. She was usually right, too, but why encourage her? "Stella," she fixed me with her soft blue eyes, "I wondered if I could ask a favor?"

"Of course, you need me to watch Chadwick, don't you?"

"Yes, the girls and I are going up to New York for a few days and I hate to put him in a kennel."

"That's fine. He can stay here. He'll keep me company."

"Good. I've got food and his water dish in the car so you won't have to go to any special trouble."

Fifteen minutes later Chadwick's worldly possessions were in a corner of my kitchen and Bertie was on her way home to pack. She had kissed and fussed over both of us enough to warrant a much more extended trip than three days.

Chev bent down to rub one of Chaddy's ears. They stuck out on each side of his massive head like brown speckled flaps. "He's a nice dog, but he is so ugly."

"Don't let Bertie hear you say that. She thinks he's a beauty."

"Do you keep him often?" Chev was savoring, in her usual fashion, the coffee I'd just put down in front of her.

"No. Usually, he goes to a place called Pet's Vacationland. He loves it. He barks and carries on like a junkyard dog."

"So he likes the kennel," Chev grinned.

"Yep, I think Chadwick is on a mission here. I think he's supposed to protect me while Bertie's away."

Chadwick opened his big brown eyes and gave me a look of complete innocence.

"That's sweet."

"Yeah. Well, all he does is eat, sleep, and pass unholy farts." I bent down and scratched Chaddy's ears for him. "But I guess it is nice to have him here." I hadn't had a pet in years because Michael didn't like animals. Then I thought of Michael's lab. Suddenly I was all in.

Chev insisted on helping me with the dishes. When she got ready to go, I extended my hand. "Thanks for the business cards. Maybe I gave up on Ann Strayer, but Stella Jones won't let you down."

"I'm counting on that," she said, shaking my hand. It felt like an official handshake. We were on our way.

S. Alden Reilly

I watched her drive down the driveway then Chaddy and I, after he made a necessary trip outside, headed up to bed. The dog's gentle snoring was a soothing sound. Soon I was asleep, too.

THE PHOENIX

CHAPTER FIFTEEN

Georgetown had really changed in the last few years. The M street strip of shops that used to cater to old money and the taste that old money dictates were being eased out one by one by Tee shirt shops, Army Navy surplus, and punk accessory stores. Blame it on the university kids that flocked there from Georgetown University and George Washington University, not to mention the half dozen other colleges in the D.C. area. It was a nice mix of clientele. Blue haired ladies in navy blue sweater sets rubbing up against kids in giant, baggy pants with icons like Bob Marley smoking a joint across their chests.

The bar Cynthia Reeves worked in was a small hideaway off Wisconsin Avenue with old wood paneling, leaded glass windows, brass bar rails and the simple designation, 'Jeff's'.

I checked my reflection in the glass. Hair pulled back, my solution to the dire need for a hair cut. Make-up covering the bruises succeeded in toning them down to an olive green shade. Gray suit, white blouse, low heeled black pumps. If you ignored the bandages, I looked like a sixth grade teacher on her first day of school. Maybe someone would give me a big red apple.

Cynthia was in the back setting up clean glasses on an antique highboy that served as the waiter's station. She was slender, of medium height with that athletic look of pure good health that was probably due to daily aerobics or good genes. Her hair was short, spiky like a boys'. Its reddish cast reflected in the freckles across her nose and on her arms. She had intelligent hazel eyes.

"Cynthia, my name is Stella. . . ah, Jones." I almost tripped over my maiden name. I handed her one of my cards. "Could I ask you a few questions about when you worked for Brody, Borman, and Tate?"

Her first expression had been curiosity, my face I guess, then it darkened. "You mean the robbery don't you," she said defensively.

"I'm not interested in the robbery particularly." She was surprised at that. "I think it's pretty apparent it was a phony anyway."

She put her towel down and motioned me toward a booth in the back. It was dark, cool. The brick floor gave off a pleasantly musty odor as if regularly washed with beer.

When we were seated, she played with my card on the tabletop. Her fingernails were short, not bitten, but clipped close. "What do you want to know?"

I'd been thinking about how I was going to handle this. I'd picked Cynthia as my first interview; maybe I should say victim, because I'd talked to kids as part of my job for years. Hey, I had kids. I still didn't feel confident.

"How did you come to work for B.B.&T.?"

"It was a summer internship. I was studying law at Georgetown University."

"Past tense?"

"Yeah, I'm taking a break for awhile."

"How much have you got left to go?"

"One year." She looked at me like she expected a comment. I ignored the opportunity to counsel. It wasn't easy, but this time it wasn't my job and I didn't want her to tune me out.

"What were your duties at the firm?"

"Filing, typing, helping Mona, research, whatever they needed me to do." She fidgeted with my card using the corner of it to dig under her fingernail. I looked away.

"Did you get to know any of the big cases they were handling?"

She shrugged. "Yeah. I was allowed to sit in on their conferences on some of them. Go to court, but as an observer. I wasn't allowed to do anything except research for them."

"What happened with the Deseeca Case?"

"Files were missing. Evidence was missing. No one directly blamed me, but I knew I was the one they suspected. Suddenly I was getting the cold shoulder from everyone. I resigned. It was easier."

"Why did they suspect you?"

"My fingerprints were on the files." She looked down at her hands as if examining the tell tale whorls herself.

"There are lot's of explanations for that." I said.

"No. Really, I should never have handled them. They were in a locked file in Mona's office for evidence and important cases. At the time I couldn't think of how it could have happened." She looked up again, but her gaze was inward remembering. "One day I came in and someone had put a whole stack of files on my desk. I took them into Mona's office to see what I was supposed to do with them."

"What happened?"

"She told me just to put them on Mr. Brody's desk. Later she came out to see me. She acted upset. She said that they should never have been left on my desk, but not to worry about it." She looked directly at me. "At the time I didn't think anything about it. They were bundled together with rubber bands. I didn't see any names or anything but I did handle them."

"Just the one on the bottom and the one on the top of the pile?"

"Well, yes," she said thoughtfully. "I had to pick them up. Then, later, I got a receipt from the bank for a ten thousand dollar deposit I didn't make." She sounded discouraged. "I never touched the money and I don't know where it came from."

I thought for a moment. "How did you like working there?"

Cynthia ran her hand through her hair. "It was okay. Everyone was pretty nice except Mona." She shrugged. "She was cool at first, but then she warmed up."

"How about Mr. Brody?"

I never really saw that much of him."

"Must have been a busy time for him."

"Yes," she flipped my card back and forth in her hand. "But he was there. He just seemed to avoid me."

"Really?" That was a surprise. Franklin Brody was the type of man who liked to flirt. It used to burn me up when he'd pull that on Layne out in public. Usually the younger the girl, the better. I couldn't see him passing up the chance to make a play for a cute kid like Cynthia. "You must have built in jerk repellent."

She laughed. She really was a beautiful girl.

"What does your Mom think about this?" I gestured at our surroundings.

"Not much. She's been really bitter about everything. She kept saying that I should confront Mr. Brody about the rumors at the firm, that he owed it to me."

"She's right. You should have had an explanation."

Cynthia placed my card flat on the table and folded her hands over it. "I think she meant more. More than just an explanation. Anyway, she was pretty obsessed about the whole thing until the other night."

"The night of the explosion?" It was just a guess.

"Yeah, she's better now."

I patted her hand.

"Don't worry. A lot of people felt better after the other night. It doesn't mean your Mom's losing it."

"You sound like my friend Suzanne." She said surprised at my knowledge of twentieth century speech.

Well, I was young at heart. "Call me if you need anything."

I looked at my dog-eared card as she twisted it in her hand. I wondered if I should have the next batch laminated.

CHAPTER SIXTEEN

I checked in with Chev from a pay phone on M Street. "Stella Jones here."

"What are you doing, practicing your name?"

"You got it."

"How'd it go with Cynthia?"

"Okay, if you don't count cardboard mutilation."

"I don't think I want to know what that means."

I laughed. "Actually, it wasn't as hard as I thought it would be, but I've still got the mother. You know, I was wondering…"

"Wondering what?"

"Why Union Station? Why did the woman call from Union Station?"

Chev paused. "I don't know it's a busy place. Maybe she didn't think anyone would notice her there."

"Yeah, but there are lots of busy places. Maybe she had business there or came in on a train from somewhere. It might be worth checking out."

"You're right. I'll call the officer who investigated the scene."

"Well, I'm off to see Mrs. Reeves." I heard a clicking sound.

"Hey, go for it. I've got another call."

"Okay, I'll call you later." I hung up and headed for my car. I'd left it at a meter. You get twenty minutes for twenty-five cents in D.C. That gives the public plenty of tickets and the district government plenty of revenue.

I was still legal so I got in and sat for a minute reviewing my notes on Mrs. Reeves. Chev and I had decided to include her on the list. After what had happened to her kid, she had plenty of motive. She lived up off Connecticut Avenue near the National Zoo. I stuck the file in my briefcase and pulled away from the curb.

Emma Reeves lived in the Prescott. It was one of those graceful old apartment buildings that were built almost a century ago and still maintained an affluent charm. You always see little gray haired ladies walking adorably dressed Scotties or Yorkies out front.

I entered an ornate lobby with Persian carpeted marble floors. Gilded cherubs hugged each other over columns of serpentine green marble. The Windsors had probably kept an apartment here for state visits.

The doorman was a small East Indian man resplendent in a uniform heavy with gold braid. He rang Mrs. Reeves then walked me to an elevator that he opened with a key. Inside he selected the floor button.

"Apartment 726," he said in a cultured voice.

I felt the schoolteacher get up had proven a plus in this case. I probably looked like an accountant making house calls. The elevator doors opened soundlessly on seven. The plush hallway carpet muffled all sound. No cooking smells or the din of whining children here. It was eerie, like being in a sensory deprivation experiment.

Emma Reeves answered the door almost immediately. She was a small woman about forty-five with a pretty, heart shaped face and dark hair that she wore gamin style close to her head. She had arresting eyes. Arresting because they were large and blue green in color. It was natural with her. Not a pair of those phony looking contact lenses. She wore a teal colored silk blouse with a Mandarin collar. Delicate silver butterfly earrings swung from her dainty ears. Her hands were small, nails perfect. All in all, one of those women that makes you feel like an oversized, graceless lump. I looked down at my own hands. I hoped I had gotten all the paint scum out from under my fingernails.

I introduced myself and handed her one of my cards. She gestured for me to come into her living room. It was beautifully done, like its owner, in a mixed motif of Oriental and Art Nouveau design. The predominant color scheme was blue green.

"Thanks for letting me come by on such short notice." I extended my hand to her. She gave it a weak little two-fingered squeeze eyeing my nose with curiosity. "I just wanted to ask you a few questions about the incident with Cynthia at Brody, Borman, and Tate."

A pained look crossed her face like a reaction to a stab wound. She recovered quickly. As we sat on identical Chinese Chippendale chairs upholstered in teal brocade, she asked, "Could you tell me why you're interested in that information?" She tapped my card on each side in succession on the small ebony table at her side. Maybe cards are a bad idea. I watched her fiddle with the little piece of cardboard. Odd, too, how some mannerisms seem almost inherited.

"My client is interested in the matter solely to see that justice is done. My client believes that the robbery was deliberately set up. That Cynthia was also a victim." I couldn't tell her that I was representing my dead husband and a murdered private detective.

She considered this for a few minutes, and then apparently she came to a decision because she leaned forward just slightly. "I considered hiring someone myself. Cynthia was devastated." She dropped my card on the table and clenched her small hands. "You know she dropped out of law school." It was a statement not a question. "But, I was afraid it would only make matters worse."

"You thought there might be repercussions if you tried to clear Cynthia's name, from the firm?"

"Possibly." She was evasive. Was it fear of Brody, Borman, and Tate or the clients?

"What are you afraid of, Mrs. Reeves?" I realized I had lowered my voice as if I might be overheard.

She flinched at the question then a small pink dot burned in each cheek. "I'm afraid of ruining my daughter's life." She stated, almost in a whisper. "I may have already done so."

I took a flyer. "Did you help get Cynthia her job at Brody's firm?"

The pink dots got bigger. "How did you know?" She wasn't really asking me, though. "I thought it would be a good experience for her. I had a friend there." She looked down at her hands. "I thought I was helping her."

"I know," I said, letting my eyes drift upward to the ornate ceiling. Clusters of plaster grapes decorated the cornices. Someone had thoughtfully painted them a bluish green. Our voices were muffled in the high-ceilinged, airless room. Emma Reeves was like a doll you kept in a fancy box. A doll for collecting. Not one you played with.

"Who was the friend?"

Her eyes fell to her lap. "I'd rather not say." She turned a ring on her left hand. It was an antique onyx in an elaborate setting.

"Did you send a retainer to Nikki Fortuna to continue the investigation of the robbery? To clear Cynthia's name?"

S. Alden Reilly

Emma's hands fluttered like the butterflies she wore on her ears. Her eyes darted to a crystal clock on the little table.

"I have another appointment so you'll have to leave soon." It was a dismissal and a confirmation. I could have pushed and probably gotten more, but on the whole I felt that my second interview had gone better than the first. I mentally squared my detective shoulders and followed Emma Reeves to the door.

She paused as she opened the door and took my hand, this time with all her fingers. "If you do find anything that will help Cynthia, please let me know. She's all I have." Her small hand trembled slightly in mine. "I want her to have a good life."

I had an overwhelming sense of pain and loneliness or maybe isolation. "Don't worry. We'll get to the bottom of this," I said, wanting to comfort her. Once on the other side of the door I breathed in deeply, filling my puffy nose with some real air while expelling the preservative atmosphere of the Reeves apartment.

I drove up Connecticut Avenue crossing over to Wisconsin Avenue at Abelmarle Street looking for a phone booth to call Chev. I found one outside a Steak and Egg kitchen. Several men were loitering around the doorway. None of them looked very upstanding.

Chev answered, "Fortuna Investigation. How may I help you?"

"You can find out who pays the rent on Mrs. Reeves' apartment."

"Hey, how are you doing?" Chev's voice tinkled into the phone.

"Well, I found out that Mrs. Reeves has a friend at B.B.&T. That's how Cynthia got her job."

"Very interesting. Did she say who this pal was?"

"No. But it's somebody she thought would watch out for Cynthia. My guess is a man. Emma Reeves doesn't look like the type to have close women friends."

"What's she like?"

"I'll tell you later. I'm going to Mona's now."

"Okay. Want to get a pizza later and go over what you need me to do?"

"Sure" I said and hung up. It was nice to have a purpose in life again.

S. Alden Reilly

CHAPTER SEVENTEEN

Mona Freeman lived up by Washington National Cathedral off of Wisconsin Avenue. I like to think of myself as an intelligent woman, but the black wrought iron gate that you had to enter to get to her front door confounded me completely. The house was an elegant brick colonial with black shutters and a two-car garage with one of the doors open. I finally gave up trying to open the gate and walked around the fence to the garage. A large box from Spiegel was just inside the door next to a black Saab Turbo convertible. The top was closed.

I walked inside. Ivy had grown over the windows on the outside so the light was bad. The space held typical garage stuff, clippers, rakes and tools that hung on the walls. I walked over to the door that led into the house and knocked. No answer. I knocked again.

"Ms. Freeman?"

No answer. I turned the knob and opened the door. Was I breaking and entering? That thought and the thought that an angry Mona Freeman might be on the other side should have made me close it again. It didn't. The door opened into a hallway with steps to go up or down. I called out her name again. There was still no answer, so I went up. The first floor landing led into the living room, dining room, and kitchen. No Mona. I headed up again.

THE PHOENIX

Mona Freeman's bedroom was a feminine fantasy. Big patterned material with red roses, pink peonies, and other large flowers covered everything. Windows, furniture, bedspreads, valances with loose cascades draped across the canopy bed. No unsightly laundry piled on the floor or make-up strewn around. This was the bedroom of a woman who expected company. I glanced quickly around the room. A picture on the mantel of the fireplace caught my eye.

It was Franklin Brody, his arm affectionately draped around the shoulder of a woman I assumed must be Mona Freeman. It was not a candid from the office party. They were dressed in resort wear. Franklin was tanned, his hair tousled. They seemed to be leaning against the railing of a ship. Mona was curved up next to his body, her black hair blowing, her striking features animated with the first flush of love.

I lifted the picture and turned it over. It was easy to slide the photo out from under the cardboard backing. 'Carnival Cruise Lines' and 'June 1994' were stamped on the back. I slipped it back into the frame and returned it to the mantel.

The Mona Freeman in the picture was a beautiful brunette in her thirties with light green eyes and a body like a Hollywood starlet. How did Franklin Brody rate the women in his life? The overweening peacock didn't deserve the love of any woman, but it wasn't nice to speak ill of the dead.

I went from the fireplace to the bedside tables. More pictures here. Mona arm in arm with a tall, dark-haired man. At first I thought 'boyfriend' but something in the likeness between them made me think it might be a brother. He was a nice looking guy a few years older than Mona. A younger Mona standing between an older couple with an arm around each of them. I guessed her parents. She looked a great deal like her mother.

S. Alden Reilly

I opened a drawer. Nothing much. Just a squeezed down tube of KY jelly. I wondered how many of those she'd gone through. I'd had one tube my entire married life. Was there a point there?

A search of her drawers was revealing. Everything in order. Even her underwear was organized in neat stacks according to color. No panties with the days of the week embroidered on them, but I sensed they'd been in her past. My underwear drawer is organized, too. I throw the panties with the holes in them on the left and the stuff I want to be wearing in the event of an accident on the right.

I left the bedroom and made a swift circuit of the house. Here I was, a nice mother of two grown girls, a representative of a respected college, and heretofore-upstanding citizen prowling around in someone else's house with absolute brazenness. I don't know. I just couldn't seem to stop myself. I was starting to feel stretched. Like any minute, a person who was supposed to be in the house would walk in and discover me. That's why I hurried. That's why I almost missed it.

Everything was neat. Neat as a pin. Except the kitchen. The latest trend is for a white or black kitchen these days. Mona had chosen white with the industrial look for her appliances. The whole thing looked like the autopsy room down at the morgue.

The only mess was right here in the kitchen. Chopped vegetables. They lay in neat piles on the granite counter top. Only the broccoli was limp, the carrots dry and the mushrooms were turning brown. I felt an uneasy sensation in the pit of my stomach.

I started for the garage and remembered the pictures I'd handled upstairs. I ran up, wiped the frames and glass with a slightly used Kleenex from my purse, and ran back downstairs.

THE PHOENIX

I gently pulled the door shut with my Kleenex again. Why would a meticulous person like Mona Freeman leave her dinner wilting on a kitchen counter? She would have put everything away in individually labeled Tupperware if the rest of her house were any indication.

I glanced around the garage wondering if the neighbors had noticed me come in. Here, too, order was evident. All the tools on the pegboard were outlined in paint. A visual guide to organization. I looked for any discrepancies. Something was missing. A flat wedge shaped thing. At least that's what the outline looked like.

I glanced over at the car. The Saab had dark tinted windows. A garden hose was twisted in an untidy heap under the rear bumper. As I got closer I could see that one end of it was taped to the tailpipe.

Bile rose in my throat. I took a deep breath forcing the bitterness back down. It was cold in the garage. I looked out at the driveway to the sunshine and wondered if I should just walk back out there. I could be wrong. Probably was.

I walked over to the car and tried the door. It was locked. The windows were so dark in the already dark light of the garage that I couldn't see anything. I fished inside my purse and found my little flashlight. A high intensity, mini flashlight I bought from the impulse racks while standing on a long line in Kmart. I flashed it through the drive's side door and nearly fell over my own feet trying to jump back.

Mona was looking at me. She'd been watching my antics the whole time with her beautiful sightless green eyes. Her face was a hideous shade of red, her mouth opened as if to scream, and her hand curled like a claw against the glass.

I ran out of the garage and threw up all over a section of the wrought iron fence. By the time I got to the neighbor's house, my hair was plastered to my head. Clammy sweat rolled down my back.

The maid who answered the door took one look at me and, being a Christian woman, overcame her urge to shut it in my face.

"Call the police, there's been an accident next door at Ms. Freeman's house." I sat down on the steps and held my briefcase and purse to my chest like someone might try to snatch them away from me.

The maid reappeared and handed me a glass of water. She was a sweet-faced Hispanic woman in her sixties

"Thank you," I said gratefully.

"Would you like to come in and sit down?" She asked kindly. I was going to refuse. I craved sunshine right now, but I thought of Chev.

"Could I just call my office, please, to let them know where I am?"

"Sure, Senora." She led me into the kitchen where I was able to use the wall phone.

"Fortuna Investigations," Chev answered brightly.

"Chev. I've got a little problem here."

"What's wrong? You sound funny." Her tone changed to concern.

"Well, I'm afraid Mona Freeman is dead."

"Gawd!" she said. "You found her?"

"Yeah."

"Did you call the police?"

"Yes. I'm at a neighbor's house." I put my hand over the mouthpiece. "What's your name?" I whispered to the maid.

"Mrs. Peralta."

I shook her hand and spoke into the telephone. "Chev, Mrs. Peralta has called the police. What should I do?"

"Well, usually it's a good idea not to get in too deep. An anonymous call from a phone booth is less messy. Now you're going to have to answer some questions."

"Well, I thought about that, but I threw up on the fence."

"Hell, honey, they can't trace that." Chev started laughing.

I guess she was right. My DNA wasn't on file anywhere that I knew of. It made me smile, too. "Okay, I'm going to wait here for the police. I'll come by later."

"No, just go on home. I'll stop by tonight and we can talk then." She started to hang up then said, "I'll bring dinner. Your just rest until I get there."

"Okay." I paused. "Uh Chev, just don't bring Chinese."

She snorted and hung up.

S. Alden Reilly

CHAPTER EIGHTEEN

The police arrived in another twenty minutes. It seemed a little slow to me. I knew Mona was past caring, but I'd said 'accident'. The first policemen parked in the driveway and came over to where Mrs. Peralta and I stood at the edge of the neighbor's porch. When I told them what I'd found, they headed for the garage in a trot. A few minutes passed then one of the officers, the fair-haired one, came out and added his lunch to mine on the fence. They'd probably have to repaint that whole section.

Two hours later the place was swarming with police. The medical examiner's wagon was there and a hearse was pulled in behind him. A young officer finally came over to where I sat on the neighbor's steps and asked me a few questions. I'd had time to think about my answers.

"Ma'am, could you tell me why you came to see Ms. Freeman today?" He was tall, thin, with very short dark hair and kind eyes.

"I came to ask her help," I said earnestly.

"Help for what?" I could tell this had caught him off guard.

"I hoped she'd be able to help me understand some of my husband's notes." I looked down. "He was killed about six months ago."

"What sort of notes?" He asked politely. Maybe he'd begin to lose interest if I faded from a possible suspect to a 'widow woman' with a mission.

"Notes concerning some work he did for Ms. Freeman's employer. I'm trying to make sure my husband's accounts are settled." I looked down at my rumpled skirt. "May I go now?" My eyes were probably circled in green again.

"Of course, let me just ask you one more thing." He said kindly. "What did you notice when you entered the garage?"

I thought a minute. "Well, when I couldn't get the gate open, I noticed the garage door was open so I went in. There was a package from Spiegel right inside the door."

"Why did you look inside the car?" It was a new voice, but one I recognized...Detective Harrison. He had walked up behind so I hadn't noticed him. His tone and demeanor were totally neutral. I couldn't decide how to react.

"When I couldn't get her to answer, I wondered if she had gone out. But then I decided she wouldn't have left her garage door open." I looked into his world-weary eyes, portraying as much nervous innocence as I could muster. "So I looked at the car. That's when I saw the hose taped to the tail pipe." I looked down at my hands. "When I saw·that I decided I'd better check the car. I tried the door. It was locked. I had a flashlight. That made it easier." I thought about her poor face and felt the bile rise up in my throat again. I was sure my whole complexion had turned green.

Harrison looked at me then at the younger man. He shoved his hands into the pants pockets of his dark gray suit and eyed my face. "Well, thank you, Mrs. Strayer. Why don't you go home? We'll call if we have any more questions." I got a feeling he wanted to say something else but not in front of his subordinate. The fear of nausea is powerful in all of us. The younger policeman seemed relieved.

I was grateful and stood up to go to my car. "What was in the box from Spiegel?"

Harrison looked at the officer. "Curtains," he said at a nod from his superior.

I walked to my car and climbed in. I was about to start the engine when Harrison walked up to my driver side window. "Are you well enough to drive home?"

I smiled although my stomach was still doing the cha-cha. "Honestly, I can't get the sight of her face out of my mind. I feel like I'm going to be sick." I gestured at the fence. "I've already done it once over there. I guess I will get hardened to this."

"I hope you never do." Then he gestured at his army of people crawling over the crime scene. "I could have one of my people drive you home." He looked into my eyes. "You're pushing yourself too hard, Mrs. Strayer."

I couldn't think of an answer. Unfocused, I looked into Harrison's eyes. I wondered what horrors they had witnessed. But the kindness I saw in them made me realize that he sincerely wished to spare me the experience. "I have to do something," was all I could come up with.

He leaned against the window for a moment, resting his hands on the doorframe. "Okay, go home, but please be careful." Then he walked away.

THE PHOENIX

CHAPTER NINETEEN

I drove home on automatic pilot. When I pulled into the driveway, I couldn't remember anything about the actual drive. My silk blouse stuck to me like a second skin. My suit smelled faintly of barf. Chadwick ambled out from the kitchen, his big jowly cheeks smiling.

"Chaddy." I gave him a big hug. It was nice to bury my face in his furry neck. Here was something clean and sweet and real. "Do you have to go outside?" I let him out the back door. Chadwick never wandered out of the yard, but he would be busy for a little while.

I checked my face in the bathroom mirror. I looked hideous. The greenish yellow bruising was moving down my face. Now my cheeks looked discolored and puffy. My eyes looked slightly better. When I got out of the shower, I blow dried my hair and twisted it into a knot on top of my head. I pulled on a clean sweatshirt and matching sweat pants in faded pink, slipped into my moccasin house slippers, and headed downstairs to the kitchen. Chaddy was sitting on the back porch leaning against the door. "Come on in, boy. I'll fix you some dinner."

Chev pulled up in the driveway while I was opening the Alpo-lite. She was dressed for jogging in some sleek shiny black number. Her hair was in a long braid down her back.

"The dog is on a diet?" She noticed the can on the counter.

"Yeah. Don't you think he needs to be?"

"You're right. No pizza for you, Mr. Chadwick."

She laid two large pizza boxes on the table. "Don't worry. You can have a few carbs every now and then."

Chadwick gave us both a scornful look and went back to inhaling his food. A few hours earlier the thought of eating would have been enough to send me to the nearest fence, but now I was famished. We polished off one pizza and were two pieces into the other one before we pushed ourselves away from the table.

I was developing a sincere appreciation for Chev Fortuna. She hadn't asked me one question about Mona Freeman. She just waited until I was ready to talk about it.

"You want me to go first?" I said.

"Sure." She pulled a legal pad out of her purse and got ready to take notes.

"Okay." I filled her in on Cynthia Reeves and her mother, Emma Reeves. I told her my theory that Emma may have been Nikki's anonymous client.

Chev looked thoughtful on that one. "If it was my kid, I wouldn't stop until I knew the truth."

"Me neither. To send the retainer anonymously would be a way to help her daughter without risking exposure."

Chev nodded, waiting. I took a deep breath and started in on Mona Freeman. It was funny how relaying the day's events made me see some things more clearly. "You know what bothers me?" I didn't wait for Chev to answer. "It was too messy. It wasn't her style." Chev just looked at me, silently. "She'd take some pills, put on her best nightie, and lay on top of her comforter like a romantic heroine in a novel."

"So you think she was murdered?"

"Yes. Harrison will probably call it suicide. Am I a nut or something because I see murderous intent everywhere? And another thing wasn't right. The hose was all tangled and bunched up under the car. Mona would have coiled it neatly and then taped it." I picked at a piece of pizza crust. "There's also that box. How did it get in her garage?"

Chev put her pen down. She folded her arms behind her neck and leaned back in her chair. "What are the options?"

"She was murdered because she knew about the robbery at the firm. Everyone that's died so far has had that robbery as the common thread. Maybe the Parnelli's wanted to clean up the mess that Franklin made."

"I can see that," Chev said. "What about the box?"

"Options." I ticked them off on my fingers. "One, she opened the door for a delivery man then forgot to shut it when she decided to commit suicide. Yeah, right," I said scornfully.

Chev laughed. "Hey. Just throw them out there. Something will stick."

"Okay. Two, the delivery man came after the fact, got the door open somehow and left the box."

"More promising, but how'd he get the door open?"

"A neighbor maybe. It has an opener. Maybe she gave one to a neighbor or even the driver. No, she wouldn't give it to the driver. You wouldn't want a stranger to have access to your house." I leaned forward, my elbows on the table. I thought for a minute. "Hey, maybe the murderer brought the box with him or her to the house..."

"And masqueraded as a delivery man." Chev finished my sentence excitedly. "That could be how he got in. She let him in through the garage."

I thought for a few minutes. "Harrison said there were curtains in the box." I shook my head. "But she had curtains in every room. The whole place was 'house beautiful' like she'd just redecorated. I wish I'd looked in the box."

Chev drew a doodle on her pad. "I'll get a copy of the police report. They might have a description." She flipped back a few pages. "You want to hear what I dug up today?"

I suddenly realized that she was excited about something. What a great observer of people I was turning out to be. "Go ahead."

"Guess who paid the rent on Emma Reeves apartment?"

"Paid, as in past tense?" I felt a pricking of the hair on my neck.

Chev nodded. "Definitely past tense unless Franklin Brody set up a trust fund for her before he died."

"Wow! No wonder she's frightened. She went up against Franklin to reopen the investigation. And look what happened to him." I reached over and grabbed another piece of pizza looked at it hard and put it back. "How'd you find that out?"

"Research." She smiled. "I called a friend down at the courthouse. The apartment is owned by F. Brody. A little more digging with the property manager and I discovered that Emma was living there rent-free. Who wasn't he screwing,Stella?"

I thought of Mona in the picture, curved into his side, happy, in love. "His wife, unless you count the dissolution of their assets."

"You're right. That skunk screwed everybody. Blowing up was too good for him." Chev banged the table with her hand.

"My sentiments exactly." I was getting a mental picture of what might have been a better punishment when the phone rang. It was Layne. "Hi, how are you feeling?" I asked, mouthing her name to Chev.

"Much better. I just have this nagging headache." Layne's voice sounded good. Stronger, more determined. "I've got some news for you."

"Shoot," I said.

"You've got an appointment with John Borman tomorrow at three o'clock. And John's asked for Deseeca and the Parnellis to see you in the morning."

"You are so efficient." I could hardly believe that Layne had accomplished so much in one day.

"No problem. John is being really nice. Is Chev there? Tell her I said 'Hi'. I'll come over tomorrow if I'm feeling better."

"Okay, thanks, Layne." We hung up and I filled Chev in.

"She didn't even ask you about Mona."

"I know. Layne doesn't read the papers or watch the news. She'll hear about it eventually. Then she'll call all excited and want to know why I didn't tell her."

Chev went to her enormous purse and pulled out a file. "Stella, this is something I picked up today. Do you think you want to take a look at it?"

She handed me a fistful of papers. I could see the Medical Examiner's office on one letterhead. It was the accident report on Michael with the M.E.'s report on Michael and Nikki.

"Yes," I said, mentally shrinking from the task. "I'll go over them."

"Good." She pulled one more file from the purse.

"Here's the diet I used in case you want to follow it. You'll see the pizza wasn't really that bad."

She placed my new eating regime on the counter then lifted the purse in a graceful arc and settled it on her shoulder. "Call me tomorrow." She said.

"I will."

She reached out and gave my arm a squeeze as she said goodbye. "Sorry you had to have the 'discover the dead body' experience on your first day."

"Hey, I guess it's like an initiation to 'detective hood'. I'm official now."

I shut the door behind her and watched her drive away, then quickly straightened up the kitchen. Part of me was anxious to look at the report, but the other part dreaded it. I let Chaddy out for one last comfort run. Then we locked up and headed upstairs to my bedroom.

CHAPTER TWENTY

When I was comfortable, I turned on my reading light and opened the accident report. It was pretty straightforward stuff. Like taking a knife and twisting it in your heart. There was a list of the official terms for the injuries, which devastated, then killed my husband. I forced myself to reread it three times pretending it was some other human being, not the moody, introverted, semi-genius I'd been married to for twenty-one years.

A lot of the information on the accident report I already knew. It appeared the driver of the pickup truck had been speeding. When he ran the stop sign and struck Michael's station wagon, he never even braked. Two days later, the truck was found abandoned five miles from the accident site.

Tears that I'd held back for six months started sliding down my face. Michael and I had been friends. Married too young, we'd eased ourselves into a relationship that was companionable, yet distant. He had his lab and I had my study. We had good times, bad times, and two great kids. The pain came from knowing we didn't really love each other, have passion for each other. I think that we both felt we'd missed something. It caused a void that made our emotional life empty, unfulfilled. I was sad that he was gone because he would never find the one person who was meant for him, but I looked forward to the prospect of a new life and a chance to find the passion that I'd been missing at the same time. This was a source of tremendous guilt.

I couldn't read anymore. I put the reports together and slid them under the bed. Something inside of me didn't want to think about what might have been. Didn't want to feel guilty. What I needed was to get on with my life, fill the void. Suddenly I realized that I was excited about what my new life could become. I got out the diet Chev had given me. I started to read the menus, but got lost in a daydream of slimness. Me, svelte in a black satin evening gown. Me, skinny and sexy in a small black string bikini. It was a pleasant daydream. When I turned off the light, I shut my mind off, too. In a few moments I was asleep.

THE PHOENIX

CHAPTER TWENTY ONE

I was locked in a car. All the electric power was off. I couldn't breathe. I wanted to get out, but all I could do was honk the horn. It didn't work. It just made a huromph, huromph sound.

I opened my eyes. Chadwick was facing the bedroom door. The hair on the back of his neck all the way to his tail was sticking straight up.

"Huromph, huromph." That was the way Chaddy barked. It came from deep in his throat, a cross between a bark and a cough.

"What is it, boy?" The hair was beginning to stand up on the top of my head, too.

He cast a look back at me that was chauvinistic in the extreme. It said 'he'd take care of it if I'd just open the damn door.'

I walked to the door and opened it a crack staying partially behind it in case someone was just waiting to fall in. Chadwick didn't crowd the door. He just waited until it was wide open then took off like a shot with a furious scraping of toenails on the hardwood floor.

I followed him down the stairs and caught a glimpse of him as he tore around the corner into the living room. There was a commotion of crashing, louder barks, muffled curses, then the sound of glass breaking.

When I got to the living room, Chadwick was at the window that faced the driveway, his big paws braced on the windowsill, barking his head off. Chadwick wasn't stupid. Shards of glass stuck up from the bottom and hung down from the top of the window casing. My intruder hadn't been as smart. Blood stained some of the shards at the bottom.

"Good boy." I patted his massive pumpkin head.

From down at the end of the driveway, I could see taillights and hear the roar of a vehicle pulling out. As soon as he was sure the unwelcome guest was gone, Chadwick jumped down and came to my side.

"Let's go get a cookie," was all I could think of to say. My hand shook as I handed Chaddy his Ritz crackers. I gave him about half a roll. Then I called the police.

I live in a small town. We share a sheriff with the entire county. Still, five minutes later, Sheriff Bartley and his two deputies were going over my living room. It truly looked under construction now. The robber had knocked over a scaffold that subsequently fell against one of the casement windows breaking out the glass. My visitor had followed the ladder through the window.

Chadwick, the hero of the house, and I were sitting in the kitchen. The men were fascinated by Chaddy. He accepted the adulation with the appropriate grace. He lay flat on his stomach under the kitchen table. He was snoring but occasionally he'd open one eye just to let us know that he was still on guard.

There was a knock at the back door and Sheriff Bartley escorted Chev into the room. I'd called her right after the sheriff. She came to me and gave me a hug. I patted her on the back.

"I'm okay. Chaddy took care of him."

Chev let go of me and sat down in the chair next to me. She took two coffees out of a 7-11 bag and handed me one. I took a sip. It was just what I needed. Some people would see her toughness and off hand manner and think they had her pegged. But Chev was one of those real salt of the earth types that hide a generous heart, tremendous guts and intelligence behind a to-hell-with-it-all façade.

"God, Stella, we've really stirred up something. Maybe we should quit before you get hurt."

Hearing her voice my own fears made me able to get rid of them. "No way. It's just getting interesting. We must be doing something right. Besides I've already had one break in. Right after Michael died."

Chev looked at me. "What did they get that time?"

"Nothing, they just trashed the place." I shrugged my shoulders. "That's when I started my renovations."

"Oh. So that's what you call it." She laughed.

"I like white," I said indignantly. "Anyway, I think Michael's lab was checked out, too. At first I thought I just didn't lock the door. That's why I jumped when you came up to me the other day."

"What do they want?" Chev asked.

I thought I knew. "Michael's notes." I explained how I'd put them in his car's trunk until I could give them to the new ME. "There's something important in them. I just don't know what it is yet."

"I bet you're right. Where are they now?"

"Under my bed. I pushed them under there the last time I read them."

"So what do you want to do next? They might try again."

I reached down and scratched Chaddy's ear. "Keep the dog a few more days and try to find out the truth."

Chev took a last drag on her coffee, savoring the brew in her usual manner. "I'm with you," was all she said.

CHAPTER TWENTY TWO

Then next morning I called a painting contractor and a window company. They both promised to come before noon. The sheriff and his boys had been kind enough to nail a piece of Masonite over the broken window, or I wouldn't have slept a wink. I put a pot of coffee on while Chadwick did his business outside. I was perusing the protein diet and had just realized that I could not eat French Fries anymore when the coffee aroma brought Chev downstairs in a matter of minutes.

Chev had insisted on spending the night in my guestroom. I was glad she stayed. Stress usually makes me sleepless, but last night had been an exception. I had put all the questions out of my mind and slept like a baby. I poured two cups of coffee and we sat down.

"What's the plan for today?" Chev asked. "Because I can reschedule your appointment with Deseeca and the Parnellis if you're not up to it after last night."

"Are you kidding? I feel like my head is finally starting to clear."

"Well, then, you'd better get going because you've got a ten-thirty and a one-thirty before you see Borman at three."

I took my coffee upstairs and got in the shower. I was back downstairs in thirty-five minutes. Clothing had been a problem. My school marm suit needed to go to the cleaners. I'd pulled out an elegant black number that I hadn't worn in months. I must have already lost a little weight because I could actually get into it, but the skirt made me look like a bunch of grapefruits in a net bag. So I dug deeper and found an off white model from a university tea ten years ago. Snug, but decent; I would look like some retro ice cream vendor with Ann Klein accessories.

"Layne called," Chev said when I came back into the kitchen. "She wanted to know why you didn't tell her about Mona." Chev grinned. "She said she'd be over tonight."

"Fine. What do you think?" I gestured at my outfit.

She studied me a moment. "I think you should hit the mall tomorrow."

"Yeah," I said, "you're right." I needed an update. My wardrobe was from another life, another career.

"Would it be all right if I worked from here today? I can have my calls forwarded." Chev asked her hands cupped around a mug of coffee. "I thought I could get the contractors in." She handed me a sheet of addresses.

"God. I forgot all about that." I grabbed up my purse and briefcase. "Thanks, Chev." It was nice to have a partner. "I'll call you later."

CHAPTER TWENTY THREE

Anthony Francis Desecca had a very plush penthouse office in the heart of Bethesda. His secretary eyed my suit, barely able to control the sneer on her face.

"Matches the bandages," I said, putting on my most beautiful smile.

She gave me a haughty look and tossed her head. It was a wasted motion. She had so much gel on her black hair it wouldn't move. Twenty minutes after our appointment time, he buzzed her and she motioned me in.

When I opened the double doors to his office, Tony Deseeca rose and came around his desk to greet me. He was a tall man in his late forties, thin, dark, and handsome in a brooding way. He clasped my hand in a firm handshake.

"Ms. Jones, what can I do for you?"

"I appreciate you seeing me on such short notice, Mr. Deseeca. I am looking into the break-in at Brody, Borman, and Tate for my client."

"Who's your client?" He said suspiciously as I took a seat in front of his desk. He returned to his own seat, a luxurious blood red leather swivel chair that fit in perfectly with the English country house décor.

"Ordinarily that would be confidential, but my client is dead. He was my husband." I said simply.

That got his attention. "I'm sorry to hear that. What did your husband have to do with the break in?"

"He investigated it along with another man. Now they're both dead and Franklin Brody was just killed in an explosion. I don't believe in coincidence."

Deseeca sat back in his chair and made a tent with his fingers. "What are you suggesting?"

"That you answer a few questions for me. That's all."

"If your question is, did I have anything to do with any of it? The answer is no."

"Actually, that was my third question."

He laughed and his face relaxed into more attractive lines. "Okay, I'll bite, Ms. Jones. What are questions one and two?" He leaned back against the soft leather and waited.

"Franklin Brody was your attorney." He nodded in agreement. "And it would seem that your case was the catalyst for the robbery. What was the evidence that was lost in the burglary?"

Deseeca looked at me like I was green. Come to think of it he looked a little green himself. "Contracts. Documents. Inspection reports."

I waited. Silence makes most people uncomfortable in conversations and they feel compelled break it. I needed him to talk. I really didn't know what question number two was going to be yet.

"To be more specific, I had proof that my building on N.W. fourteenth Street in Washington D.C. was scammed. I hired the Parnellis as contractors. We broke ground about six years ago. It was supposed to be completed in two years, but the Parnellis cut deals with their subcontractors to do substandard work. That building isn't up to code on any level. It's cost me millions to put it right."

"But the inspectors?" He made a face like 'who are you kidding lady'? "Okay, so I won't lease an office there."

He smiled. "Oh, you could lease an office there now. I had to tear out most of it and rebuild, but it's safe."

I sensed that he had opened up a little. I worked to see if I could get anymore. "Did you have any way to reconstruct the evidence that was stolen?"

"No. It cost a man his life to get it in the first place." He frowned.

"And three more since it disappeared," I said, almost to myself.

"Who was the other man? I'm sorry, you said that your husband had been killed and Franklin. Who was the other man?"

"Nicholas Fortuna. He was working the investigation for Franklin Brody and came to my husband for help."

"I knew Nick Fortuna. Knew him when he was a cop." He shook his head. "I remember reading about his death." He paused. "I'm sorry for your loss and for Nick, but Franklin Brody, I can't shed any tears for."

"I never had any use for him, either. In fact, I think my husband was suspicious of him when the break in occurred."

"He was right." He swiveled sideways in his leather chair and looked at the ceiling. "My theory is that Brody took the papers for the Parnellis himself. But he wouldn't just turn them over to them. He would use them like an insurance policy."

"He must have forgotten a premium."

"Yes. I guess he did."

I thought for a minute. "Do you think Brody was capable of killing someone?"

"Sure, but only if he couldn't get someone else to do it for him." He leaned forward resting his elbows on his desk. "That wouldn't be too hard given the set of playmates he ran with." He thought for a moment. "Unless it was personal. Unless it mattered to him on a personal level. Then I think he would be quite capable of murdering someone himself. He was that cold. That calculating."

"Or maybe just that evil," I wondered out loud.

Deseeca nodded. He understood. I looked at him behind the big sleek desk.

"What was the cost?" I said, "for bringing the suit in the first place."

"You mean why am I still around?" I nodded. "I settled. Dropped the suit. What choice did I have without the documents? But I don't think it's really done yet." I must have looked slightly horrified because he added. "Don't look so worried, I have a few more Aces up my sleeve."

I had had enough for now. I asked him if I could call again if I had more questions. He graciously assented as he stood and took my hand. He peered into my eyes for a moment. I wondered if he was trying to decipher my face under all the bruises and bandages. 'Good luck,' I thought. Deseeca was an attractive man. I really did hope he had those Aces.

CHAPTER TWENTY-FOUR

It was only eleven-thirty when I got back to my car. I decided to check in with Chev at a pay phone on the corner. When she answered I could hear pounding in the background.

"What's going on?" I asked.

"It's what's going in, namely your new window." I could hear her muffling the phone. When she came back on, the pounding was fainter. "I'm in the closet. Can you hear me better?"

I laughed. "The pantry, the girls used that for a phone booth for years."

"I've got some interesting news." I waited for her to go on. "Mona Freeman didn't order anything from Spiegel."

"How'd you find that out?" I asked in amazement.

"It's amazing how helpful catalogue companies are. I called them and said that I had received an order in error. I gave Mona's name and address and asked them to confirm the billing. The girl checked everything in her records and…nothing. Mona hadn't ordered anything since last Christmas."

"That is interesting. We were right, then. The killer brought the box."

"I should have a copy of the police report tomorrow."

"Maybe we're getting somewhere." I filled her in briefly on my visit to Deseeca. "Can you find out anything about the building on fourteenth?"

"I'll give it a try. I also found out that there is a bank ATM machine that faces the phone booth that the woman who contacted Nikki called from. I asked the detective in charge to see if there is videotape from that day. They time everything so they should be able to pinpoint it."

"Hey, that's a great idea! If we could just find her."

"I know. God, it's getting hot in here."

"I'll let you go. See you later."

When I hung up I stood for a few minutes thinking about the Parnellis. I wanted to be sharp witted. I needed some coffee.

I drove downtown from Bethesda, parking at a meter on Sixteenth Street not far from the Parnelli construction office in an old mansion.

There was a small coffee shop around the corner from their building. I went in. The place was dingy, dirty, and practically empty except for two men at the counter. I opted for a booth with a cracked gray Formica table.

The man behind the counter looked like an ex-prize fighter with callused ears and a nose that must have made breathing a challenge. His faded green tee shirt and the dingy white apron around his middle were streaked with grease. I decided to forego food of any kind.

"Tighe, how about some more coffee down here?" The guy who yelled had greased back gray hair and a gold ring on his right hand that looked like a lump of polished ore. His companion was a dark haired, younger version who preferred his gold in a thick chain around his neck.

Tighe walked down the length of the counter and served them. "How come Jerry hasn't been in lately?" Tighe asked the older one.

S. Alden Reilly

"Jerry? Yeah well, Mr. Jerry is AWOL, old man. If you see him you'd better tell him that the boss don't like it."

My waitress arrived with a steaming black plastic mug. She was short, dumpy, and had dirty two-toned orange and black hair. It was pulled into a ponytail. Her skin was in an adolescent frenzy of acne, but she had glommed on at least an inch of pancake makeup to even out the surface.

"Anything else?" She sneered in that offhand manner that seems appropriate from the age of sixteen until maturity sets in. She was staring at my nose.

"No, thanks. Just some cream, please."

She pulled two creamers from her apron pocket and left them next to the mug. They were lukewarm. I peeled back the soggy paper on one of them. The inside looked too oily to add to my coffee, so I drank it black. Not the best, but not the worst coffee I'd ever had, either.

I watched the two men at the counter over the top of my coffee mug. They had dropped the subject of the missing Jerry and were in a hot debate with Tighe over the outcome of last night's welterweight fight. I tried to think through the questions that I wanted to ask the Parnellis. I admit I was a little nervous. I'd never had much contact with purported members of organized crime in my role as a college administrator, or at least not that I was aware of.

I took out a note pad and started writing down the facts I knew to date. Not a lot of those. Then I wrote down my questions. Many of those and some theories I was developing. I was deep into a reverie of past events, so when my waitress approached with the coffeepot and started to pour, I jumped.

"Sorry, lady. I just thought you'd like some more coffee." I guess I startled her into courtesy.

THE PHOENIX

"Thanks." I checked my watch as she retreated. I had fifteen minutes to walk around the corner. I drank the rest of my coffee and left.

S. Alden Reilly

CHAPTER TWENTY-FIVE

The Parnelli Brothers office oozed power, money, and the skill of a high priced decorator right down to the tasteful oil painting of the brothers on the wall behind the receptionist. I waited in a wing-backed chair upholstered in a tapestry fabric that had to be over a hundred dollars a yard. The receptionist sat at an antique desk. She was a cool blonde in an impeccable gray suit. I bet a clothing allowance was part of her salary.

She hadn't been too impressed by my looks, but she'd had the skill to hide it. I didn't blame her. I wasn't too impressed, either. A subdued buzzing sound from a black box on her desk apparently indicated that I was to go in because she nodded to me and got up to open the door.

Evidently, I was only to see one Parnelli. Robert, the younger brother, rose to shake my hand. Younger and more elegant looking than his brother Leo, if the portrait could be trusted, Robert was of medium height, not heavy but a workout enthusiast. All that bunched muscle around his neck gave him away.

"Please, sit down, Ms. Jones. John called and asked me to see you." Robert folded his arms on the desk. He had thin gold-rimmed glasses. His suit was a dark navy. He looked more like a banker than a hood. "He didn't explain what it was you needed."

"Just the answers to a few questions."

"Oh?" His dark eyes got a little colder.

"Yes, actually, I'm looking into the break-in at Brody, Borman, and Tate a few months back."

"I'm sorry. I know nothing about that matter, Ms. Jones." His manner was urbane but the temperature kept dropping in his eyes.

"That's surprising since your firm directly benefited from the events there." He started to say something, but I cut him off. "Now that Franklin Brody is dead, you may feel that the issue is moot, but I am investigating the deaths of . ." I flipped through my notes as if I needed reminding, "Michael Strayer and Nicolas Fortuna. I believe there was a connection."

"I'm sorry." He leaned back in his chair. The lenses in his glasses made his eyes look smaller. They looked like slits now. "I've never heard of either one of those people."

I didn't think he had, either. The look of surprise had been genuine. "Both men investigated the break-in. Both are dead now along with Mr. Brody and Mona Freeman. Don't you think that's suspicious?"

"I think that you, Ms. Jones, are on a wild goose chase." He stood up indicating that our meeting was over.

"I don't think so, Mr. Parnelli. I think that I'm going to find evidence that the same person or persons killed all three men." I stood up. We were almost eye-to-eye. "If I find that it leads here, I'll be back."

"Like I said, a wild goose chase. You should drop it, Ms. Jones. Wild goose chases can leave someone hurt."

I looked into his eyes and felt like I'd seen through a window into Hell. It was a very cold place indeed. I had never experienced the veiled menace that underlined

Parnelli's comment. It frightened me. It made me damn mad, too.

"Only if they're not careful, and prepared. Don't worry about me."

I left walking briskly through the reception area to the elevator. I'm careful and prepared? What a retort. They guy probably thought I had myself confused with a Boy Scout. Just once I'd like to say something clever. A real come back at the right moment that would set my opponent back on his butt. I always thought of brilliant things about a week later.

The elevator door opened to let off the two characters from the coffee shop. They barely glanced at me. I got on, hit the L button, and leaned against the wall all the way down. I was shivering when I got back to the car. I had to put the heater on to get warm again.

THE PHOENIX

CHAPTER TWENTY SIX

The appointment with John Borman was the only thing that kept me in town. All I wanted to do was to fly up Interstate 270 from Washington DC to my house, lock all the doors, get Chaddy close, and eat French fries with catsup until I exploded. Instead I had an hour to kill before meeting Borman at his office on L Street.

I was near Adams Morgan so I drove a few blocks. I parked the car and ate Thai noodles in a café that had tables on the street. The day was one of those balmy fall days that fill you with vitality. Good cleaning-out-the- garage weather. I wondered when all that would feel normal again. I drank the whole pot of hot tea. It tasted like gardenias smell. I started to feel better.

I got back in the car and drove down Twenty-first Street, turned left on L Street, parked in an all day garage, and walked the block over to Brody, Borman, and Tate. The receptionist showed me right in. I was beginning to realize that the receptionist and her surroundings were supposed to set the tone, get the public ready to bite on whatever image the company was trying to project. Okay, so this isn't new to most people, but I had been in more reception areas in the last two days than in the past five years.

The entry to B. B. & T.'s suite was supposed to evoke serene, stable, dependable trust. A beautiful silver haired woman showed me through to John's office. Like the reception area, it was decorated in earth tones, pewter, and gray. It was very conservative, very secure.

John Borman himself was sort of a study in earth tones. Sandy hair, graying at the temples, gray suit with subtle pin striping, and light brown eyes. He was a handsome man with no extremes: not too tall, not too muscular, not too overbearing. In fact, he seemed nice. It was an odd trait for a partner of Franklin Brody.

"How is it going?" he asked.

He seated me in front of his desk. The base was stone. The top a big piece of cypress with resin poured over it. I looked, but no plastic clock parts were embedded in the urethane. The effect was beautiful. Nature preserved for eternity, thanks to chemistry.

"Let's just say it's going for now."

He laughed. "Layne told me that you were investigating this on your own. Do you think it wise?" he said with lawyerly concern.

"The wisdom is probably not apparent to the professionals who have already covered the ground, but we feel we're bringing a fresh viewpoint." I was beginning to sound like a lawyer myself.

"Sometimes that can be valuable."

He toyed with a number two pencil on his desk. "Layne seems to be doing pretty well." He watched me react. He was obviously more than casually interested in Layne. It was there in the forced nonchalance. I wondered if she even knew that John Borman had a thing for her. Probably not. Franklin had blinded her with his artificial brilliance for so long it would probably take a while for her to recover her sight.

"Yes. She's better every day. I just worry that she's lonely." I can't help it. I'm an inveterate matchmaker, besides I wanted to see if he'd take the bait.

"I should really stop by to see how she's doing."

"I think that would be very thoughtful, John." A happy expression relaxed his features and he went off into a daydream. I let it go for a few seconds then I brought him back to reality. "I really appreciate your help in getting me in to see Anthony Deseeca and Robert Parnelli."

That brought him around. "I really can't take credit for that. Layne used her influence to press for the interviews." Layne again. He had it bad.

"Well, thank you, anyway. I'm afraid Mr. Parnelli was not pleased to see me reopen this investigation, but I think he understood my point of view when I left." Understatement is sometimes the best way to handle bad news. No need to say Robert Parnelli would like to squash me like a bug.

John looked thoughtful. "I know Robert and Leo were very sensitive about the way that break-in looked to everyone."

No kidding, John. Lawyers could make anything sound abstract. "Yes, I could see that," was all I said.

"Is there any way I can help you?" He folded his hands together lacing the knuckles like he was playing the church game.

I wondered if he would show me all the people. I was tired. "As a matter of fact, John, I was wondering if you noticed anything odd about Franklin's behavior at the time of the robbery?"

"Yes, I did." He wasn't going to waffle on this. He looked me in the eye. "He wasn't himself. Hyper, I guess you could call it. He couldn't concentrate. He was irritable and difficult."

"Did he get over it? That behavior I mean?"

"Not really, the best way I can describe it is on edge, right up until his death."

"All due to the robbery?"

"No." John paused. "I think his life was getting too complicated."

"How was it complicated?" John squirmed in his seat.

"You know that I think Layne is a fine person," he began.

"Yes." Of course I knew.

"Well, I think Frank was involved with another woman." The regret in his eyes was sincere. My estimation of John Borman was going steadily up. He was a little naïve perhaps, but a nice man.

"Do you know who it was?"

"Not really." He said. "It's all irrelevant now, anyway, but I think the woman was really driving him crazy." He knew or at least had a suspicion, but he wasn't going to be a cad and rat the lady out.

"Why do you say that?" I asked, intrigued.

"Because he'd get phone calls almost every day and then he'd rush off or blow up at someone. He acted like a crazy man these last few months." It was hard to think of the cool headed, silver haired Brody machine breaking down in any way.

"Well, if you think of anything else or learn the lady's name, give me a call," I said, rising. "Thanks for your help, John." I started to leave then stopped. "You should really call Layne. I know she'd like that." She needed an alternative to Elliott anyway.

CHAPTER TWENTY SEVEN

I drove home on automatic pilot again. When I pulled into the driveway I didn't remember any of the trip, just the theories that were beginning to form in my head. The window damaged in last night's melee looked okay from the road. I couldn't believe it. The repairman had actually come and fixed it. I was living right.

When I opened the door into the kitchen, Chaddy was waiting on the doorstep. He went into a spasm of wiggles until I had thoroughly petted him, then he headed for the kitchen table to lie down.

"Chev?" I expected her to be at the table drinking coffee. There was a fresh pot on, but no Chev.

"In here," she called from what seemed like the vicinity of the living room.

The dining room leads from the kitchen into the foyer and the living room. I headed in that direction. The floor was strewn with paper strips that made a pathway through the room. I was just figuring this out when I came into the living room. All the scaffolding was gone. The walls were painted a soft white. The wood work a shade deeper. Chev, dressed in jeans, was standing by the window seat of the window that had been broken.

"What do you think?"

I turned again. It was all done, painted, complete.
Then I realized how clean everything was. The wood floors
gleamed. The rugs had been shampooed. I wandered into
the family room and my study. All was orderly, clean, sane.

"Wow!" Was all I could say.

"Good. I hoped you'd be happy," she said with a
chuckle. "I just called in a crew and had the whole place put
right."

"Chev, I don't know how to thank you," I said
gratefully.

"Don't worry about it. You can afford it, can't you?"
She added quickly. "Because I can take care of it."

"No way. Michael had a ton of life insurance. I was
just too. . " I searched for the word. " . . .too."

"Preoccupied," she offered.

"Exactly. I couldn't concentrate." I had a twinge of
panic. Chev had single-handedly resolved the chaos that I
had been hiding behind for the last six months. I was naked.
I was standing under a spotlight and the question was 'Now
what would I do?'

"You know you're going to need some furniture."
Chev looked around at the soft walls, the light wood floors,
the pale carpet. "It's like a blank slate, Stella. You can do
whatever you want."

"If I can just figure out what that is," I said quietly.

"You're getting there," was all Chev said as she
walked toward the kitchen.

"Thanks again, Chev." I followed her.

"You're welcome," she laughed. "Don't be so serious
about it. Come and sit. Tell me how your day went." We sat
down at my kitchen table and Chev got out her note pad.

"Coffee?" I said jumping up to grab two cups and
the coffeepot.

"The answer is always 'yes'." Chev accepted her cup gratefully.

"Well," I settled into my chair, "Deseeca is very interesting, kind of nice, too. Sort of sexy. Robert Parnelli threatened me," I hurried on. "John Borman was gracious. Seems to be interested in Layne. Very helpful." I was yammering.

"Whoa, wait a minute. Did you say Parnelli threatened you?"

I looked at Chev and took a sip of coffee. "Yes. I think I can definitely say that."

"That piece of . . ."

"Now, Chev." I cut into her description of Robert Parnelli as manure. "He didn't care for my questions, but I let him know that I'd be back."

"You and Arnold, I suppose." She smiled, but her eyes were serious. "He's a dangerous man, Stella. Don't get him too riled up."

"I know. I'll be wearing cement sandals on the bottom of the Potomac or sucking carbon monoxide from he tailpipe of my Trooper." I felt lighter now. Parnelli had really frightened me, but now it was manageable. "I don't really think he knew anything directly about Nikki or Michael. But, I think he's threatened because we're on to something."

"You're right, but which something are we on to?"

I laughed. "That is the sixty-four thousand dollar question. But if I keep stirring it up, something will come to the surface." I sipped my coffee. "John Borman knows something." She looked at me quizzically. "I think it's about the women Franklin was seeing, but he thinks he's being gallant by not revealing it."

"Can you get him to tell you?"

"I think so. I let it go because I didn't want to push him too hard."

"Well, here's something to think about . . .I found out who is looking for Damon Edwards. A woman named Alexa Grant."

"All right! How did that happen?"

"Palmer Detective agency. She was the client on the missing persons case. The one that Nikki and Michael worked the fingerprints on for Palmer. I convinced Palmer to turn it over to us." She grinned. "Steve Palmer owes me a favor, or maybe several. Besides, she'd dropped the investigation with them anyway."

I felt a rush of excitement. "Did you get her address?"

"Yes, and a phone number. I called and actually talked to her. I told her we had some evidence relating to Damon Edwards and could she come in?"

I drew a blank for a moment then realized. "But we don't have anything on Damon Edwards."

"Well, we'll have to make something up." Chev laughed. "That's your department. The glib private eye stuff."

"Thanks. What have you found out about her?"

"Absolutely nothing." Chev shook her head. "Nothing comes up in the computer. We're going to need some evidence to find out who she is."

"Such as?"

"Such as finger prints." Chev looked at me.

"Well, this ought to be a fun project. Got any ideas?"

"Did you see that Al Pacino movie where they kept taking the drink glasses back to the kitchen?"

"Yes, but don't you think that's a little elaborate for us?"

"Trust me, honey, it'll work. I've got her scheduled for tomorrow afternoon."

"Okay. I've got to go to the doctor tomorrow morning."

"The unveiling?" Chev smiled. I felt the bandage on my nose.

"Yeah, the unveiling. God, I hope I like the way it looks. It's very weird to look one way all your life then suddenly have a new face for the rest."

"Oh, I don't know, some people get an overhaul every few years."

"I'm not some people," I said darkly.

"Boy honey, you've got that right." Chev refused to be intimidated. "You've got more directions to go in than exits off the beltway. Your trouble is you don't know which one to take."

I blinked. It was hateful of her to always tell me exactly what my problem was.

"Now don't give me those dark looks, Stella, you know I'm right." She had given a perfect impression of Bertie. She laughed. Her laugh was hearty and infectious.

I laughed, too. "Okay. I guess having too many choices is better than none. What do you want for dinner?"

CHAPTER TWENTY EIGHT

We were putting the finishing touches on a pot of eye- tearing Chili when there was a knock at the back door. It was Layne.

"Are you alone?" I looked for Elliott behind her.

"Yes, completely." She sounded relieved. She also looked much better. Her bruises, like mine, were fading to pale discolorations. She looked brighter, her eyes snapping with energy. I had never seen her like that.

"Come in. It's chili night." I pulled a chair out for her at the table. She and Chev exchanged greetings. I looked at the two of them in their trim jeans, Layne's red sweater complementing the color in her cheeks. I looked down at the faded yellow sweat pants and navy sweatshirt I was wearing. I would hit the mall tomorrow.

Chaddy had his own dish by the back door, but ignored it, hoping for better fare at our table. No way was I going to let him have any beans. Methane is a deadly gas. I wiped tears from my eyes. I didn't realize we'd added quite that many peppers.

"This stuff will clean out your pipes," Chev laughed.

"Yeah, in all directions, I'm afraid." Internal phenomena aside, I felt good. Like someone who's been in a coma coming back to consciousness. I was starting to get bits and pieces, but I was afraid to push it. Slow was better. I could be sure it would stick.

Layne looked at me. We had finished dinner and were drinking coffee. "You probably don't know this but I used to be a lawyer. I gave it up when I married Franklin. He wanted me to focus on our marriage." She made a face. "Anyway, I've decided to practice law again."

She said it so quietly, so matter-of-factly that it hit me like a foreign language. Layne had been a lawyer? What else didn't I know about her? "Great! I think that's great, Layne. Don't you think that's great, Chev?"

I looked at her. She was as surprised as I was. "It's wonderful," Chev said kindly. "What made you decide to do it?"

Layne blushed a little." Well, John Borman gave me a call and we got to talking." She ducked her head like a bashful kid. "Anyway, I told him I was ready to practice again, and he suggested that I call a friend of his at another firm. And," she paused, "they want me to start next week." She smiled, obviously happy. "I've got to work hard to be reinstated, but I'm ready."

I couldn't believe the transformation in Layne. All traces of ditsyness were gone. The only clue that it was the old Layne was a streak of blue ink across one knuckle.

"I think this deserves a toast!" I went to my pantry and brought out a couple of bottles of Cold Duck I'd confiscated from a kid at Zara's last party. I got out three champagne glasses and poured. It was weird but wonderful tasting. We made several toasts until we killed the bottles.

"Why did you marry Franklin anyway?" I asked Layne. "I'm sorry, it's the wine but I've always wanted to know."

"Sex."

I thought Chev would loose it. She choked on her cheap champagne. "It must have been good," she said with a straight face.

"It was tremendous. I never met a man with an appetite like Franklin's. It was exciting. We'd check into hotels as if we were strangers having an affair." She snickered with a slight hick-up. "We were even members of the mile high club."

I guess my mouth must have been open for a long time because Chev started laughing and clucked under my chin with her finger. "Wow," I said.

Layne smiled. "I know you never thought of me that way, but I was caught up in it. Franklin made me feel like I was the center of his universe. Like we were the only two people in the room at a crowded party. It was incredible how he could focus on just you, the sexual tension."

She smiled, remembering, and I could see regret for the loss of that feeling. Layne circled her champagne flute with her hands tilting it to look into the liquid as if she could read something there. "Our life was very superficial and hedonistic for a long time. Everything was fine, intense, but fine until I wanted to go back to work. He threw a fit. It was like I had broken some spell. He withdrew."

She set the champagne stem on the table and looked up. "Then it got ugly," she sighed. "One evening, we were supposed to meet at a hotel for a romantic weekend. To try to rekindle our love." She looked at us both. "I've never told this to anyone, but when I went to the room, Franklin was already there, but he wasn't alone. There was another woman with him. They were in bed and wanted me to join them. I just turned and ran out of there."

"Why didn't you leave him?" I couldn't believe the betrayal.

"I should have." A tear rolled down her face. "I guess I thought it was my fault that I couldn't hold him. I spent the next couple of years trying to be woman enough for him." She rubbed the tear away with a fierce gesture. "I stayed, trying to figure out what to do, but finally, I couldn't take it anymore. His womanizing, his contempt. I realized that he would never be happy with just one woman. That he didn't value me. That he didn't love me. That it was over." She shrugged her shoulders. "I've come to think that he probably never really loved me. Just some ideal of a woman he had created."

She looked at us her eyes clear, tearless. "When I got the courage to divorce him, I went to him. Went to his office. His secretary made me feel like I needed an appointment to see my own husband."

Chev stifled a snort of disgust and gave me a look. I knew she felt the same way I did hearing this story. Downright homicidal.

Layne didn't notice. "When I walked in, I was so nervous that I just blurted out that I was leaving him. He glanced up at me with an expression that was indescribable. Like he was looking at some little bug. Then he just went back to the papers he was reading." She shuddered a little. "He never said a word. He was so cold. He was like a stranger to me."

Chev had tears in her eyes. "I know what some of that feels like," she said. "Nikki cheated on me for a long time before I realized it. I finally understood it was Nikki's sickness, that I wasn't to blame. I left him for two years even though I loved him. He came to me and asked for a second chance. We went to counseling. At the very end I think he was faithful. He had conquered his demons. That's why losing him was so hard."

I looked at both of them. "I want to clear up something that you said the other day." I looked at Layne. "You said that I got a good one. But I didn't." There, it was out. Chev looked at me with the kindest expression on her face. It made me go on. "Michael was my first real boyfriend. He was the relationship I should have had in high school. But I was too shy. When we met in college, I was impressed with him, his intellect, his self-possession. I was so naïve because I had never really dated. I didn't know anything about men." I laughed and felt my face get red. "I've never experienced the passion you guys are talking about. Michael didn't love me in that way. After a time I realized that it wasn't my fault because I didn't love him that way, either. I felt like his mother, his roommate, his friend, never his lover. I've spent all these years trying to be the perfect wife hoping that I could make up for not loving him." I'd said it. It felt like a great weight had come off my chest. Tears rolled down my face.

Chev leaned across the table and clasped my hand then she took Layne's hand, too. I smiled and grasped Layne's other hand, making a ring. We held hands laughing and crying at the same time.

"Chili and champagne therapy is very effective," I said when we finally let go.

"Men suck," Layne said laughing. "Let's have some coffee."

"You read my mind." Chev headed to the coffeepot to make a new batch.

I couldn't stop smiling. "I want to get whoever killed Michael. Then I can put him to rest."

"That's what we all want," Chev said. "We need to put our men to rest."

When midnight rolled around Layne left and Chev was right behind her. I locked up, and Chaddy and I went to bed. The whole house was peaceful, serene. It felt like life was getting in order. I was asleep minutes after my head hit the pillow.

THE PHOENIX

CHAPTER TWENTY NINE

I was on my way to the doctor's office. The day was brisk. The kind of day that fills me with more ambition than ten corporate raiders. I'd worn a comfortable outfit. A black jersey jumper with a hot pink oversized shirt underneath and black suede boots. I'd dredged it from Zara's closet. I was tired of the dumpy array of my fat clothes and I had lost five pounds. I actually looked decent for a change. I'd pulled my hair into a ponytail low on my neck.

Dr. Gonzalez's office was an attempt at a Tudor revival that made you wonder when the madrigal singers would show up. White stuccoed walls were crisscrossed with dark timbers. The furniture looked like it had been finished with a dull ax. I sat in one of the comfy wooden chairs and waited like an obedient serf.

The nurse finally called me into an examining room where I sat on the papered table for another fifteen minutes. When the doctor bustled in he took one look at me and said, "Very good, the bruises are going. What are you so unhappy about, Ms. Strayer?"

"Call me Stella," I said before I even thought. I guess I was getting used to it. "I'm a little worried about what I'll look like."

"What confidence you have in your surgeon, Stella." He said with a gentle smile. He was applying alcohol to the edges of the tape. Several deft moves of his hand and I could feel the bandages were gone. He tilted my head from side to side looking at his handiwork.

"Tell me what you think." He handed me a mirror.

I lifted the mirror slowly, watching my forehead disappear as my eyes came into view. The top of my nose seemed fine. I tilted the mirror. I could see the whole thing.

I couldn't believe it. It was beautiful. Pretty much my old nose only straighter and thinner. I looked at my profile. It was Grecian in proportion. I undoubtedly had the best looking nose in the Mid-Atlantic States. I beamed.

"Now that's more like it." Dr. Gonzalez smiled. "It's still a little swollen. Why don't you check back in about two weeks?" He tilted my head looking at his handiwork. "And you were worried about looking like Frankenstein." He grinned at me.

I just kept looking at my nose. It was still me but I looked better, prettier. "I don't know what to say, Dr. Gonzalez, except thank you."

"My pleasure, Stella. You should be able to see the real result in a few weeks. It takes a while for the tissues to heal and the swelling to go down. In about six months, it will be completely healed. Your cuts and scrapes are minor. They should completely fade in about the same time."

I left his office in a state of mild euphoria. I headed straight for the mall. I wandered around for a while getting my bearings, then walked into a trendy looking hair salon. I usually had my hair trimmed at Sara Lynn's in Circe, but I didn't think Sara Lynn would approve of what I was about to do.

The girl at the counter looked like she'd just completed a Robert Palmer video. White skin, dark hair, red lips. I was about to open my mouth to explain that I didn't have an appointment, but she cut me off. "Haircut?" I guess I looked like a woman who needed help.

"Color, too."

That must have been her next suggestion because she smiled broadly. "Raphael has some time before his next appointment."

Raphael turned out to be a pleasant older man with a New York accent. He wore his short gray hair in a ponytail. "What did you have in mind?" He pronounced 'you' as 'use'.

"The works. Bring me into the millennium."

He liked that. "Why don't we cut it about here?" He tilted my head then held his hands out flat on each side of my head to illustrate. God, it looked short.

I decided to go for it. Raphael led me to a sink where a small oriental woman with three inch, blood red finger nails sat me down to wash my hair. It was like having Freddie Kreuger give you a scalp massage. In the next hour I was colored, my hair in little pieces of aluminum foil, washed, and cut. When it was over, I did not even remotely resemble Ann Strayer, dignified college administrator. I looked like a lead singer with a Swedish rock band.

My hair was short, icy blonde on the tips, full on top, and tapered down my neck. With a little pomade, I could look like an albino version of Elvis. I expected to hate it, but I actually looked nice. Even better than nice, I looked sexy.

"You are pleased?" He showed me the back in the mirror.

"Definitely."

I gave Raphael a generous tip. I couldn't wait to get back out in the mall. In a frenzy, I hit store after store. I had always been a decisive buyer, but I'd tried to get things on clearance and mix them into a wardrobe by sticking to a few colors. Now, driven by my new look, my new identity, I found myself picking out things I would never have looked at before. Less conservative, more stylish, than anything I used to wear.

I pulled up to Fortuna Investigations at about a quarter to two. When I walked in Chev's mouth dropped open.

"Gawd! Don't you look great!" She came out from behind her desk to check me out. "Stella, you look wonderful. Of course, I don't know what you looked like before the accident," she teased.

"Take my word for it. Not this good."

She looked at my outfit. A slim black skirt, size eight I might add, with a long black jacket. I wore a thin silver chain at my throat. "You've been to the mall."

"Stella Jones needed clothes. The Ivy league-Junior league look just didn't cut it," I said. "She needs to lose a little more weight, though."

Chev guided me back to Nikki's office. "Don't tell me why you don't deserve a compliment, just take it." She was a bossy little thing.

"Yes, ma'am."

She eyed me as we walked down the hall. "You've got a pretty face and a good figure. It's about time you showed it off."

I was about to protest with one of my usual self-effacing comments, but caught myself. "You're right. Maybe I can get work as an exotic dancer in my spare time."

Chev laughed and pinched my arm. "You don't have any spare time. Come on." She led me into one of the rooms down the hall. It was an office decorated in masculine touches, dark furniture, and a green shaded lamp on the desk. "I want you to feel free to use Nikki's office whenever you want. I've got Mrs. Grant's file. It was a mess when Palmer sent it over, but I've organized it for you," she said, sorting the folders nervously. "I told her you were taking over

Nikki's cases and wanted to interview her yourself about Damon Edwards."

I touched her hand for a moment. "If she had anything to do with Nikki getting shot, we'll find out. She may not know anything and if she did it may be like Nikki said: she really never showed up. It could have even been another woman, but we'll find out."

"I know we will." Chev smoothed the skirt of her electric blue suit with black trim. She had French braided her long hair so it hung in a tail down her back.

"You look exceptionally nice today. Is there a special occasion?"

She blushed a faint pink. "Well, I'm going to dinner with one of Nikki's old friends from the Department."

I arched an eyebrow at her. She hurried on, "It's in the line of duty. His name is Dan Phillips. He works in the missing persons department."

"Missing persons?"

"Yeah, I thought he could help us with this Damon Edwards thing."

"I wish he had something for me in the next fifteen minutes. I have no idea what I'm going to say."

"You'll think of something. She has to go along because she doesn't want trouble. She just wants information." She was bustling around me, arranging the things on the desk in a way that gave the impression that I'd been pouring over files for days. "Hopefully, I'll get something tonight." I must have looked skeptical. "Dan's had a crush on me for years, but there aren't any strings."

"Good. We do have standards to uphold, you know. Of course if Harrison Ford knew something pertinent to our case, I might consider going above and beyond."

"Who says he has to know anything?" she said, laughing. Then she pointed a crimson tipped finger at me. "Hush." She commanded with mock seriousness.

The front door buzzed.

THE PHOENIX

CHAPTER THIRTY

Alexa Grant was one of the most striking women I had ever met. I guessed her to be in her late forties. Dark hair, almost black, fell in smooth wings from a central part to her chin. Her eyes were dark brown. Her brows were full and arched. With her flawless, cream-colored skin and full lips, she could have been a doe-eyed beauty from the pages of Vogue. It was the steel in her gaze that gave her an edge. Somehow it made me think about the danger of swimming in shark-infested waters.

I shook her hand as I introduced myself. She was wearing a supple, rust colored leather coat with matching gloves. She slipped the coat off but left the gloves on. I looked at Chev as she stood at the door with a shrug of my shoulders that asked non-verbally. 'What are we going to do now?'

Chev responded by offering Mrs. Grant and me a cup of tea. Mrs. Grant declined. She also declined coffee, soda, and ice water. I could see our plan was going in the toilet.

"Thanks, Chev. I'll have coffee please." I needed a cup. Maybe even something stronger. "Mrs. Grant, I've been going over your file. First, I have a few questions then I have some information for you."

She smiled. Her teeth were perfect, white. The incisors were pointed like little fangs. "Of course. I'm here because I am anxious to resolve this matter." Her voice was husky for a woman. That sexy kind men like.

"Good. I wasn't sure if you still wanted to pursue it." I said in a businesslike tone while shuffling papers in her folder. I pulled out a list of notes Chev had made on the contents. "You are looking for a man who has been missing for twenty years. Mr. Fortuna was asked to help another agency analyze old fingerprinted documents. Can you tell me why you are looking for this man?" I paused, pen ready, an expectant look on my face.

"Well, I am trying to help a family friend." It was awkward at first, but then the story started to come easier. "Damon Edwards was killed in a boating accident in 1976, in Mississippi. It was very tragic, no body was ever found. He left a wife and child."

She explained that she was trying to help the family sort out an estate that was complicated by the missing man. Now she was really into it. I made notes conscientiously although I was sure that I was recording lies and half-truths.

I took a big swig of coffee when she paused for breath. "Why don't you just have Damon Edwards declared dead? It seems the easiest solution. Or do you really think he is alive?"

The question took her by surprise. "Well, I don't know. I really hadn't . . . I mean I just want this resolved. For the family," she added. It had the ring of truth. Somebody had done her wrong. She was worried about something. I wondered who she was and what she was up to.

I went for the tough question. "You had an appointment with Mr. Fortuna the day he died, didn't you?"

Her face went pale. "No. No, I didn't. You must have me confused with someone else." She seemed the slightest bit uncomfortable.

"You didn't call Mr. Fortuna from a phone booth at Union Station on March 15th?"

"No. As I said you have me confused with someone else." She summoned up some indignation. "Look I've answered your questions. You're supposed to have some information for me."

Here it was. Time to stir things up. "I do. I can't give you anything official yet, but we may have found Damon Edwards."

The effect was electric. She leaned forward, a dangerous gleam in her eyes. "I knew it! I knew he was alive. Where is he?" She was naked. The predator was ready to pounce on her prey.

I was a little dismayed at her reaction. But hey, I'd started this. "As I said, it's not definitely confirmed. I wanted to make sure that you were still interested in pursuing this matter." I paused. "There is also the financial consideration. You had a relationship with another agency. You dropped that case. Why?"

"They weren't getting anywhere. It was a waste of my money. However," She opened her purse and pulled out a wad of cash. "Would five thousand dollars take care of a retainer? I'd like to hire your firm to continue."

"Of course. I'll ask my partner to give you a receipt and I will let you know the minute we've firmed this information up." I stood up. "Thank you for coming in today," I said, shaking her hand inside the glove. "I'll keep in touch."

I guided her back out into our living room-reception area and explained to Chev that Mrs. Grant had just retained our services. If Chev was surprised when I handed her the cash, she hid it well. She wrote out a receipt and contract for Mrs. Grant, and we were saying our good-byes when Chev came around her desk.

"Mrs. Grant, I'm sorry, I don't mean to be rude." She leaned closer to her. "But you've got a little speck of something on your tooth." She pointed to her own right incisor. "It's right about here."

Alex Grant looked blank for a moment then she pulled the glove off her right hand. She used one of her nails to pick at her tooth.

"I think it's still there." Chev said very concerned. She obviously didn't want the poor woman to be walking around with food on her teeth. "Here honey, try this." She said just as Alexa began to fumble in her purse. Chev leaned over her desk and pulled a small metal edged mirror out of the middle drawer. Alex grasped the mirror and looked at her mouth. She smiled at her reflection examining first one side then the other.

"Good, you did get it." Chev was all smiles.

"Thank you." Mrs. Grant placed the mirror on the edge of the desk. She picked up her glove.

"You're welcome." Chev said ushering her out. "Have a nice day."

We waited, practically holding our breath, until she pulled away from the curb. Then Chev flipped the sign on the door to 'closed' and locked it. She took a plastic baggie out of a file cabinet then used a small pair of tongs to lift the mirror into the bag.

I could see the prints through the plastic. "God, I hope these come out."

"They will." She said. "They have to after all that trouble."

She slipped the bag into an envelope then she locked it in her desk.

I looked at her. "Would you like a cup of tea, soda, ice water, Gatorade, a rum and coke, or perhaps some coffee?"

"I'm dying for a cup." She laughed.

We sat at the little jellybean table to drink our coffee. "So what did you make up to tell Mrs. Grant?" Chev said as she stirred her coffee. "In the heat of the mission to get her prints, I forgot all about it."

"I told her we'd found Damon Edwards."

"No way."

"Way." I laughed then I got serious. "She scared me a little. She's got a vengeance thing going on somehow."

"Well I hope we can produce him, especially since we've got five thousand dollars of her money."

"We will. I think we're close, but we should put the money in the escrow account until we get something concrete."

"Two retainers from questionable women." Chev twirled a strand of hair.

"And one of them might have murdered Nikki or led to his getting murdered," I finished the thought for her.

She looked immeasurably sad. "I wish Nikki had dropped the whole thing." She folded her grief back up and put it away. Locked it in her heart.

"Hey. We're on a mission here. Remember?" I said squeezing her hand. "Besides, I think that Michael and Nikki were marked from the day Franklin called them about his robbery."

"I know you are right. I just regret. . ." She looked at me and let it drop. "You know, you're getting very cocky. Do you hear yourself? It would appear some self-esteem has started to take up residence in Ms. Jones' psyche. You really believe we're going to figure this out."

"We are. As a matter of fact I'm going to shake things up a little more." I was feeling more confident lately, why not use it. I finished my coffee and cleaned my cup at the sink.

"I'm going by Mrs. Grants on my way home."

"Why? Thought of another whopper to tell her?" Chev laughed.

"I want to see where she lives. See if I can get a feel for her and what she's up to." I grinned. "I'll make something up. That's my department, you know, the glib lies department. You want to call me later or will it be a late night?"

"Don't worry. I'm not looking to get laid," she said warmly.

"Fine. Call me later then." I started to leave then remembered the mirror. "I've got my own 'Dan' who could help us on this."

She handed me the envelope. "Go for it."

CHAPTER THIRTY ONE

Alexa Grant, or whatever her real name was, lived in a town house near Germantown, Maryland. Germantown is a booming bedroom community of Washington D.C. full of condos, townhouses, and single-family homes that feeds a steady stream of commuters into downtown D.C.

I climbed the steps to the narrow front door. Each townhouse was finished in an early American color scheme. Hers was Wedgwood blue with gray trim and burgundy shutters. I rang the bell and waited. I was surprised at how calm I was. Once, when I was a student in college, I got a job as a field marketer for a survey company. I was supposed to go door to door handing out samples of diapers and feminine hygiene products and give a little spiel. After several rude comments, I began hanging the sample bags on the doorknob and skipping the attempt for dialogue. Needless to say, I was fired in a week's time. Hey, I figured most people could use the stuff, and if they couldn't they'd pass it along. So much for market research.

I rang the bell again. This time I got an answer. "Hello. Ms. Grant?"

"Yes." She was obviously surprised to see me. Why not, she had just left my office.

"I'm sorry. I just had a few more questions."

She had been stumped by her own name. I knew how hard it was to keep a new identity straight. I had the same problem. I moved to a sofa in the narrow, early American style living room and sat down. Her coat lay across the back of it as if she'd just thrown it there. The room had a temporary feel to it. I wondered if the furniture was rented.

"Have you lived here long?" I decided on the way over to try to get a little more information on the Mississippi story.

"No, not really." She looked uncomfortable.

"Oh? Have you moved here from Mississippi recently?"

"No, not recently, not from Mississippi." She didn't elaborate.

"You said that you are acting for the Edmond family because they are trying to settle an estate. Who died recently?"

"Jack Edmonds. Damon's father. He passed away about nine months ago." A tear slipped from the corner of her eye and rolled down her cheek.

"I'm sorry."

She used her other hand to shield her eyes for a moment. "That's okay. He was a special man. I'm starting to get used to it. That's why the family wants to get everything cleared up."

"I understand," I said reassuringly. "Why did you think that Damon Edwards is alive? You've believed that always haven't you?"

"I don't know. The lack of a body and the fact that he was too mean to die" She said with thinly veiled contempt.

"You said you were a friend of the Edmonds family? How do you know them?"

That threw her. "I can't say." She got that look on her face my students would get when they were trying to think of a way to bullshit their way through a tough question in class, but she took the high road. "It's a private matter." She stood up. "Please excuse me for a moment." She went down the hallway toward the back of the house.

I looked around while she was gone. From the sofa you could see into the kitchen and dining nook. Salad fixings were laid out on the counter. I had a weird sense of déjà vu. Mona Freeman was making a salad before she died.

Alexa reappeared with a wad of Kleenex in her hand. I certainly didn't want to upset her anymore. "Do you know the names Franklin Brody or Michael Strayer?" I it was a wild card but I thought I'd throw it out.

Her face turned so white that I thought she was going to be sick. I stood up ready for anything, but I couldn't take my eyes off her face.

"No, I'm sorry, I don't," she whispered, regaining her composure.

"Sorry you're not feeling well. Is there anything I can do?" I said moving toward the door.

"No, I'm fine. Just not over Jack's death yet." She waited, watching me as I closed the door behind me.

I wondered if grief gave you that dead look I'd seen in her eyes. Maybe it did.

S. Alden Reilly

CHAPTER THIRTY TWO

I walked down the steps feeling like Super Detective. I just wished I knew what I had detected. Alexa Grant's reaction to Franklin and Michael's names told me she knew something, but what? I was still puzzling over the whole conversation when I got in my car and pulled away from the curb in one smooth motion. I merged onto Interstate 270 going north and joined a line of cars passing a semi on the left. A blue pickup was right on my tail. It was a fancy truck. Lots of chrome and the words 'Big Blue' on one of those plastic strips across the hood.

I tapped my brakes a couple of times to warn him. He didn't seem to take the hint. The sight of him looming in my rear view mirror was getting on my nerves. I put my foot to the floor and passed the semi. When I dropped into the lane in front of him, the pickup came level with me and tried to squeeze in behind me, but I slowed a little to close the space. I couldn't see who was in the truck except that I was sure it was a man. He finally pulled in front of me and began to slow down. I slowed, too. The poor guy in the semi blared his horn, annoyed by our petty car games.

The semi made a move into the left lane to pass me. I let him go. The creep in the pickup slowed again. I waited until the semi was clear of me then I swung out behind him. When we passed a slower semi-trailer truck moving up the mountain, I merged to the right behind the semi I was following, dropping into the lane between the two trucks. The pickup passed me and started to merge into the lane ahead of me again but the semi in front of me slowed down and cut him off. I was in the slingshot position between two huge trucks with only a few feet separating our bumpers. At first I was uncomfortable with their closeness, but then I realized that they were escorting me. The pickup stayed with us, hanging in the passing lane for a few miles then pulled away doing about ninety. The sun glinted on his mud flaps with the Dolly Parton cutouts.

I rode between the two semis for several miles. There is a popular truck stop where Interstates 270 and 70 meet. I figured we might be heading there. When the lead truck pulled off the road into the truck stop, I followed and parked by the restaurant. I sat in the car for a minute.

A tap on my window startled me out of my reverie. A man smiled. "Hey lady, I'm from that rig over there." He pointed to one of my escort trucks.

I rolled my window down. "Thanks for helping me out there. Could I buy you and your friend a cup of coffee?"

"Naw, that's okay. Me and Ernie have to get on to Cumberland before it gets dark." He was an older man with a weathered face and a missing front tooth. "Did you know that guy?"

"No, I didn't get a good look at him."

"Well, here's his plate number if you need it." He handed me a grimy slip of paper with 'FNJ 694' written on it.

"Thanks. I guess I'll get on home. I really appreciate your help Mr.?"

"Just call me Dave," he said. "No problem. Just be careful, there's a lot of whackos out there." He grinned and headed over to the two big trucks where a smaller man waited.

S. Alden Reilly

I waved as I pulled out of the parking lot. My knight-errants were still standing next to their eighteen-wheelers. They gave me a wave back.

THE PHOENIX

CHAPTER THIRTY THREE

The rest of the ride home was uneventful. I pulled into the driveway behind a silver Buick. Bertie was back.

"Hello," I called as I opened the back door. Chaddy came bounding up to me wiggling in excitement. "Your Momma's back, isn't she?" I bent to scratch his ears.

Bertie came into the kitchen and gave me a big hug. She was wearing white polyester slacks with a navy and red top. Big red, white, and blue earrings in the shape of anchors hung from her ears.

"Is it the Fourth of July already?" I grinned.

"Hush," she laughed. Her blue eyes crinkled at the corners. I gave her another hug. I really loved this woman. Bertie and I sat down at the kitchen table. "We're having a dinner at church tonight for the 'All American Family'." Bertie's church auxiliary liked to have theme dinners. It gave the ladies an excuse to decorate and dress up.

"Tell me about New York."

"Tell me what's happened to you first." She tilted my face from side to side. "You look beautiful."

"Thank you." The flattering words pleased me even from a biased source. I was beginning to feel different. "A new haircut, new clothes, a new nose. Nothing major. Now, tell me about New York."

"Well, we took a helicopter ride. All of us except Vivian. She chickened out."

"I bet it was neat to fly over Manhattan in a helicopter."

It was. She filled me in on the dinner in Little Italy, the Met, the Hanson cab ride, and the Tavern on the Green. I don't think New York will ever be the same.

When Bertie wound down, her blue eyes fastened on me. "I know you've had a lot on your mind lately, but Zara just called while you were out. She said that she hadn't heard from you for a week and that Ari hadn't either."

God, has it been that long? "It hasn't been a week. She's exaggerating." I started to feel guilty, but I just couldn't bring it up. The girls were busy in their lives. I would call, but I was busy in my life, too.

"It's been interesting since you left."

"Now it's your turn, tell me all about it and don't leave anything out," Bertie said excitedly.

I went over it all. The connection I believed existed between Michael, Nikki, and Franklin's deaths. The possible ties with Cynthia and her Mother, Emma. The missing persons case that Nikki was working on when he died, and discovering Mona Freeman. I went over everything, not only because I respected Bertie's opinion on things, but also it was helping me to get the big picture again. "I think everything is connected. I just don't know how yet."

Bertie nodded thoughtfully. "What do the police say about Mona Freeman's murder?"

"Officially, I don't know. Chev heard that it is probably going down as a suicide." I thought of Chev and Dan at dinner. I couldn't help smiling. "We're getting the police report, but I want to see what the M.E. said."

"I bet it was murder." Bertie's voice was low, her eyes big.

"I think so, too." I said just as solemnly. "I just have to figure out why."

Bertie patted my hand. "You will, dear." Bertie always believed I could do anything. That confidence has kept me going in rough times, just because I didn't want to let her down.

I ran my hand through my hair distractedly. I was surprised for a moment when I felt no hair. God, I was getting confused. "I'm starting to feel like I know too much. I've got too much data. I don't have a handle on it yet."

"Well, you'll get it sorted out, dear. I've got to go. Will you keep Chaddy for me for a few more days? I've got a lot of cleaning to do and it just upsets him so."

"Sure," I smiled to myself. "He's good company."

Bertie walked to the back door. Chaddy followed, eager to go with her. Bertie sank down on her knees until she was on Chaddy's ear level. I could see her talk to him, his tail was wagging, and then all of a sudden he came back to stand by me. After a hug and kiss, Bertie was on her way.

"You're supposed to protect me, right?" Chaddy just tilted his head at me like he was considering whether to admit it or not.

I fixed myself a small salad with tuna on top with tarragon vinegar dressing and went into my study to call the girls. Zara was full of psychological advice, but love, too. I could sense her concern.

"Zara honey, by the time you get me all figured out, I'll probably be in an old folks home. My biggest problem will be finding someone to push my wheelchair."

"Mother!" She laughed.

"Don't worry. I'll get a motorized one."

We talked about school, her boy friends, and my hair until I finally said goodbye.

Arianne was either in the throes of PMS or she'd had a really bad day. "Honey, you sound depressed."

"Oh, Mom, Jon and I broke up."

God, here was another installment in the saga of Jonathan, the boomerang boyfriend. Throw him away and he keeps coming back. I listened to a few minutes of her eighteen-year old's heartbreak, then I told Arianne about my nose and hair.

"Mom, you didn't." She wailed.

God, did I need a keeper already? "Don't worry, I'll hold a name card in front of my face the next time I pick you up at the train station." That brightened her a little.

We chatted for a few more minutes and when we hung up, she sounded happier. Being a mother is rough work. All in all maybe it was just as well I had my girls at a fairly young age. If I'd waited any longer, I don't think I would have had the stamina to survive their adolescence.

CHAPTER THIRTY FOUR

I was still musing on my worthiness as a mother when the phone rang. It was Chev.

"What are you doing, or can't you say?" I teased.

"Ha, Ha, very funny. Danny went home an hour ago." There was a don't-go-there tone in her voice.

"What are you doing?"

"Sitting here, trying to decide if I've been a good mother or not."

"They're still alive aren't they?" She asked.

"Yeah."

"Then you've done your job."

"I've heard that joke."

"Okay, here's some news for you. The curtains from Spiegel."

"What did they look like?"

"Ornate, turquoise fleur-de-lis pattern, damask fabric."

"Turquoise?" I said. "Turquoise, as in blue-green?"

"You got it."

I could see in my mind's eye an ornate room with a blue green color scheme.

"Emma Reeves."

"What about her?"

"She has blue-green eyes. Her whole house is in that color."

"Jeeze."

"Did Danny know anything about the M.E.'s report on Mona Freeman?"

"He's going to try to find out for me tomorrow. And he's checking out the Damon Edwards case."

I thought for a few seconds. "Chev, could we get some photographs of anyone connected with the Edwards case? Alexa Grant knows something about the murders that she is afraid . . . let me take that back, she isn't afraid of anything. That she is reluctant to tell."

"Do you think she saw Nikki's killer?" Chev asked, a catch in her voice.

"I don't know if she is the woman who was supposed to meet Nikki. But I think she knows something about Franklin, Michael and Nikki's deaths."

"Well, I'll call the library and see if they can help me get newspapers from Mississippi from about the time of Damon Edwards' death."

"Great. I'm going back to see Mrs. Reeves tomorrow. I want to verify that the curtains from Mona's garage belonged to Emma and ask her if she has any clue how they turned up at a murder scene." I remembered the mirror. "Oh, and I'm going to see about our fingerprints, too."

"Okay, call me if you think of anything else."

I hung up after we agreed to meet the next day at the office. I fixed myself a glass of iced tea and headed upstairs to my bedroom, Chaddy dutifully at my heels. I pulled all the files out from under my bed and sat down on the floor. I stacked them then went through them one by one.

I read the medical examiners report on Nikki. He was shot in the chest. The bullet entered his back just under his right ribcage and moved upward exiting through the left chest. It ripped the aorta. He was dead in minutes. There were photos of the scene. He had slumped over in the seat on his back. His right hand was over the wound as if he was trying to stem the flow or reach for his gun in its shoulder holster.

I stared at the pictures for a while then put them away. Nikki had been a handsome man. He had dark, curly hair, a strong face and dark eyes. After knowing Chev it was even harder to look at them.

The last file was Michael's. It was his notes and the journal of his special cases. I reread all of it. It was easier this time. I found I was beginning to understand some of his weird shorthand, too.

When I came to the notes on the break-in at Brody, Bowman, and Tate. I felt something nag at me. I couldn't figure out what was bothering me, so I kept flipping pages. On the last page was a note I'd read before. The initials D.E. and fingerprints circled with his little stars running off to the edge of the page. The words 'one and the same' underlined. I had no idea what he was talking about.

I sat on the floor with my back against the bed. I closed my eyes. I must have dozed off because when the phone rang I jumped so badly my heart was racing.

"Hello."

"Ann! Ann! It's Layne." At first my old name threw me. But the suppressed excitement in her voice was like having ice water thrown in your face. I was completely alert. "There's something funny about the M.E.'s report on Franklin."

CHAPTER THIRTY FIVE

I held on to the phone while I pulled myself to my feet. "What's funny about it?" I sat on the edge of my bed.

"They say it's definitely Franklin. They identified his dental records, but they didn't find all of his teeth."

"I thought teeth didn't melt or deteriorate when there was a fire."

"Me, too, but they didn't find some of them," Layne said quietly.

"Well, Franklin did have all his teeth, didn't he?" The thought of the silver haired, extremely patrician Franklin Brody with sunken cheeks gumming his food was a real gut buster.

"Of course, he did," she said snappishly. 'God, did I really believe she'd fool with some toothless asshole?' was in her tone.

"Well, then what happened to them?"

"Exactly."

"Exactly," I echoed, my voice trailing off as I thought of the implications of the missing dental work.

"Ann! Ann!" I came back from my reverie.

"Could you make that Stella please?"

"Stella?"

"Yep. It's too hard to explain now, but it would make my life simpler if all my friends would get into one camp."

"What in Heaven's name are you talking about?"

"I told you it was complicated."

"Okay. Okay." She stumbled over it. "Stella. What should we do?"

Without hesitation, I said, "I'll look into it. Don't worry."

I was as surprised by the authority in my voice as Layne seemed to be, but she accepted it without question. "There's something else." I waited. "John Borman wants to talk to you."

"Okay. Tell him I'll call him tomorrow afternoon."

"Thanks Ann, uh Stella." Layne didn't seem to want to chat. I didn't either.

When we hung up I pushed the files back under my bed. I took my notebook and wrote down the key points that I needed answers for. My eyes were stinging when I lay down. In spite of my fatigue, my mind was racing. Sleep finally came. I don't remember what I dreamed.

The next morning was one of those gray fall days when cold mist covers everything. The dullness of the atmosphere intensified the vivid colors of the rest of the world. I stood at the kitchen window mesmerized by the red leaves of an elderly oak tree outside.

I was washing my breakfast dishes, ready to go and see Emma Reeves again, but the warm water, the gray mist and the red leaves were holding me still. Something was running around in my brain like a name I couldn't remember or a title less song. I shook my head, drained the sink and rinsed my hands.

I went upstairs to my bedroom, took a shower, and began to dress. I chose a straight black skirt with a black silk blouse. I put on my new black and gray tweed jacket. My stockings were off black. I wore low-heeled black leather pumps. I'd been the high-heeled route when I was younger, trying to improve on my small stature. I'd finally accepted being short. Now I was strictly into comfort, stylish comfort that is.

I was still learning how to deal with my hair. I moussed up my hands and slicked it back. My daughter did this on a daily basis. I would probably master the technique in a few years. I put on a pair of silver hoop earrings. I was ready to go.

I looked around my bedroom. I needed curtains, furniture, and accessories. I had a lot of work ahead of me on the home front. When I knew why Michael died, I would make it my next priority. I picked up the phone from the nightstand and punched in Chev's number.

"Fortuna Investigations."

"This is your ace investigator about to begin a day of the relentless pursuit of truth."

"Justice, and the American way. Good, Superwoman, will you be flying by here sometime this afternoon?"

"You bet cha," I laughed. "In the meantime, can you get any of your friends down at headquarters to comment on the M.E.'s report on Franklin Brody? Specifically the fact that he apparently was missing some teeth."

"What?"

"That's right. Not enough teeth. Layne called me last night. She insists that the man she was married to had a full set."

"God, that's bizarre. I'll see what I can find out."

"Okay, I'll see you later."

"Ten-four."

CHAPTER THIRTY SIX

The drive in was pleasant enough. I wasn't in a big hurry, but traffic was fairly light on I-270 and I breezed into D.C. with no problems. I found a parking space on Connecticut Avenue about a block above Emma Reeves' building and walked down.

The same doorman was there. He didn't recognize me. When he rang Emma Reeves apartment, no one answered. I had already thought this one through.

"That's funny. She is expecting me." I fumed a little for his benefit. "Emma never forgets an appointment. Something must be wrong."

"Well, ma'am, I haven't seen her today," he began, but I cut him off.

"We've got to check on her. Have you got a key?" I just needed a look at the apartment. I wanted to check the curtains. I kept pushing until he finally relented.

"Okay, Ma'am. If it will put your mind at rest."

We took the elevator to the seventh floor together. The doorman led the way to number 726 and pressed his hands down the front of this uniform. I imagine his palms were a little sweaty. He knocked on Emma Reeve's door, paused, and knocked again. I thought he'd be knocking for the next ten minutes, but he reached up under his coat and unhooked a set of keys that extended on a chain from his belt. His movements were slow and measured. At long last, he retrieved a single key from the bunch in his hand and unlocked Emma Reeves' door.

"Mrs. Reeves," he called discretely. No answer. He opened the door and stepped in motioning for me to join him. The living room looked the same. The floor to ceiling windows, the heavy damask curtains in turquoise fleur-de-lis pattern. I felt a surge of electricity travel up my body from my toes. Pride. I had actually detected something.

The light was strong in here. I crossed to the window and fingered the material. It was slightly faded. Not enough to be replaced in my world of housekeeping, but intolerable, I'm sure, to someone with no money worries or perhaps not enough to do.

If the doorman wondered why I was so easily distracted by the feel of brocade, he didn't let on. He continued through to the kitchen calling for Mrs. Reeves. I recovered myself and followed him. The apartment up to this point had appeared immaculate, but the kitchen made me apprehensive. A large Dutch-oven type pot lay on the floor at the entrance in a puddle of water. Not much water, though. The pattern on the shiny tile floor showed that a great deal of it had evaporated. Utensils were scattered in a path to a door leading out of the kitchen. The little man looked at me, resignation in his eye. He was, after all, the one in charge.

He opened the door and immediately swayed backwards. The stench was hideous. I grabbed him and half carried, half dragged him to the sink. He fell into it heaving from his shoulders.

I grabbed a dishtowel from a hook and covered my new nose. I went to the door and looked in. The room had hand painted walls in a Rousseau type forest scene. Emma's bed was a cascade of fabric in an abstract leaf pattern with a few flowers thrown in for color. Emma Reeves lay in the middle of the impossibly romantic canopy bed like a mottled brown bug. The one earth tone in a sea of green. At least, I think it was Emma Reeves. The body was so puffed up it was hard to tell. There was a greenish blue scarf tangled around her neck. It looked like the belt from the negligee she wore. A soft teal-colored long silk gown. The skirt had been arranged to cover her legs. Her arms were extended like she was making a snow angel. In fact her whole body had been straightened, arranged in almost a loving, reverential way. It gave me the creeps. I didn't look at her eyes.

I backed up and shut the door. My stomach heaved like an alien thing was trying to break out through my chest just north of my belly button. I fought it down. I collared my elderly guide, helping him through the apartment until we were out the door. I pulled it shut behind us.

"You better call the police," I said as we stepped into the elevator. He still seemed a little woozy, but by the time we reached the lobby, he was back in control. He walked briskly to his desk and phoned the police. When he was done, he sat down heavily on his high-backed stool.

"I've got to go, Mr.?"

"Khouri." He nodded as if we'd been formally introduced.

"Mr. Khouri, please give this to the detective in charge." I wrote a note to Harrison, asking him to call me, on the back and handed it to him. "Are you all right?" He nodded again. I thought speech was going to be difficult for a while. "Here, keep this one for yourself. If you need to call, I'm not in the book." I tucked another of my cards in his pocket. He just blinked.

CHAPTER THIRTY SEVEN

I walked back to my car then changed my mind and crossed Connecticut Avenue to a phone booth outside a fast food restaurant directly across the street.

"Fortuna Investigations," Chev answered smoothly.

"There's been another one," I said solemnly.

"Another what? Gawd, another murder?" She answered her own question.

"Yes, Emma Reeves. I don't think they'll call it suicide, either."

"Tell me everything." I could imagine her, pen poised, ready to get everything down on paper.

"The curtains are hers, by the way."

"All right, Sherlock!" Chev's voice was a blend of concern and humor. She had a knack of keeping the right emotional balance.

"I didn't throw up this time. The doorman did, but I didn't."

"You're getting to be pretty tough, Stella. What happened?" I told her about the mess in the kitchen. Emma's body in the bedroom.

"But why?" was all she said after I finished. I was asking myself that question.

"The only link I can see is the robbery at B. B. and T. And if that's the common thread here, then we need to get a hold of Cynthia Reeves as soon as possible."

"You're right. Let me take care of it." I could hear the worry in her voice.

"You're going to see your friend at the forensic lab next, right?"

"That's where I'm headed. I'll call you in about an hour."

I could hear sirens from a distance. It was time to go. I gave her the number at the forensic lab. I told her to ask for David Ramsey if she needed me. When I pulled away from the curb, I could see the flashing blues in my rear view mirror.

I parked my car behind the lab building. The surrounding woods and rolling hills a gentle contrast to the business conducted inside the brick and glass building. I went through an entryway that reminded me of my daughter's elementary school except no kids' artwork lined the tan tile walls. Forensics was a complex of green glass cubicles with glimpses of chemistry type labs in between.

David Ramsey had been Michael's classmate at the FBI academy years ago. Both of them were mavericks. Now David was Chief pathologist for the District of Columbia. He and Michael had continued to compare notes and trade professional services right up until Michael's death.

The surprised look on David's face reminded me that he was expecting Ann Strayer not Stella Jones. "I'm sorry, David. I should have prepared you on the phone. There have been a few changes in the last six months."

"All good ones," he said gallantly. Gallant. That was a good word to describe David Ramsey. He was the type of man who was extremely kind to women, animals, and small children. He was tall and lean with wiry black hair, liberally peppered with gray. He had a nice face with dark blue eyes, long nose, and wide mouth.

"Thanks for letting me come by." I pulled the envelope with the mirror and Michael's notebook from my briefcase. "I need some help, David. I'm going to tell you my idea and I don't want you to laugh, or smile, or think I'm cute because I'm dead serious." I opened the notebook and showed him the entries about the break-in. "I think that Michael, Franklin, and another man were killed because of some information they had about the break-in that would threaten Leo and Robert Parnelli. I think that two more recent deaths are also related." I decided to keep it simple. Emma Reeves wasn't common knowledge yet. I didn't need to worry. Instead of pooh-poohing my whole theory, he actually listened.

"I'll do what I can." He looked at the mirror. "What's this about?"

"I don't know yet." I looked down at the filmy prints. "I just need to know who this is."

"I'll feed it into our database, but I don't know if I'll come up with anything." He was a kind man who just happened to get better looking as he got older.

"Thanks for taking me seriously."

"Well, I still think you're cute." He smiled.

I blushed like an adolescent. I couldn't think of the last time that I'd felt cute. "You always were a smooth talker." I opened the journal and pointed to Michael's notes about the fingerprints. "You know Michael's chicken scratches better than I do. Would you look this over if you have time?"

"Will do." He piled everything in the center of the gleaming steel lab table. "I'll call you in a day or two when I know something." He walked me to the door.

"I expect to discuss this over dinner," he added. Gallant. He was fussing over me because he sensed I needed it. We both knew that ours was just a friendship. But it felt nice just the same.

CHAPTER THIRTY EIGHT

I didn't fly to Chev's office, but I did a four-wheeled drive impression of it. When I pulled up outside, I noticed a beat up, blue Chevy caprice in the space ahead. An unmarked police car was my guess.

Harrison was sitting at Chev's desk enjoying a cup of coffee. Chev was wearing a very flattering dark brown suit with a leopard-patterned scarf around her neck. It complimented her big brown eyes and her blonde hair that she had plied into a French twist. She put down her cup.

"Here she is. Stella, Detective Harrison wanted to ask us a few questions." Chev's tone was light, unconcerned. She was the soul of innocence.

"Hello, Detective Harrison. I see you got my note." I shook hands and sat in the naugahyde chair on his left.

"Coffee?" Chev asked me.

"Yes, please."

Chev bustled out of the room. I could hear the clatter of dishes from the kitchenette.

"You've done something different to yourself." Harrison had a way of streamlining conversation. He stated the obvious and avoided the polite question. He looked a little less weary today, nicely dressed in a navy blue suit with a white on white shirt and reddish tie.

I brushed my hand through my hair. I kept forgetting I didn't have any. "It's the haircut." I could play this game myself.

The barest hint of a grin flirted across his mouth transforming his face, making it handsome. But he was all seriousness as he pulled out his notebook.

"What were you doing at Emma Reeves apartment? The doorman said that you insisted you had an appointment."

"I lied. I just wanted to see her curtains."

Harrison had a great poker face. "So you didn't have an appointment after all?"

"No, just a theory."

Chev had returned with my coffee. She freshened Harrison's and fixed her own. I waited until she was done and comfortable in her chair.

"We found out that the curtains in Mona Freeman's garage were blue-green. I remembered that Emma Reeves was a nut for blue-green." I looked at Chev. "You see, I'd gone to interview her a few days ago. And, well, we just decided to check it out," I ended brightly.

"What does that connection tell you?" He was like a teacher in school trying to lead me through the problem.

"That the murderer had access to both women's homes."

"What day did you see Mrs. Reeves?"

"Monday."

"Well, you might have been the last person to see her alive. I'm going to need a statement from you."

Chev turned in her chair and pulled a file from the in basket on her desk. "Here are the notes on the interview. We always keep records of each one." She handed Harrison a sheaf of papers.

"If you'd like me to go over it," I started to say, but Harrison waved his hand and began to read.

"You thought that she was frightened?"

"Yes and angry, too. We think she retained Nikki's services after Brody cancelled the investigation."

"We received an anonymous retainer to keep looking into the robbery. I told Nikki I didn't like it but we put it in the escrow account and he kept going. Franklin Brody was not happy."

"So she was trying to clear her daughter? That's your theory?" Harrison asked.

"Franklin Brody was paying the rent on her apartment. We're not sure what their relationship was, but we have a guess," Chev added darkly.

"Both of the murdered women, Mona and Emma," I paused, and gave Harrison a look, "had bedrooms that were out of this world. Obviously to impress a man, who by good authority, was a fifteen on a scale from one to ten in the lovemaking department."

He didn't dispute me, didn't dispute that they had been murdered. An indescribable expression played across Harrison's face. Finally he chuckled. "You two are incredible. Finding motives in draperies. I guess I need to pay more attention to interior decorating styles."

"Hey, I don't think the assumption that Franklin Brody was the lover of these two women should be a stretch," I said, somewhat defensively.

"Okay, okay. I agree. It would appear that he may have had some sort of relationship with both women," Harrison said in an attempt to placate our feelings.

"And that's why they're dead," Chev finished.

"Well, I can't assume that yet, but it certainly is an idea worth checking out." He asked me a few more questions then asked Chev for a copy of the file. While she made the copies, he said, "Mrs. Strayer, I know you want to help. It's understandable after the shock you've had, but why don't you let the police handle this? You could get hurt. You both could get hurt."

I felt my face flush. Hey, I'd figured out the curtains. How could he just brush me off like this? "It's Stella Jones, now. I'm working as a freelance investigator for Mrs. Fortuna."

"That's right." Chev turned and handed him his copies. "Stella is helping me finish off a few of Nikki's cases. They just seem to be getting her in the wrong place at the wrong time."

Harrison looked from one to the other of us with the indulgent skepticism of a parent listening to a kid's lame excuse for wrongdoing. "Where's your license?"

Chev said smoothly, "It's applied for. She has temporary status with the firm until it's official."

"Okay Chev, just don't get yourself and your friend killed. I don't need the pressure." He got up and shrugged back into his raincoat. "I might need you to come down to the station. I'll let you know." He seemed as if he wanted to say something else, but just shook his head and walked out the door.

I put my head down on the edge of Chev's desk and took a deep breath.

"What's wrong?" Chev said as she locked the front door.

"I'm just letting go a little." Tears ran down my face. "I don't like finding dead bodies. It's awful, and I keep thinking it will be like Perry Mason. That someone will suspect me."

"Well honey, you know better than to grab the murder weapon, get your fingerprints all over it, then stand by the body and hold it up for the police to see like all Perry's dumb ass clients do."

I had to chuckle at that one. "They do all act like dumb asses." I wiped my face with a paper napkin. "I am beginning to think we've stirred this one up a little too good." I shook my head.

"Are you thinking you may have caused Emma Reeves death?" She said quietly.

"Yes."

"Have you considered that if we'd stirred this up sooner she might be alive?"

"No." I hadn't thought about that at all.

"Hey, we're partners in this thing. I'll do whatever you want to do, but Emma may have been doomed anyway. At least we can make sure she gets some justice." She paused and looked at me. "This can be a dangerous business. Most of the time it is tedious and boring, but other times, it's deadly." She quit talking. Just sat drinking her coffee. Waiting for me to make the decision.

"You're right. We may do some good. So it's worth it to keep trying."

THE PHOENIX

CHAPTER THIRTY NINE

I was helping Chev clean up when I remembered. "My God, I forgot about Cynthia."

Chev handed me a cup to dry. "She's gone to her grandmother's house. The old lady lives on a farm outside of Frederick."

"Will she be safe there?"

"I hope so since we're the only ones who know she's there."

I dried the next cup. "Is it her mother's mother or her father's?"

"Neither." Chev said sudsing the coffeepot. "Her maternal grandmother is dead and she never met her father's mother." She paused and looked at me. "She never met her father, either."

"Or maybe she met her father but she didn't know it." Chev gave me a long look. "So who is this woman?" I asked.

"Her name is Sarah Porter. She is the lady who used to baby sit her when she was little."

"Good. I hope it's not a widely known fact. It should be obscure enough to protect her." I put the last dish away and hung up my towel. "How did she take the news about her mother? By the way, I'm sorry you had to be the one to break it to her."

S. Alden Reilly

Chev smiled. "Thanks." Then her face saddened. "She took it pretty well at first, but I had a feeling she was just waiting to get to her grandma's to let go."

We were quiet as we finished in the kitchenette, each busy with our own thoughts. When the phone rang in the outer office, I jumped a mile. "I'll get it." I headed for her desk. "Hello, Stella Jones, may I help you?"

The voice on the other end faltered then said, "I thought I should tell you whom Franklin was seeing." It was John Borman. "I'll make it easy for you, John. It was Emma Reeves."

His surprise was genuine. "How did you know?"

"We tracked it down. He held the deed on her apartment. He was supporting Mona Freeman, too."

Borman paused then cautiously said, "Yes. I guessed that they had had an affair."

A guess confirmed. He was speaking slowly, like the words had to be dragged out of him. I didn't think it had anything to do with loyalty to Franklin. "John, Layne's better off now. This won't hurt her anymore."

That was just the cue he needed. "Even though he was my partner, I hated what he did to Layne. I thought the Reeves woman and Mona were bad enough. I wanted to fire Mona, but he fought me over it." He was unburdening himself. It kept pouring out. "Then he started getting calls from some new woman."

My attention was completely focused. "Who?"

"I don't know, but she called collect a few times. My secretary put one of her calls through to me when Frank was out of the office. She sounded very young. Later, I saw the bills. It was Tennessee, I think."

"Do you still have the bills?" I kept my voice calm.

"Well, I can have my secretary look them up."

"Good. It would be a great help, John." I hung up and went looking for Chev. She was in Nikki's office arranging some files on the desk.

"That was John Borman. He confirmed that Franklin was involved with Emma and Mona."

"We already knew that," she grinned. "We're just too damned good," she said, motioning me to come around to Nikki's chair.

I laughed. "Well there may be another woman in the picture, from Tennessee."

"Wow, I knew the guy was an A-hole, but is there a limit?" She shook her head. "Here, sit down and look at what I found today. Your hunch was right."

I sat in Nikki's chair and opened the top file. It contained faxed copies of newspaper clippings. "What are these?"

"Newspaper clippings from Oak Ridge, Mississippi." She picked up the first clipping and handed it to me. "Remember when you said some of Mrs. Grant's story might be true? You were right. I called the nearest library, which happened to be in Jackson, and got them to look up a boating accident twenty-three years ago. The librarian even remembered it because the family is the local version of royalty. Big money, they own half the town."

"So what is her real name?"

"Here, look at these pictures." She fanned the papers out. One clipping had two photos. The fax quality was poor, but Damon Edwards appeared to be a handsome man. High forehead, slightly hooked nose, he looked like someone I'd seen before, a movie actor maybe. The other picture showed a young woman cradling a baby. They were standing on the steps of a church. The caption read 'Martine Edwards leaves the funeral services for her husband, prominent attorney,

Damon Edwards with daughter Aurora, nine months.' It was Alexa Grant holding the baby.

"So Damon Edwards was her husband. Why couldn't she just be honest about her name?"

"Who knows why people lie. I can't believe she didn't think we'd figure it out," Chev sighed. "By the way, Danny's getting a copy of the Oak Ridge police report."

I read through the clippings again slowly. "Boating accident. His companion washes up on shore three days later. Damon Edwards never does." I was lost in thought. Chev just stood beside me and waited. "So the Damon Edwards of Michael's notes was the late husband of Martine Edwards, better known to us as Alexa Grant. Whew!" I shook my head.

"Sounds like it," Chev said matter-of-factly.

"What is she up to? She really believes that Damon Edwards is still alive. Is that who she is looking for or is it someone else?"

"All good questions," Chev grinned. "I never said this was going to be easy."

"Well, at least you found out who she really is. Good work partner!" I said closing the file.

"Are you ready for this?" she said, handing me another file when I came back from my reverie. It was Franklin's autopsy report. I leaned back in the chair and read it through. The medical examiner had done a thorough job. The body had practically disintegrated from the blast and fire, but the estimated height, weight, and other vitals were there, as well as teeth and metal pieces described as dental appliance material.

I looked at Chev. She had gone to sit in the client chair in front of the desk. I underlined an item and handed it to her. "Look at his notes on the jawbone," I said to Chev. "See where it says the bony ridge was perforated?"

"Is that what that says?" she said, looking at the Latin terms.

"It's the fifty-cent version. Anyway, that indicated that the man had implanted teeth." I explained, "If you have your teeth knocked out the dentist can implant a false one in the space and the bone will grow around it and it has a natural appearance."

"So what does that mean?"

"It means that either Franklin did have implants because his teeth were knocked out at some point in time, or that jawbone does not belong to Franklin."

"Well, Layne would know that kind of thing wouldn't she? I mean, if her husband got his teeth knocked out or not?"

"Maybe it happened before they met and he never told her about it. Let's check with Layne and get the name of their dentist." I picked up the phone to call Layne. Her phone rang four times. Her answering machine picked up. I left a message. I turned back to Chev. "There are several options here. A. We have bad information about the state of Franklin's dental health, B. the coroner's report is wrong, or C. the dead guy isn't Franklin Brody."

Chev looked at me. "Well dog my cats."

"My sentiments, exactly."

CHAPTER FORTY

By the time I left the office I was dead tired. I toyed with the idea of stopping to see Cynthia Reeves, but since it was dark, I decided to head straight for home instead. I was in my automatic pilot mode when I hit Interstate 70.

Ordinarily, I would get off at the first exit, but when I moved to the right to get into the exit lane, a truck came barreling up from nowhere and cut me off. I swung my Trooper back into the left lane, my knees shaking.

The driver was in shadow, but the truck was a familiar blue pickup. 'Big Blue' was on the plastic guard across the front. The hands on the steering wheel were obviously a man's.

Fear settled over me like a cold clammy fog. I tried to shake the feeling, but my hands and armpits were already sweaty. I gripped the steering wheel like it was a lifeline and stepped on the gas. My car shot forward, but I tapped the overdrive button for good measure. Not warp speed, but a reasonable substitute. Interstate 70 is usually one long speed trap, but I didn't see a single state trooper as I raced along. Where were the cops when you needed them?

We flew up the mountain and down the other side practically neck and neck. I wondered why the blue pickup didn't try to force me off the road with a sideswipe, but I guess he didn't want to scratch his truck.

I tried to think through my panic, taking deep breaths, willing myself to calm down. The road made a fairly straight shot west through the mountains of the panhandle of Western Maryland. The medians were wide and full of rock or mounded up in small hills. Not much hope there unless. ..

I put my foot to the floor as we careened into the first valley. I managed to gain about six car lengths on him as we came into the curve. I remembered a spot. A place where the median between the roads widened and a swampy area provided a break in the hills that separated the east and west lanes of the highway. As I came into the curve, I started braking. My car bucked as I pushed down hard on the brakes. I turned my lights off and hit my four-wheel drive button as I coasted into the grass of the median. The trooper hovered at the edge like a reluctant swimmer testing the water, and then plunged down the incline into the marshy water just as 'Big Blue' came into view.

I felt my car sinking into the mud as the blue pickup squealed his brakes. The moon was only a sliver. He didn't see me, but he knew something was wrong. All of a sudden, the night lit up. He had a set of headlights mounted on the top of the truck. His brakes squealed as he tried to slow down. My heart skipped a beat. I didn't want to be bogged down in the mud in case he doubled back. I gave the Trooper a little more gas but she sank in a little deeper. Sweat broke out on my forehead. I realized I was rocking back and forth in my seat, unconsciously willing us up and out. Finally, with a weird sucking sound, she rolled a little forward and waddled up out of the water like a boxy duck. I drove her like a tank through the ravine and up the other side. A guardrail cut me off but ended with a gap on the left. I was just squeezing through when I heard a distant roar. The pickup was speeding away.

I came out on the shoulder, switched back into normal drive and hit the gas. Chunks of mud flew in every direction as I accelerated to ninety miles per hour in a very respectable time. I figured 'Big Blue' would try to double back on the next exit. I intended to be long gone.

My knees didn't want to work when I pulled up in my driveway. The sight of a familiar silver Buick made tears come to my eyes. I wanted to run into the house. Run to Bertie like I did when I was five and the neighbor kids had been mean to me. Instead I walked calmly into the kitchen picked the phone and called Chev.

"Stella. What is it?" She sensed something was wrong?

"I need you to check something out for me." I rummaged in my purse until I found the slip of paper my Knights from the other evening had given me. "A license plate number. FNJ 694. Maryland.

"What's up?"

"Just one too many run-ins with a very aggressive driver." I described the truck and the two incidents. "It may be the same truck that was at Franklin Brody's just before the big bang. I forgot about it after everything that happened today."

"No problem." I could tell that this news had rocked her, but she calmed me with her voice. "I've got good news. Danny's got some more information on the Mississippi case. You want to come by tomorrow morning and we can go over it?"

"Sure, see you about ten o'clock." I hung up the phone and turned around. Bertie was standing by the kitchen table. Chaddy at her feet. Both of them were looking at me reproachfully.

"Okay, I'm sorry," I said flinging my arms out dramatically. "I am trying to be careful." My knees were still shaking.

Bertie walked up to me and put her arms around me. Chaddy came and sat on my feet. Oddly the weight of his big body relaxed my legs, took the shake out of them. "Honey, I know. I just didn't like hearing about that monster following you, intimidating you."

I leaned on her shoulder wondering at the strength in her fragile frame. "I think you and Chaddy ought to go home. It's getting too crazy and I don't want anything to happen to you two." I reached down to pat the dog's massive head.

"Nonsense. We're staying here until you're out of danger." Bertie looked like a sweet little grandma in her pink polyester pantsuit, but her eyes were chips of blue ice. I knew my highway harasser would be in serious trouble if he showed up at my house while these bodyguards were on duty.

"I'm starved. Let's eat something." I headed for the fridge.

"It's in the oven." Bertie announced. "Why don't you get comfortable? I'll have it ready when you come down."

I showered and changed into a big terry caftan. When I sat down at the table, Bertie placed a juicy steak and salad in front of me. I ate like a starving person for the next few minutes until I realized what I was doing and slowed down.

Bertie was full of the success of her church dinner. The older people at the church really looked forward to these bi-weekly dinners because so many of them had lost spouses or were distant from family members.

"It is so rewarding to see their faces relaxed and happy," Bertie smiled with an inner glow. "And it keeps the girls busy."

I smiled at Bertie's term 'the girls', and the fact that Bertie excluded herself from the need to keep busy. She was completely honest. She had never stopped moving since the day she was born.

Chadwick snored under the table while I basked in the details of the menu and conversations. It was a return to decency and normalcy that made all the day's events recede. That is until a knock on the door startled all three of us.

THE PHOENIX

CHAPTER FORTY-ONE

It was Layne. Layne like I'd never seen her before. She was wearing a pair of old jeans with a man's long sleeved blue shirt that hung to her knees. Her shoes were battered penny loafers with two dull pennies stuck in the slots. Her hair was windblown, or else she had been running her hands through it. As if to resolve that question, she ran her left hand nervously through her hair.

"Come in." I took her arm and helped her inside. She was so obviously upset that I was concerned. When I gripped her arm, I realized it was excitement, not fear driving her.

"Bertie, Layne's here. Why don't you pour her some tea?"

"I'm sorry An. . .Stella, I just had to see you. I hope I'm not intruding."

"Of course not, come and sit down."

Bertie gave me a look. I shrugged my shoulders. I didn't know what was going on. "Here, dear." Bertie placed a cup of tea in front of Layne. "Why don't you tell us what's happened," she said soothingly.

We all sat down. Layne gripped her teacup with both hands and took a sip, and then she set it down and looked at me.

"I was checking on restarting my law practice," she began. I nodded encouragingly. "Well, I had to send a letter to the Bar and they sent me back a bunch of paperwork to fill out," she paused. "I was going through my records to get the dates and everything, and I found some old papers of Franklin's." She shrugged her shoulders. "Okay, when I moved into my apartment I took all my papers and Franklin's, too. They're still all in boxes. I know it wasn't nice, but I was sure he was going to try to cheat me. So I took all his stuff, too." She laughed. "A lot of good it did me. Anyway, I found the original application Franklin had submitted to the D.C. Bar. The form had 'Franklin Brody' on it with nearest relative listed as 'Emma Brody, sister.'"

"What?" I said at full attention.

"Yes. It said that Franklin had a sister named Emma and gave an address in Cumberland, Maryland." She turned to Bertie as she explained the point. "Franklin always said that he only had one brother and that he was dead."

"What explanation could there be?" I began.

"I don't know, but when I heard the news this afternoon about Emma Reeves's body being discovered, I called the hall of records and asked about her." She looked back at me. "They said that she was born Emma Mae Brody. That she'd been married to a Charles S. Reeves and that she had an older brother named Franklin."

"Well, dog my cats," I said. "What birth date did they give you for her brother?"

"July 17, 1946."

"What was Franklin's birthday?"

"May 26, 1948." She looked at her teacup. "At least that's what he said it was."

"What did the application say?"

She gave me a blank look. "Oh, I never thought to check that." She reached down into her purse. "I've got it out in the car. I'll go get it."

Bertie looked at me when Layne went outside.

"Dog my cats?"

"It's a Chevism. I picked it up."

Bertie shook her head. "I always thought you needed a good kick in the behind to get you going, but this is a little too much."

"Yeah, kind of like a run-away roller coaster." I put my hand over hers on the table. "What doesn't kill us makes us stronger. Nietzsche said that and I believe it."

She was sputtering, trying to think of a reply when Layne came back in. She opened the file on the table. The yellowed application form was dated June 1, 1979. Franklin's birth date was typed in on the application. July 17, 1946.

"Why would a man have two birthdays?" Bertie asked the obvious.

"That's a good question," I said. "I'll get Chev to add it to the list of things we need to find out."

"Franklin always said the problem with our relationship was that he was a Gemini and that Geminis are easily bored." Layne spoke like a robot. Evidently the memory of that conversation wasn't a pleasant one.

"Maybe Gemini's like Franklin are just two faced assholes," I said angrily. I hated the way even the memory of that slime ball affected her. "Layne, I need you to look into this."

"What?" She said coming around. Her eyes lost the glazed look I'd just seen.

"I need you to follow up on this."

She set her face like a person about to whine, 'but I can't.' Instead she just said, "How?"

I went over to where I dumped my briefcase on the counter. I got out my notebook and wrote on a piece of paper.

"Here." I handed it to her. "This is Cynthia Reeves address. I need the two of you to go to her mother's apartment and sort through her personal papers, legal documents, old letters, photos, you know. Anyway, find anything you can that might help us clear up this two-birthday thing. Can you do that?"

She looked at me quietly for just a second. "Sure."

"Good. I'll call Cynthia in the morning and tell her to expect you. If she has better ideas about where to look, help her out, okay?"

"Okay, she'll have to clear it with the police, but they will probably let her have access. She'll need some of the documents so she can make arrangements for her mother." She was thinking again. Getting better.

I put my hand on her arm. "Here, call Detective Harrison. I scratched out his phone number on the piece of paper from the card he'd given me. I put the card back on the counter next to the phone. Please watch out for Cynthia and yourself. It's not too safe these days."

"I will." She looked down at the pennies in her loafers.

I gestured toward them. "Want me to polish those for you?"

Layne laughed. "No way. It took me years to get that tarnish on there. I haven't worn these since college."

"I knew you looked familiar. I've seen this fashion statement on Zara and her friends. Those pennies might be collectors items by now."

Layne smiled, "I'm not that old, but if you wait long enough, everything comes back in style."

THE PHOENIX

Bertie chimed in.   "What goes around, comes around."

How true, I thought. Especially when it's murder.

CHAPTER FORTY-TWO

I found out later that evening that Bertie was going to be my bodyguard for the duration of whatever my investigation led to.

Layne had gone home. A forty-three year old college student with a mission. Now my elderly aunt was going to sidekick with Chaddy to keep me safe from various and assorted villains.

I sighed and carried her heavy suitcase up to Zara's room. I'd left the girls' rooms intact. I didn't need to inflict my trauma-induced redecorating on them. Zara's room was the more acceptable guestroom only because her tastes were a little more mature. Arianne's room looked like a video rental store had exploded inside. Every square inch of space, including the ceiling, was filled with movie posters. I didn't think Bertie was ready for the cinema verite school of interior design.

Bertie came out of the bathroom in a fuzzy pink bathrobe. She sat on the bed and patted the covers next to her. "Come here, honey. I want to talk to you."

I had been putting her things into the drawers of Zara's dresser. I went and sat next to her and held her hand. "What is it? Is something wrong?"

"No, not unless you count the danger you seem to be in lately." She rubbed the bridge of her nose thoughtfully.

Her blue eyes looked bigger when she didn't have her glasses on. She looked more vulnerable too.

"No, I just wanted you to know that I love you." She stroked my hand with her fingers. "But I'm not going to be around forever."

"Bertie! Is something wrong? Don't you feel well?" I looked at her eyes. Trying to discover the hint of a secret in them. There was only concern.

"No, dear. I'm not going anywhere yet, but someday I won't be here and I worry about you. You need a partner. A life partner." I must have had a skeptical look on my face because she hurried on. "Stella, I know you were married to Michael for a long time, but he wasn't the right man for you. You need someone completely different."

"I never thought . . . you knew," I said incoherently.

"I knew you didn't really love him. And I knew that you had the girls to raise and that your focus was on them. But you're still young. You have the best years ahead of you. You deserve someone wonderful. Someone who will appreciate your spirit and return the passion I see inside of you."

It was such a deeply personal statement that it touched me and made me unable to answer for a moment. "I never believed that I had any passion or spirit," I finally muttered. It was my greatest fear. The fear that I was only capable of a half-hearted response to life. Although I had enjoyed my job, I had no passion for it, no passion for my husband, no passion to pursue an answer to the perpetual feeling of being disconnected. I'd always felt like a voyeur, not a participant in life. The only thing I had cared about was being a good mother to my kids, and, of course, the precious little woman who sat next to me. At least until now.

Bertie pulled my head down onto her shoulder and stroked my hair. "Michael getting killed was horrible dear, but it has set you free. You're going to find yourself. Then you will be able to recognize your love," she paused. "I don't just mean a person, although I think that you will find someone special. I mean recognizing what you love about your life, what makes you feel alive, what connects you to this earth." She gave me a tight hug. "Now, go get some rest. You've got a lot to do tomorrow." She shooed me off the bed and got under the covers.

I laid her robe across the end of the bed and kissed her forehead. "I love you, Bertie, more than you could ever know." I kissed her again on the cheek. "Goodnight, sleep tight."

She kissed my cheek. "Goodnight, baby."

Chaddy, who had been napping by the door jumped up and looked at Bertie, then, mindful of his responsibility and unwilling to play favorites, took up his station at the top of the stairs. He flopped down flat on his stomach, his massive head perfectly centered on the landing. He could open his eyes at any time for a quick survey down the stairway. I patted his head and went to bed.

The smell of fresh coffee was my wake up call. I showered, dressed in black slacks and a deep violet purple tunic. I added a black patterned scarf at my throat, silver earrings and low-heeled black leather boots.

I was getting pretty good at handling my hair. I had it spiked a little on top. My nose looked thinner, too. I hoped for a good day. "What are you doing today?" I asked Bertie as I downed my calcium tablets and multiple vitamins with a swallow of 'light' grape juice.

"I don't know." She was toasting a couple of bagels.

"Why don't you have the girls over for bridge?"

She shook her head. "No, I'll be fine. Just call me later so I'll know when you're coming home."

"Okay." I thought I'd better get to the bottom of things very quickly. Bertie would be like a caged animal in a couple of days. I couldn't think of a better incentive to sharpen the old brain cells.

I made it to Chev's in record time. I was anxious to see what she'd learned from the ever-hopeful Danny. When I opened the door she looked up from her desk. She didn't look good.

"What's wrong?" I walked quickly to her side. "Are you ill?"

"No. Just worried. About you."

I felt a chill in my stomach. "What is it?"

"The truck that tried to cream you twice?"

"Yeah?" I wouldn't forget 'Big blue' anytime soon.

"It's registered to the Parnelli Brothers Construction Company."

I sat down on the client chair. "Good."

"Good?"

I stood up and leaned over her desk. "We wanted to find out why Michael and Nikki died. We know the truck was at Brody's house before he died. I know we're very close. This just confirms it. Besides," I stood up, "this fear thing is how they get you. We're not going to buy into it. We're not going to worry."

"Me worry?" She grinned a slow grin. "Your nose looks better."

"Thanks. I feel like doing some snooping today."

"You're good, but from now on you're going to have company."

"Great, first Bertie and now you."

"Chadwick was the first." She picked up her giant purse. She had on a pretty raw silk skirt and long blouse in a khaki color that set off her blonde hair.

"Who are we going to see first? Dr. Lazaro?" She was the Brody's dentist. I had remembered to get her name from Layne before I left the house and called Chev.

"Don't need to. Franklin changed dentists. Dr. Lazaro hadn't seen him in a year. Transferred all his records to a new dentist. I checked the name and it isn't in the local area."

"How did the police identify him then?"

"Don't know. I have a call in to a friend at the precinct." She was obviously frustrated by the whole thing.

"You know that's just a little too weird. Didn't she keep anything, you know in case of a lawsuit?"

"Apparently nothing she wants to share at this time." Chev shook her head. "I got real cold vibes from her office. They said that if the patient signs a release they forward the records no questions asked."

"Well, the police got some records from someone. I hope your friend can help us out." We locked the office and got into the car.

"What did Danny have to say about the Mississippi case?"

"The guy with Damon Edwards, his fishing buddy, the one who washed up on shore? Well, he didn't drown, he was strangled."

"What?" I froze, my hands on the steering wheel. "He was murdered?"

"You got it. Choked with a piece of rope they used to tie the boat."

"I bet if Damon Edwards hadn't disappeared he would have been the number one suspect."

"There was money, too." Chev fastened her seat belt. "The Edwards family is worth millions. There were two sons. Damon, the oldest, and Beau. Beau was killed about a year before Damon's accident. His death was an accident, too. Accidentally shot with his own gun while on a hunting trip with his brother and some friends." She reached into her black purse and pulled out a newspaper clipping. "I asked my librarian friend to fax me anything on Beau."

The article detailed Beau Edward's accident. His gun had misfired and blown up in his face. The accompanying photo that showed a handsome man with classic features almost Grecian in proportion.

"God," I said. "Doesn't that seem like an excessive amount of tragedy for one family?"

"That's what I thought. Tennessee Williams aside." She gave me a sly grin. "It does seem like overkill." She handed me an envelope. "Here's one last thing."

"What?" I said opening the envelope.

"Remember when you had the idea about the ATM camera across from the phone booth that the mystery woman called Nikki from?"

I nodded as I pulled a grainy black and white photo from the envelope. "Mona Freeman!"

"Exactly." Chev hugged her arms.

"I'm beginning to understand why she was killed." I looked at Chev. "I think she was killed because of what she knew about Franklin. I think he had her make that call to Nikki to lure him to a place that Franklin could get rid of him. He thought she was completely under his control but she couldn't accept being a part of Nikki's murder. I think they fought about it and she got scared. I think she was trying to dig up dirt on Franklin. She was trying to get some insurance for herself but maybe she went too far and Franklin found out."

"Well, she's dead now." Chev seemed sad.

I took her hand. "I know that Mona didn't kill Nikki and I also know that he was not seeing her or any other woman when he died."

Chev gave me a brave little smile. "I want to believe you're right, but she was so beautiful."

"Bull. You're ten times the woman she ever was in looks, smarts, everything." I was emphatic. "Nikki had finally figured that out."

Chev patted my arm. "Thanks, dear partner. Don't worry. I'm not usually the insecure type, I guess I just got jealous for a minute." She put the photo back into the envelope and slipped it into her bag. "Let's go. We're going to be late."

I started the car and backed into traffic. "Where are we going first? David Ramsey can't see us until after lunch." Chev adjusted her seat belt then folded her hands in her lap.

"I have a little surprise," Chev said, "We've been invited to meet with an expert."

"An expert on what?"

"Wiseguys."

I pulled away from the curb. "This ought to be interesting."

"And educational."

I gave her a look. "I watch movies, I read, I know what the term 'wiseguy' means."

Chev laughed. "God, you are so touchy. "

"Sorry, I think it's my new look. It makes me edgy."

We were meeting the 'expert' at a vegetarian Chinese restaurant at a trendy mall in Rockville.

"What is this guy's name?" I asked as we rode a neon-outlined escalator up to the restaurant level.

"Tony."

"Tony who?" I said as I followed her into the restaurant. The décor was subtle. Soft mauve walls with delicate Chinese prints and hand painted fans hung over each booth. Chev waved to a man in a booth in the back. He was partially obscured by a black lacquered screen.

"Tony Deseeca. He claims to be an expert on wise guys." Chev whispered.

I tried to retain my cool, not act surprised. He rose to greet us both. Today he was dressed casually in a long sleeved black sweater and gray slacks. The thin gold watch on his wrist looked very expensive. He was just a little over six feet tall. He looked more approachable than when we met in his office. He had dark hair, almost black in color. His lips were full enough to be sensual without looking feminine. His eyes were a goldish green color, like the pieces of jade in a scarab bracelet I used to wear, and were framed by strong black eyebrows. He was slim but muscular; his handshake was firm.

"Stella, Tony called and asked to see us. He wants to help us find Nikki and Michael's killer," she paused, "Stella's husband," she said by way of explanation to Deeseca as we slid into the booth.

"He says he knew Nikki from years ago. He wants to help."

Tony Deeseca looked at me. For some reason today he made me nervous. "When you came to see me in my office the other day I didn't really give you much to go on. Maybe I can change that. Have you turned up anything?"

My stomach felt queasy. I looked at my hands. I could still see the indentation where my wedding ring used to be. I started rubbing my finger. "Yes, actually we've uncovered a lot."

I could feel myself claming up. I didn't want to share our discoveries yet. I hadn't figured everything out, but I would eventually, and without his help. Was he an expert because he was a mob guy, too?

Deeseca reached across the table and took my hand. "I'd like to help you." I realized he was rubbing the same indentation on my finger I had just noticed. "Both of you."

He glanced at Chev with a smile. "Of course, I have selfish reasons." He released my hand. "If I help you, maybe I can clear my name."

Chev looked at me. I was still looking at my hand. I couldn't seem to think of anything to say. Then I got a grip on myself. "What I'd like to know is anything you can tell me about the Parnelli Brothers."

He leaned forward on his elbows and looked at me, his eyes taking in every line of my face with such intensity that I thought he intended to counsel me on some more plastic surgery.

"You look great. I didn't realize what a pretty woman you were under all those bandages." He smiled at me. His face was handsome, his expression sardonic. Almost menacing, but somehow sexy.

It was beginning to feel stuffy in the restaurant. "Chev," I muttered under my breath.

"Relax," Chev whispered. "Tony, you said you knew my husband when he was a cop. How did you meet?"

Tony smiled and relaxed again. "He brought me in for questioning."

Chev laughed. "For what?" I guess my face must have had a strange expression on it because Chev said, "You're shattering Stella's image of you."

He actually looked concerned. "I got called in for questioning when my foreman was murdered." Chev glanced at me, her eyebrows raised.

I remembered. "The man who was killed over the papers Franklin was holding?"

"Yes. He fell down the construction elevator from about five stories up. The coroner found some injuries that occurred before the fall. It looked like he'd had a terrible fight then was thrown down the shaft."

Chev shuddered. "I remember when that happened. Wasn't it about five years ago?"

"Yes. Larry called me from the site. He said he had evidence for me of a scam the Parnelli's were running with some of the sub-contractors on the building on Fourteenth Street. Said he had forged documents that had been given to the inspectors." He looked down at his hands. "I told him to wait, that I would be right over." He shrugged his shoulders. "I left and drove straight to the site. I found him there. Broken and bloody. We'd worked together for twenty years."

His eyes looked misty. Tony cleared his throat. "Evidently, the police thought maybe he and I had a fight and that I pushed him. They couldn't find the papers that Larry had for me and I guess that made it hard for them to believe my story, but then they let me go."

Tony glanced at Chev. "Your husband was straight up with me. Said that he didn't think I was involved."

Chev smiled. "He was a good cop. He quit the force right after that and started his own agency."

Tony smiled. "I know. That's why I recommended him to Franklin after the break-in. I knew he was good." He looked from one to the other of us. "What did I say?"

"Nothing." I said quietly. "It's just that we think that everyone who has died was tied to that investigation."

Tony Deseeca shook his head. "And I started it. I'm sorry. Really, I am. None of this was worth anyone's life."

I believed him. He sounded sincere. I relaxed a little. "Look, Chev said you might be able to help us connect the Parnellis to Franklin Brody and all of this."

"Like Stella just said. We've got a list of people who were connected to the Brody break-in who are dead now." Chev ticked them off for him. "Michael Strayer, Mona Freeman, Emma Reeves," She took a deep breath. "Nikki, and a man with dental implants."

That got his attention. "Whoa, wait a minute. What's this about false teeth?"

Chev explained about the body found in the explosion and our theory. "Stella has to be close because some thug in a blue pickup has been following her for days."

He looked at me for an explanation. "I'm afraid I've been playing bumper tag with a guy in an eighteen wheeler cross dressing as a pick up truck. Better know as 'Big Blue.'"

"Registered to Parnelli Construction Company," Chev chimed in. "Driven by one Jerry Derr, a small time button man for the P. brothers. He's been with them for the last seventeen years. He always visited my site in that blue monster. I should say past tense. The word is that Jerry's been missing for the last two weeks."

Wheels began to turn in my head. "Did he have all his teeth?" I asked.

If Tony thought my question was strange, he didn't show it. "He used to be a prizefighter. There's a good chance he might have lost a few teeth."

I thought that one over for a second. I knew something. It was in my brain. I should be able to pull it out, but my brain was forty years old now and the information retrieval system had developed a few bugs.

"Stella?" I realized Chev was poking me in the ribs.

"Sorry." I looked at Tony. "You hired Franklin Brody to pursue a case with the Parnelli's. Why did you do that? I thought you said that the papers were gone when you got to the site. How could you pursue anything?"

"Franklin called me to tell me he had heard that the papers were still around. That he could help me get them back. That's why I hired him. It was a condition of getting my evidence back."

"What?" I shook my head. "He got them back for you then they were stolen again. That's just too weird."

Tony smiled. "I know. I think the whole thing was orchestrated to keep me from going to the FBI with what I knew about the Parnellis."

"What did you know?" Chev asked.

"I wish I could tell you."

"I know." Chev laughed. "You'd tell me, but then you'd have to kill me, right?"

Tony smiled, but it wasn't humor I saw in his eyes." No, I wouldn't have to kill you, but someone else would," he said quietly.

A cold chill went down my back. "What can you tell us about Franklin Brody and his association with the Parnellis?" I asked.

"I thought about it some more after you left the other day. I think I have most of it put together." His tone was serious and businesslike. "Like I said, the whole thing was set up to get me in line. I'm not sure how, but Franklin got the papers. Then he approached me with a deal to get my papers back. But he was working a deal with the Parnellis at the same time. I don't see Franklin Brody as the victim. I think he approached the Parnellis just like he approached me. He got me on board and then used the evidence and me as bait to get the Parnellis as clients."

"Why?" I looked at Chev. She was studying Deseeca's face intently.

"For the influence. To gain an allegiance with an important family," he said, fixing me with his jade eyes. "He staged a fake robbery to hide the evidence. That's how he neutralized me for the Parnellis, but he kept the papers for himself to have a hold over them."

"So what happened? Did they get rid of him?"

"No, I don't think so because they were looking for him right before the explosion."

Great, I thought. Chev and I had gotten ourselves in right up to our armpits. I remembered Harrison's warnings. I think my heart actually slowed down for a beat or two. "Got any suggestions?" I said when my heart kicked back in.

"No. Just try to have an ace up your sleeve." He looked at each one of us. "Or stay out of it." He shook his head. "It's not worth anymore lives."

He stood and graciously shook hands with Chev, then me. He held onto my hand for a moment. "Forget about what I said about clearing my name," he said earnestly. "You two keep safe instead."

I tried not to inhale his cologne, but got a good whiff of something clean and sexy, anyway. My face flamed up when he walked away.

The waiter came immediately with glasses of water and the food we had ordered. I moved over to where Deseeca had been sitting. "He must meet people here all the time," I said, as I ate Hunan gluten, supposedly a vegetarian alternative to beef or chicken.

"I bet you're right. That's why the waiter was holding off." Chev dug into her mock Kung Pao chicken. "What did you think of him?"

"Interesting." I was suddenly very interested in the texture of my food.

"Uh huh." Chev had that know-it-all tone of hers. "I think he got under your skin, Ms. Jones. With a blowtorch yet." I refused to react. "I know you got under his," she laughed. "And you thought you were matronly looking."

I ignored her and continued to push the little pieces of tofu paste around on my plate. "I don't think I'm ready for this."

"What, sex?"

I choked on my tofu.

"Well, I was thinking of something more preliminary, like dating. Like trying to get to know someone better. Like having conversation. Like feeling interested in someone. I haven't even thought about, you know, 'it'."

"It? Oh brother. We've got a long way to go." Chev shook her head. I ignored her.

CHAPTER FORTY-THREE

The drive to David Ramsey's lab was pleasant. The weather had produced a brisk fall day with a clarity and brightness that etched each leaf on each tree.

"Let's drive up to New York and see the girls when this is all over. I'd like you to meet them."

"It's a date," Chev grinned. "I've been curious about them since the other day."

"You mean when I couldn't decide if I was a good mother or not?"

"Yeah, I never know either."

I was shocked. "You mean you've got kids?"

"Two boys. One's in the Marines and one's in the Army's Special Forces."

"God, I can't believe we've been so single minded we didn't even talk about our families."

"So, we'll do it now," Chev laughed. "Noah is my oldest. He looks just like Nikki." She smiled. "It gives my heart a jump every time I see him. He's a good boy. He's had a little trouble dealing with Nikki's death, but I spoke to his commanding officer and they are looking out for him." She rubbed her hands together. "Troy, he looks like me, only taller, thank God. Troy takes it out in his job, on the surface he looks fine, but he's just postponing his grief." She looked out the window like she wanted to say more, but didn't.

"My girls weren't as close to Michael as your boys probably were to their father. He didn't give them much of his time," I offered to break the silence. "In a way it has helped and hurt them. They seem to be dealing with the grief, but I think they miss what might have been." I turned into the parking lot and pulled up outside of David Ramsey's office. "They are always talking about the good times, but there weren't enough good times."

"They'll be enough good times to come to make up for it." Chev patted my arm as we got out of the car and headed up the walk.

I led Chev into the lab. "This is my expert." I introduced Chev to David Ramsey. David clasped Chev's hand and in just that second I knew he was gone. Talk about a thunderbolt. I couldn't believe the change that came over him. He pulled a chair out for Chev and helped her into it. After a minute I grabbed a stool next to his drawing board and dragged it over as he sat down at his desk. I felt like a baby in a high chair at the dinner table.

"What have you found out?" David looked up at me, went through his memory bank, and remembered who I was.

"Oh, sorry, Ann."

"Stella Ann, but that's not important. What did you find out?"

"Well." He began then faltered. I cleared my throat as his eyes began to wander back to Chev. It got his attention. "Uh, well, here you'd better take a look at this." He was getting himself together.

I jumped down and came around to his side of the desk. "What?" I asked.

"Right here." He had marked the book with post-it-notes. "See this finger print? It is from the group of prints Michael lifted at Brody, Borman and Tate. This is Franklin Brody's set." He said flipping to the next marker.

I looked at the whorls and loops nodding. "Now, look at this." He flipped back to a set of prints that Michael had written the notes around. "This is the same print identified as Brody's on the earlier page." He pointed to the line underneath the print. "Do you know who D.E. is?"

I felt my heart beat against my rib cage like it was trying to get out. Chev choked out, "Damon Edwards."

David looked at her with loving pride." Exactly, they are the same man." He pointed to the notes. "This is the last case he worked on. It was brought to him by a Mr. Fortuna."

"My husband." Chev looked down at her rings.

"Late husband." I said under my breath for David's benefit. "One and the same. Michael knew. Franklin Brody was really Damon Edwards."

I imagined Michael in his lab out in back of the house. I wondered what he thought when he made the connection. Wondered if he had decided to speak to someone, or never had the chance. Maybe Franklin-Damon made that choice for him. Poor Michael.

I went back to my stool and perched on the edge. "Can you pull up another ID for us?"

"Sure." He swung to his right and waited, fingers poised over the keyboard. "Franklin Brody?"

David paused, looked confused for a moment then he realized what I was getting at. "Let's see what we come up with. If the real Brody never had a job where he got fingerprinted and no criminal record, we'll be out of luck." He punched in a series of information then waited.

It came up. The real Franklin Brody's prints and personal data. The birthday was July 17, 1946. Even to my unprofessional eye, the whorls on the fingerprints were different.

"What do we have for Damon Edward's date of birth?"

David retrieved the file from his desk. He opened it and read, "May 26, 1948."

I turned to Chev. "We need pictures of these men."

"Well, I can oblige you on Mr. Edwards." He handed Chev a photograph. She took it gingerly as if his fingers might burn hers. It was an excellent black and white portrait. It showed what the faxed newspaper clipping did not. I put my hand across the nose and chin of the man in the picture. "What do you see?"

"Franklin Brody," Chev said, pleased with our cleverness, "Who is really Damon Edwards after major plastic surgery."

"May we keep this David?" I asked.

"Sure, but that's not all." He handed me another photograph.

"Martine Edwards. Better known as our client Alexa Grant," Chev said.

Although Chev had stolen his moment, David looked at her benignly. "How did you know?"

I jumped in. "Chev is an excellent researcher. She got copies of twenty three year old newspapers and we figured it out."

David reached in an envelope and pulled out a plastic bag with our mirror in it. "Was this your idea, too?" he asked Chev.

"Yes." She looked everywhere but at him.

"Very clever," he said admiringly.

I was getting a little nervous. Chev was becoming downright antisocial. David was in danger of loosing his dignity. "Well, we really appreciate the help, David. You've confirmed several theories for us." I stood down from my stool and grabbed Chev's arm. "We've got another appointment. I can't tell you how much you've helped." I picked up the folder with the pictures and Michael's journal from his desk as I propelled Chev to the door.

"Thanks for the information. We'll do dinner soon." I knew I was babbling, but I couldn't think of anything else to do. David gave me a bewildered look as I shut the door behind us. "What is wrong, Chev?" My tone was a little tough. I liked David, and I admit my matchmaking juices had been flowing.

"I don't want to talk about it." She mumbled, head down. I peeked under her hair. I'd never seen such a stubborn look on another human being's face in my life. Not being totally brain dead, I let it drop. We drove downtown in complete silence. Chev didn't say a word when I pulled up on Sixteenth Street and parked.

"I'll be right out," I said. She just nodded. Her mood had apparently deteriorated into melancholy. I ran into the coffee shop around the corner from the Parnelli's and ordered two cups of coffee to go.

Tighe was there. His apron had a few streaks of dried blood on top of the grease. I forced myself to look away as my stomach rolled. "My friend isn't feeling too well, but she really likes coffee."

"Yeah?" He managed to keep a cigarette hanging from his bottom lip while he talked. "Maybe this will pick her up."

He poured coffee into two Styrofoam cups. He snapped a paper bag with one hand, then with practiced ease he set the two coffees down in the bag.

I grabbed a few creamers and tossed them in, too.

"Are you Tiger. . .?" I snapped my fingers like I was trying to remember.

"Moran," he said, obviously pleased. "Everyone calls me Tighe."

"Right. Right. I've got to tell my dad." I picked up two coffee stirrers. "My dad is a big fight fan." I dropped them into the bag. I leaned toward Tighe. "My dad's a dentist. He told me that he replaced those teeth that Jerry Derr lost in that big fight. Didn't want to take a penny, either, said it was the least he could do for a talented fighter like that."

Tighe nodded, his battered face animated. "Yeah, Jerry was on his way. That fight with Ricki Payne was a killer. Knocked out so many teeth that Jerry said he just told the Doc to yank em all out. But the Doc made him some fake teeth, put them right into his jaw, and made it look like he'd never lost a one. Of course, Jerry didn't fight no more or he would have lost them again for sure. He'd lost the edge. Ricki saw to that." Tighe was lost in thought for a moment. He flipped his tongue and revealed his upper denture as if momentarily offering it to me. "I should have seen your Dad. Got a full upper set now. Give him my regards."

I pulled out my wallet. "Thanks, I will. He'll be thrilled."

"No charge, honey." He said with a wink. I thanked him and left the shop.

Chev was still in a blue mood when I got back to the Trooper. I handed her the bag. "I got us some coffee." She took the bag and held it in her lap. This was more serious than I thought. I pulled away from the curb. "Okay, where next?" I asked reaching or my coffee.

She hardly noticed. "I'd like to go home," was all she said.

CHAPTER FORTY-FOUR

We rode up Sixteenth Street in silence. I sneaked a look at Chev. She had opened her coffee, creamed it and begun to take a few sips. I said a prayer to the coffee god to do his stuff.

"So what did you find out?" She finally said.

"Find out?" I asked innocently.

"Look, I'm not a fool. You didn't drive halfway across town just to get coffee at Ruby D's."

"Well, it's pretty good coffee."

She smiled. "Oh, cut the crap. I know you found something out. You've got that look."

"What look?" Chev made a groaning noise so I decided no to push it. "Jerry had dental implants. Evidently setting a trend among the younger boxing set."

"Oh, the false teeth," she said, the light coming on.

"Exactly."

"Good work, Sherlock."

"Are you getting over your attack of the shitties?"

"Yes," she said grudgingly.

"Still want to go home?"

"Yeah. I want to show you something."

We connected with the beltway and headed North on Interstate 270. Chev was quiet for a while. When we exited to Davidson, she began to give me directions. We passed the office and turned right onto a street that headed up a hill. We made another right and pulled up outside a comfortable looking ranch style house of yellow brick and cedar.

"Aren't we on the street behind the office?" I asked as we got out of the car.

"Yeah. It's right down the hill." She led me to the side yard and pointed. Down the hill through the thinning leaves of the trees I could just make out the roof of the little gray house. A series of steps cut into the hillside led to a walk- way around the back of the office.

"This is great," I said. "How did you manage it?" We walked back to the front porch.

"We had the house first. Then the little house came available and we bought it."

She put her key in the lock and opened the door. I followed her inside. It was a comfortable house. Overstuffed furniture, colorful rugs, craftsy doodads, but something was wrong. I noticed a man's sweater draped across the back of one of the couches in the living room. There was clutter on every surface. Mail was stacked in piles. I noticed the top piece on a pile on the foyer table. It was addressed to Mr. Nicholas Fortuna.

Chev went to the kitchen to throw out our coffee containers. She came back in and sat on the couch, her weariness apparent.

"You have a lovely home." I sat on the loveseat opposite her.

"No, I don't. Look around you, doesn't it look weird to you?"

It's always hard to answer a question like that. You don't know if you're expected to agree or disagree. I decided to agree. "Well, yes a little."

"Don't try to be so polite. It's a lot weird." She sounded belligerent, but it wasn't directed at me. "I haven't

S. Alden Reilly

changed anything since Nikki died. I haven't even run the sweeper. You know, he's been dead six months and he gets more mail than I do. At work, I used to set two cups of coffee out." Tears started rolling down her cheeks. "I'm not coping. I'm just pretending."

I swallowed the lump that was starting to form in my throat. "But that is coping," I said. "Everyone handles their grief in a different way. I emptied my house. You filled yours up. We're both in chaos. But we're starting to put some order in our lives."

"When you came to the office, you burst the little bubble I was using to hide the pain. I guess it hurt so much because it looked like we might have made it this time. Nikki and me. And then I had the doubts again. You know, about other women. I've felt so guilty and hurt. At least I don't think he was cheating again anymore. Now I'm just sorry that we didn't get our chance."

Tears rolled down her face. "But I'm glad you came. I need to move on, especially for Troy. It might help him."

"Hey, you did get your chance. You had worked it out. That is something you'll always have." I looked around the room, then at Chev. I got up.

"Time to clear out the ghosts." I went to the kitchen. It was on the other side of the dining room. I fumbled around until I found some plastic garbage bags. I went back to the living room.

"Come on," I said, motioning to her.

We started filling the bags with mail, the sweater, anything that had obviously been Nikki's. I dragged the filled bags into the dining room and came back. I'd managed to locate the sweeper and began running it over the rugs. Chev took a bag into the master bedroom off the hallway leading from the living room. She opened closets and drawers filling bags with Nikki's belongings. I could see her from the living room. At first, she had to stop and look at each item. I could see her wrestling with herself. Finally, she began stuffing things in more quickly.

The day was brisk but not too cold. Fresh air would be good, I thought, opening windows as I progressed. I followed her from room to room dusting and sweeping. In two hours we had dragged the last bag out to the garage. Then we stood and looked at the pile of Nikki effects.

"I'll let the boys go through these things. They'll probably want some of the clothes." Chev put her arm around me. "Thanks, Stella," she said softly.

"You did it for me. I just returned the favor." I gave her a quick hug. "Want any painting done?"

He big smile returned. "No thanks, lady. I like my house just the way it is."

We walked back inside. She'd said 'my' house. I knew she would be all right.

CHAPTER FORTY-FIVE

We walked down the hillside steps to the office. Chev made us fresh coffee while I went through the files on Damon Edwards and the information that David had given us. In the file was a copy of a marriage license. I glanced at it idly until I saw Martine's name on the certificate listed as Martine Edwards. She was an Edwards before her marriage to Damon.

"Chev, look at this."

She came in with the coffee and sat down.

"That's funny." She looked up from the license. "Unless they were cousins."

"Can we call someone and check?"

"Sure, let me have it." She left to go to her own desk. In a few minutes I heard her on the phone.

I picked up my phone and called Layne's number. There was no answer. I started to call Cynthia's grandmother and thought better of it. I had just gone out to ask Chev if we'd gotten any messages when Layne and Cynthia walked up to the front door.

"Hi, I was just thinking about you guys," I said, opening the door for them. They were both subdued. It seemed that melancholia was the mood of the day. I took them into Nikki's office. Chev waved her hand to let me know she was in the middle of something.

"What's wrong?" I said to Layne.

"Nothing. I've spent the last twelve years living a lie. A lie inside another lie." Her voice was flat. She handed me a small packet of papers in an aging manila folder.

I unwound the string from the little paper wheel. Cynthia winced as I opened the folder. Her eyes were glazed over like a wounded animal, her short reddish hair disheveled. Inside were photographs, a letter, and documents. One photograph was a formal portrait of a man and a beautiful young woman. The woman was Emma Reeves. I turned the picture over. Franklin and Emma Brody, 1976.

I handed Layne the picture of Damon Edwards. Her face turned white. "This is the man I married?"

I sat looking at it for a few minutes. "They really did resemble each other, Damon and the real Franklin Brody, that is."

Both men were handsome; both had high foreheads, dark brown hair, and the same basic facial structure.

I opened the letter. It read, "Dear Cynthia, I may not be alive when you read this letter." I looked at Layne. She glanced at Cynthia then back at me. I kept reading. Emma had written it all out. She hadn't spared a detail no matter how unflattering to herself. It was a courageous final chapter to a very sad story: a young beautiful girl, recently widowed, living with her abusive brother. And meeting her brother's old law school chum, who had suddenly turned up for a visit.

Emma had fallen head over heels in love with Damon Edwards when he appeared. Together they had done away with her brutal brother Franklin so Damon could assume his identity. Happy and pregnant with Damon's child, Emma had been able to rationalize her role in the murder of her brother. Even though she would have to keep up the pretense of being a sister to the man she loved, she thought it would all be worth it. They could live together and raise their child. People would think the baby belonged to her late husband. They could pull it off. The regret came later. When Damon, in his new identity of Franklin Brody, had moved on to other women, and eventually to Layne.

She couldn't speak up, couldn't protest, because she had to protect herself and her child. But Franklin never really abandoned her. He kept his pretty doll safely wrapped up in her box and even visited her now and then. That's why Emma thought he would help Cynthia, but he used his own child to cover one of his schemes. By the time she had died, Emma had been terribly afraid. Afraid of the evil, was how she put it.

"Well, that clears up that question," I said quietly, replacing the letter in the envelopes. I looked at the documents. They were copies of birth certificates: Emma's, her brother's, and Cynthia's.

I looked at Cynthia's with interest. Her father was listed as Frankin Brody, her mother as Emma Reeves. The parents' thumbprints were on the certificate as well as a tiny set of baby footprints. I tapped my finger on the page.

"Would you mind if we hold on to these papers for a few days, Cynthia?" She looked at me woodenly. Her expression was a combination of grief and defiance. "Don't worry. I won't disclose any of this unless it is necessary. Your mom suffered enough."

She looked down at her hands in her lap. "Thanks," came out in a cracked voice.

Chev came into the office. She had a notebook in one hand. "Stella, you're going to want to look at this." She handed me the notebook. When she noticed Cynthia, she went to stand behind her and began kneading her shoulders. Cynthia gave her a grateful look and relaxed a little.

I handed Chev Emma's packet. "Could you lock this up, Chev?" We exchanged looks as she took the envelope.

I read the notes she'd penciled in on the notebook page. Martine married to Beau Edwards. Shooting accident kills Beau. She marries his brother Damon. "Good God," I said. "What is it with this family? Do they think they're characters in a Faulkner novel?" I knew I was going to have to make another visit to the townhouse in Germantown. I looked at Layne. "Could you see that Cynthia gets back to her Grandmother's safely?"

"Sure," Layne said. "Oh, by the way, John sent these for you." She handed me an envelope from her purse.

I raised my eyebrows, but she ignored me. I put the envelope in my pocket. When they stood up, Layne gave Cynthia an affectionate squeeze. Poor girl. She was going to be completely black and blue before she got out of our office.

CHAPTER FORTY-SIX

It was getting to be suppertime when I pulled up outside Alexa Grant's townhouse. I ran up the steps past banks of purple mums. The air was getting crisp. It would be cold tonight.

Martine answered, my visit surprised her but I didn't sense any reservation as she let me in the door. She didn't say a word just motioned to me as she moved to the sofa in the small living room and sat down.

"I guess I should call you Mrs. Edwards," I said. I took a seat opposite her in an overstuffed armchair.

She was dressed completely in black; slim pants, a turtleneck sweater, black boots. Her face was luminous in all that black, like a disembodied moon in a night sky. There was tension in every aspect of her body, gestures, and posture. Something was up. She didn't play dumb. "How much do you know?"

"Well, I know that you married two brothers and were apparently widowed each time."

"Apparently?"

"I'm not sure what happened to your second husband."

"Neither am I," she said. Her large sloe eyes were polished ebony.

"So why are you here?"

"My daughter's missing."

I had to admit that wasn't the response I'd expected. "Aurora?"

"Yes, she's been missing for over a month now."

"Why do you think she's here?"

"I got a phone call." She pierced me with her cold eyes. "It's been a long time, but I recognized the voice."

"Damon?"

She nodded. "He told me to back off or I'd never see Aurora again."

"When did he call?"

"Right after Aurora disappeared. Almost a month ago."

"You've been after him for awhile. You hired the Palmer firm to look into his identity. What made you come looking for him in the first place?"

She laughed a short bitter laugh. "I'm on a mission from God. Or at least from my Father-in-law, may he rest in peace."

"To find Damon Edwards?"

"Yes. My father-in-law refused to have Damon declared dead which, as you said to me, would have been the simplest solution." She sighed and looked at her hands in her lap. "He was convinced that Damon was alive. Jack, my father-in-law, didn't want it to be too easy for Damon to fade away. He wanted to find him and expose him. Unfortunately, when Jack died, it got to be a priority because I needed to settle the estate. Then Aurora disappeared."

She watched me. "I didn't really know where to start so I checked with the Bar association in each state. Damon was a lawyer in Mississippi. I figured he wouldn't give up the profession. But I hadn't gotten anywhere. Then I got a call from a woman claiming to know what had happened to Damon Edwards."

"Did you know her?"

"No. And when I tried to follow up, she disappeared. That's why I had to hire a private detective." She looked down seeming to stare at my shoes. For a minute I thought there was something wrong with them, that maybe I'd worn one brown and one black. I looked down to double check.

"Aurora was in graduate school. William and Mary. I thought she'd be safe. I came up here and hired Mr. Palmer. He seemed to be making progress then Aurora disappeared."

I recognized the universal mother's lament. How could we mothers raise our children so carefully, nurture them, protect them, only to see them go out into the world and go slap up against the ugliness. Where did we go wrong? The guilt was overpowering.

"Mrs. Edwards?" Martine blinked then she refocused from my shoes to my face. I just hoped she wouldn't give it the same scrutiny. "Has Aurora tried to contact you at all?"

"No, and that's why something is wrong. She would never want me to worry."

"Are you close?"

"Yes." She said fiercely, "We are very close."

I didn't want to be the one who came between this Momma lion and her cub. I slipped my hands into the pockets of my jacket. My left hand toyed with the envelope from John Borman. I'd forgotten I'd shoved it in there. "Look, Mrs. Edwards, my partner and I are actively pursuing this case. We'll let you know if we find out anything pertaining to your daughter.

"Thank you," she said, her voice low and husky. Martine was a spring coiled almost the breaking point. When she let go, it would be one hell of a force.

I got in my Trooper and pulled away from the curb. I drove a couple of miles, stopped at a 7-eleven, and got a cup of coffee. I was really coffeed out, but I found it comforting to hold the warm cup in my hands while I thought things over. I sat in my car in the parking lot.

I read the billing invoices for the phone calls for B. B. and T. There were a few calls to the south. John had been confused. The calls were to and from Virginia, not Tennessee. Franklin had been in touch with Aurora. I checked through all the out of state and calling card calls. I pulled a highlighter from my purse and marked several entries. Edwards had called New York several times, too.

I was tempted to call Chev from the pay phone, but she was tired. It could wait until tomorrow. The rest of the ride home was uneventful. I kept a look out for 'Big Blue,' but I didn't see anything. I wondered what Franklin had been up to.

CHAPTER FORTY-SEVEN

I saw a battered blue Chevy Caprice parked in front of my house when I pulled into the driveway. I ran to the back door, my heart thudding inside my chest.

Harrison and Bertie were deep in conversation at the kitchen table. Chaddy was fast asleep under the table. Harrison rose, stretching to his full height and gave me a slight nod of greeting. He was dressed in a pair of snug blue jeans, Air Jordans, and a black Henley-collared knit shirt that emphasized his muscular chest.

"Hello, Ms. Jones, I hope you don't mind, I was going to wait in the car until you were home, but your Aunt insisted I come inside."

Bertie looked at him as he sat back down on the other side of the table. "We've had a very nice conversation while we waited for you."

"What's happened? Is everything alright?" I looked from him to Bertie and back again.

"Well, Ms. Jones, Bertie", he nodded in her direction with a smile, "had a little run in with that blue truck."

"What!" I came to sit by Bertie at the kitchen table. I put my arms around her. "Did he hurt you?"

"No, nothing like that. I just saw the truck at the Produce Market. I got back into my car, came here and called Detective Harrison. And even though he was off duty, he came over to see me." She gave him a beatific smile.

The Produce Market was a little grocery store at one end of Circe. He had figured out where we lived, but I guess I should have foreseen that.

"I don't want you in this." I must have sounded a little hysterical because Harrison reached over and put his hand on my arm.

"Calm down. I can have your local sheriff get involved. Or maybe you both should stay with Chev."

I looked into his kind face. He didn't seem so sad today. He was relaxed, and his smile actually reached to his eyes. Maybe spending time with Bertie was good for him. It was usually good for me, too.

"That's ridiculous," Bertie said defiantly. "Stella and I aren't going to be chased out of our homes, our town." Chaddy roused himself at Bertie's tone and came to sit between us.

"There is no shame in being careful," Harrison said in that deep calm voice of his.

"He's right, Bertie. Maybe we should go to a hotel for awhile or stay with Chev." I looked at Harrison. "I think someone is getting desperate."

"Who is getting desperate?" Harrison looked at me closely.

"I'm not sure. Right now it could be. . ."

"Franklin Brody?"

I stared at him. "Hey! I'm trying to tell you my theory."

He laughed. "You should see your face. I just threw out something I've suspected for awhile. My guess is that you have the same theory."

"Yes, It could be Franklin Brody, or at least a man we've known as Franklin Brody. But there're some other people in this as well."

Harrison nodded his head. "I think you're right."

"Well, we have the proof, too." His face was all business then. I went over the discovery of Emma's papers and the links we found in Michael's notes. I filled him in on the work Chev had done to dig up Franklin's past. When I finished a slow smile crossed his face.

"All right, Ms. Stella Jones! I am very impressed. I guess I'm going to have to get used to having you and Chev around."

Bertie beamed. "Stella is going to surprise you Vin, she's just getting started." So he and Bertie were on a first name basis. How long had they been talking? He probably knew every embarrassing detail of my life. I could feel myself blushing.

"Chev and I can come by tomorrow, if you want, and show you what we've got."

"That would be a big help." He looked at his watch. "It's getting late. I should let you ladies get to bed."

He stood up and shrugged into his jacket. God, he was tall. "Do you think you'll be alright if I leave you alone?" He waved a hand at Bertie. "No offense, Bertie. I know you and Stella are tough ladies."

"We'll be alright, but thanks for coming by and keeping me company." Bertie stood and walked with us to the door. Chaddy came and sat at his feet, his big head cocked to one side. When Harrison bent down to give Chaddy a pat on the head Bertie reached up and gave him a little kiss on his cheek. A sheepish grin of pure pleasure spread over his face.

"Goodnight, ladies. I'll check around the house before I leave so don't be alarmed." Then he was gone. We could see his flashlight as he made a circle around the yard then a little later we heard him pull away.

"He's a very nice man." Bertie said as we locked up and walked upstairs. "But he's going through a rough time right now." He did know everything about me.

"I'm going to get jealous soon. Every handsome man that comes to this house falls in love with you," I teased.

"You flatterer. No, really, the poor man is going through a nasty divorce. I think his heart is broken. Haven't you noticed how miserable he looks?"

"I guess I just thought all policemen looked miserable," I said as I walked her to her room.

"Stella. You've really got to become more open to other people. Especially men." She said wisely. I kept forgetting that Bertie had been happily married for thirty years before Uncle Frank passed away. She had been a career woman. When she met Frank, she'd fallen in love, but she'd kept her maiden name and her independence, something unheard of when she was a young woman. She had been devastated when my uncle died, but she had gone on, persevered these last ten years. Obviously, she was still open to men. Harrison was practically eating out of her hand.

"I'm fine. I'm open. Don't worry about me," I said as we stood on the upstairs landing.

"You're not fine. That's just something you say to defer confronting things." She grinned. "You've been using that since you were old enough to talk." She hugged me tight. "You are a fine woman though, Stella Jones." She released me and shooed me to my bedroom door. "Now, get some rest."

S. Alden Reilly

CHAPTER FORTY-EIGHT

Chev answered the phone the next day with her usual cheery "Fortuna Investigations. May I help you?"

"Hey, We've got a date with Harrison today."

"Why? Do you think we have enough?" I explained about last evening. "Stella, I am so sorry about Bertie," she said anxiously.

I watched Bertie feeding Chaddy as I stood in the kitchen. "I'm worried, but she won't back off. She's just as stubborn as we are."

"You come from good stock. What did Harrison say?"

"He is on the same track. He was actually impressed at the work we'd done."

"Well, we've done a good job. He should be. Want me to call and let him know we'll be there about eleven?"

"Great. I'm on my way."

I hung up the phone and looked over at Bertie and Chaddy eating their breakfast. Bertie was still in her nightgown. Chaddy was chasing little kibbles of dog food over the floor with his big rubbery tongue. Bertie daintily ate a bowl of oatmeal with brown sugar over it.

"I want you guys to go visit someone today or have them visit you, but I don't want you to be alone all day."

Bertie looked up at me. "Okay, we'll go see Pauline, but I'll come back and make us some dinner later. Just call me when you're on your way home."

"Good." I walked over and gave them both a kiss. Bertie first, of course. "Okay, guys, Please be careful. I love you more than anything."

I grabbed my purse and slung it over my shoulder. I had opted for the blue-jean look today. I had bought myself a pair of slim blue jeans and a fitted rib-knit blue sweater that reminded me of one I had in college. The fact that the color made my eyes look really blue was also a plus. I had on new sneakers that were supposed to be my running shoes whenever I started my health program. I felt they looked sporty.

Chev was waiting for me. "I've got all our files ready. Do you want to take him the originals or copies?"

"I don't know. I've never done this before. What do you usually do?"

"Take copies and originals. Layne should probably be there too to protect Cynthia's interests. We promised to keep her mother out of it."

I picked up the phone. "I think you're right. But I don't think Harrison is a bad guy. I think he would help us on that." Layne's answering machine picked up so I left her a message. "I asked her to meet us at Harrison's office if she can get away."

"Let's roll." Chev picked up her heavy purse. Files bulged its sides. She had on jeans, too, slim black ones that flattered her figure. Her cherry colored sweater would have gotten her discovered in Hollywood.

"You look great today." I said as we pulled into traffic.

"I was going to say the same about you. You've already lost a lot of weight haven't you?" She said with a slow smile.

"That is probably the nicest thing anyone has said to me in months. Yes, I think I have, but I refuse to weigh myself. I just keep getting more comfortable in my clothes." I was getting more comfortable in Stella's skin, too. I paused. "Hey, I'm sorry about David Ramsey, I like him a lot and he seemed to really like you."

She ducked her head. "Don't be sorry. He's very handsome and he seems sweet." She smiled. "But, I don't think I'm ready yet either."

"Ready? Just not ready in general? Or not ready for 'it'?"

"Okay, okay." Chev laughed. "Not ready for anything. How's that Ms. Smart ass?"

"There's nothing wrong with that," I said. "We'll get there."

For once I really believed it. We would get through this. We would feel normal again. I felt good today.

THE PHOENIX

CHAPTER FORTY-NINE

I had never been inside a police station before. Sure, I watch the police dramas on TV so I was prepared for the battered metal desks and gray color scheme. Harrison's office was actually more beige and cream colored. His desk wasn't made of metal and it didn't look battered, either. He had his own glassed-in office overlooking a bullpen of desks in the center of the room where men and women seemed busy with a variety of paperwork.

"Come in, ladies. Can I get you some coffee?" Harrison indicated two chairs in front of his desk.

"Of course," Chev said. What other answer could there be?

"Yes, please," I joined in. I watched Harrison pick up the phone and order three coffees. A few moments later a young male officer with sandy hair came in holding a cardboard tray with coffee, creamers, sugars, and little wooden stirrers.

We all spent a little time getting our drinks to our liking, then Harrison leaned back in his chair. He had on a brownish tweed suit with a blue shirt and blue and gray patterned tie. He looked sad again. I admit he fascinated me now because I had seen the other side of him, the potentially happy side of him, last night. I kept waiting for the transforming smile that reached his eyes.

"What have you got?"

Chev looked at me. "Go for it, Stella."

I took a sip of my coffee and began. "It started with some notes my husband made in his journal." I explained how I had found Nikki's name and followed up with Chev. "I saw you after I found Mona. Then I found Emma. We think that the body in the fire may have been Jerry Derr, owner of the blue truck that keeps trying to run me off the road."

Harrison looked at me sharply. "And how do you deduce that?" His tone seemed a little harsh.

"The dental implants." I felt my pride rise up. "We checked with a boxing buddy of Jerry's, he had implants done after he lost several teeth in a big fight."

I could hear a slight edge in my own voice. I wasn't sure why I felt defensive but Chev and I weren't children. We were grown women who had made a decision to get to the truth. The fact that I felt we had been damn clever about it and Harrison didn't seem to want to acknowledge it made me mad.

As if he could see my backbone stiffening, Harrison lightened up. "Hey I'm sorry, it's been a bad day." He paused as if he would elaborate but smiled instead. "You've obviously done a lot of good theorizing about this and may even be right, but we've got evidence that Franklin may have had dental implants as well," he added. "Don't worry though, we'll look into Jerry Derr's dental records because it is a viable possibility."

I guess Chev had stiffened up too because she relaxed against the back of her chair as she finished. "You know why we've been pursing this, Vin."

"I know, Chev. If I had lost members of my family, I would want to see justice done, too." The frown returned. "I still don't like the risks you both are taking." He rubbed the bridge of his nose as if he had an ache there. "And I am entitled to worry about the citizens we serve."

I decided to change the subject. "Here are the notes we've been keeping," I said, motioning to the thick file in Chev's lap. "Why don't you read through them and ask us any questions you might have."

Chev put the file in front of him and then we both waited. Harrison sat and read page by page. He took a small, yellow post-it note pad and tabbed a page every so often. Sometimes he would stop and go back and reread a section. Finally, he sat back and looked at both of us.

"Thank you for sharing this with me. You've both done as fine a job of putting a case together as any of my detectives here could do. However, at considerable risk to yourselves." He looked from one to the other of us like a parent chiding a kid that has run into the street after a ball.

"What is the next step?" Chev said leaning forward.

Harrison closed the file. "We'll put an APB out on Franklin Brody, Damon Edwards, and Jerry Derr to cover our bases. We'll also check the identity of our remains from the explosion. We'll verify the dental records on both men. I'll have a couple of detectives concentrate on locating their dentists. It would probably be a good idea to see if they visited more than one in the past few years." He picked at one of the post-it notes. "The records we used to identify the remains are very new."

Chev nodded. "From that bitchy dentist who wouldn't give me the time of day?"

Harrison grinned. "She did seem unnecessarily unpleasant when we questioned her."

"Do you think the Parnellis are involved?" I asked.

"They might be. Jerry wouldn't be working for anyone but the Parnellis, no matter how much money was involved."

I looked at Chev. "Then we want to get them, too," she said.

"You're not the only ones. I've wanted to shut them down for years. It won't be easy, though. They're like the Teflon Don. Of course, good police work finally nailed him." He looked at both of us. "Can you wait a minute while I make copies of these notes? And I assume that you have the originals of Emma's letter to her daughter."

Chev nodded. "We told her we'd try to protect her mother."

"It's still evidence. We'll need it eventually. But we can cross that bridge when we come to it." He got up from his desk, all six foot three inches of him, and left the room with our file.

"Well, what do you think?" I said to Chev.

She put her had on my arm. "It's a little like giving birth. It's hard to let it go, but its got a life of it's own now. They're going to have enough to get the killer and bring him to justice. Is it enough for you?"

"I think so."

THE PHOENIX

CHAPTER FIFTY

It was beginning to get dark when we finally left the police station. When we got to the office, I called Bertie. "How did it go?" She asked.

"Pretty good. Harrison thought we did a professional job."

"Of course, you did. What do you want for dinner?"

"Why don't we get something out when I get there?" I looked at Chev. "Want to come over?"

"Maybe a little later. I wanted to call the boys first." She was right; I needed to call my daughters. At least I could tell them what happened. Heal some wounds.

I drove Chev up the hill to her house. "Okay, call me later." I pulled out of her driveway and headed home. I was uneasy. Something didn't feel right. Maybe my pride wouldn't let me let go. It wasn't settled. Having the police involved was a relief, but frustrating, too. I wouldn't get to end it, confront the killer and revenge our loved ones.

When I drove up to my house it was dark. That surprised me. Maybe Bertie had gone to the store. When I pulled around to the back and saw her car, I got a sick feeling deep down in my gut.

I jumped out of the car and ran for the back door. It was slightly ajar when I got to it. I started screaming. "Bertie!

Bertie!" I flipped on lights, running from room to room like a crazy person. But she wasn't there.

I ran back outside searching around the house. Maybe she'd fallen or had a stroke while she was outside with the dog. Chaddy. I stopped in my tracks. Chaddy. Where was the dog? He'd never leave Bertie. And she'd never leave him of her own free will. "Chaddy!" I called, moving out into the back yard. Trying to sweep back and forth so that I could cover every inch of the ground. The moonlight helped. I could distinguish some features. Everything was in shades of gray.

Suddenly, ahead I saw a white patch. The moonlight glowed on the rounded white form as I ran toward it. It was Chaddy. Chaddy, my protector, was lying in the cold damp grass. Bertie was gone. I knew that now. My heart rolled over in my chest as I leaned my face down to his. His eyes were open, glassy.

"Chaddy, Chaddy what happened to you?" I whispered. His tongue lolled out of his mouth, but I felt a gentle breath on my face. "Chaddy, don't you die." I rubbed his big belly. "I'll be right back."

I ran back to the house grabbing the phone as I came inside the back door. I'd punched a couple of buttons before I realized there wasn't a dial tone. Only dead air. "Damn!" I said, getting ready to hang up.

"So, Ann, are you ready for the next move?" The voice from the receiver in my hand shocked me. In spite of my suspicions, having them confirmed so suddenly took my rational thought away for a moment.

"What?"

"Come on, Ann. Don't act so surprised. You figured out I was alive didn't you?" Franklin was on the phone. I would never be able to call him Damon.

"What have you done with Bertie?" I said, my voice sounded borderline hysterical, even to me.

"All in good time," he said mockingly. "I want you to meet me. Nine o'clock." He gave me an address off Guide Drive in Rockville. I knew the area, industrial, and lots of warehouses. "And don't bring the police or your aunt will pay for it."

"Look, Franklin, if you hurt my aunt in any way, I'll cut your balls off and feed them to you for dinner."

"Such talk, and from an English professor, too," his mocking voice continued. "Just be there at nine o'clock."

Just then, in the background, I heard Bertie say calmly, "tell her to look after Chaddy."

The phone went dead. Relief, then cold anger chilled my system. I was deadly calm.

I looked at my watch. Seven o'clock. The phone seemed to be working so I called Chaddy's vet. She agreed to meet me at her clinic. I called Chev at home. Her voice was groggy. She had dozed off in front of the TV, but when I told her about Bertie, she snapped out of it.

"Where should I meet you?"

"Hey, why should both of us get in a bind? Who's going to tell the police where I am and help them nail the bastard?"

"We're in this together," she said stubbornly. She wouldn't budge.

"Okay." I told her to meet me at a gas station on the corner of Gude and Frederick road. I left the lights blazing and ran back out to Chaddy. He was still breathing. I tried to lift him and realized that I'd never make it to the car with him.

I backed the Trooper onto the grass next to him and opened the back door. I knelt beside him and circled him with my arms. I shut my eyes and with all my strength, lifted him. Stars and bursts of fireworks were flashing behind my eyes, but I got him inside. Adrenaline is a great thing.

I drove the five miles to the vet's in about two minutes. Dr. Patricia Peters was waiting. She was a little, wiry woman. Perpetually tan, she had short dark hair with the kind of good honest face that inspired confidence. Between the two of us, we got the big dog on the examining table.

"I think he's been poisoned," I said, my words tumbling out incoherently.

Dr. Peters was checking Chaddy's eyes, listening to his heart. "Yes, he's been drugged. Any idea as to what was used?" I shook my head no. "Well, I'll pump his stomach right away."

She got busy and in a few minutes Chaddy was cleaned out. The doctor took a specimen and went into her lab. I just stood by Chaddy and stroked his head. At first he just laid there, then his tail wagged a little. "You're going to be all right, boy," I whispered in his ear. I kissed the side of his big ugly face.

"Got it." Dr. Peters came back in. "It's an animal tranquilizer. Used enough to knock out a Clydesdale. It was in some steak, see?" She indicated a chunk of something she'd retrieved from Chaddy's digestive system.

"I'll take your word for it," I said. I was already squeamish enough. "Is he going to be all right?"

"Maybe. He should be dead, but I guess he doesn't know that." She grinned, selecting a vial and a needle from her dispensing cabinet. "This should bring him back around if he's able to."

I looked at my watch. "I've got to go, Dr. Peters." She looked surprised. "I'm sorry, but my aunt is the other side of the same mess. I've got to go to her before she's as bad off as Chaddy."

"Go. I'll take care of him," she said firmly. I looked at Chaddy again and patted his head. "Don't worry too much. He's a tough old boy," she said before I left. I promised to call as soon as I could.

CHAPTER FIFTY-ONE

The drive down to Rockville calmed me a little. I slipped into the rhythm of Interstate 270 and began piecing it all together. I knew Franklin had to be feeling desperate. He was trapped. I wasn't sure what his next move would be, but the number of bodies to date was obscene. Whether he had murdered them or not, he was the root cause of all the mayhem. The knot in the pit of my stomach turned over. The man had to be certifiably insane.

I must have been doing ninety because I pulled into the gas station with a half-hour to spare. It had one of those mini mart things so I got a cup of coffee and some of those tiny powdered white donuts and sat in my car. The fluorescent glow of the station's lights made an artificial daytime. Cars passed by in the blackness, their taillights identifying their species. I was in the safe zone, the island of light in a dark sinister world.

I got out of the car, pitched my empty coffee cup and headed for the ladies room. Crisis is like a water pill to me. When I came back, Chev was standing by my car.

"Ready?" She asked.

"Yes," I said climbing into the car. "Chev, I'd like you to stay behind, to watch my back."

"No way. It's your front that's going to get shot off. What good am I going to do in the back?"

"I'll feel better knowing that I don't have to worry about the unknown. I'm not afraid to face Franklin."

"We've got to get this low life piece of scum."

"We're going to." I pulled out a pad of paper and a street map from my glove compartment.

"Here," I said. "This is the street. I'm going in here to park away from the building. You wait two minutes, then follow me. We'll go up on foot."

"Okay."

I turned the key and the Trooper roared to life. I pulled out of the gas station, made a right, and headed into an industrial wasteland. Body shops vied with junkyards for space. It was a giant processing plant for that symbol of the American dream, the car. Of course, if your car needed to come to one of these establishments, the dream had been tarnished.

I took another right an headed back into a wooded area. The road forked at a moldy cemetery. I took the right fork then pulled up into the cemetery. It was a sad, neglected place. Weeds grayed in the night-light softened the jumbled headstones. One grave had a Styrofoam ring with a faded red, white, and blue ribbon dangling from the bottom. Dead brown flowers were still stuck into the Styrofoam for some forgotten Memorial Day.

Chev pulled around the curve in her little navy blue econo-box. I motioned to her to pull in behind me. We continued on foot, following the road, keeping within the shelter of the trees until we came to a huge junkyard.

The chain link fence had a double gate. The kind that rolls back against the fence instead of swinging open or shut. A small space had been left open. I hoped the dog had already escaped. We slipped through and picked our way around the two story high stacks of cars. There were several buildings inside the fence. Only one showed light around the edges of its windows. We headed for it.

"Chev," I said urgently, "come here." I showed her the hulk of an old 57 Chevy. "Slip in here. You can keep your eye on anyone coming or going."

Chev opened the door and slipped in. "Hey, it's really nice in here."

I glanced inside. The interior was upholstered in dark red crushed velvet. The dash held a dual cassette tape and CD player.

"They must use this for their office," Chev said.

"Great. Stay here and keep down." I handed her the bag of donuts. "Just in case the dog shows up."

"What a relief. I thought you were committing diet suicide." Suddenly there was a thudding sound from the direction of the building. "What was that?" Chev whispered.

"I don't know. It could have been gun fire."

"Well, I'm not staying here and let you get your butt shot off," she said fiercely.

"I thought it was my front you were worrying about." She gave me a dirty look. "Okay. I need you out here. It gives us an extra card to play. Give me seven minutes, then make a diversion and come on in."

"What kind of diversion?"

"Whatever. You've got seven minutes to think of one," I said as I slipped away.

THE PHOENIX

CHAPTER FIFTY-TWO

The building we'd spotted was a long skinny shed-like structure that went back about six bays deep. The outside was painted in an array of colors, like a monument to the art of graffiti. I realized as I approached a narrow door in the middle that the colors were the result of random test sprays of the lacquer used in auto painting. The building was one big color sample.

Franklin must have been watching for me because the door swung open as I approached. I stopped, waited.

"Come in slowly." It was Franklin's voice. He sounded strung out, like he had his teeth gritted together.

"Okay." I tried to keep my voice calm. I walked to the door and stepped over the threshold. At first I couldn't see anything. The inside was very dark. The only light came from a single light bulb that was suspended from the ceiling. Probably a forty watter from the dim glow.

Franklin stepped in front of me and grabbed my arm. It was Franklin's voice, but his face was unfamiliar. He had bluish circles under his eyes. The same eyes, predator's eyes, gleamed in the light, but in a different face. This face had high cheekbones, skin stretched taunt over a chiseled chin, and a thin aquiline nose. He was leaner, too. He'd shed that sleek, well-fed, politician's façade.

His new exterior aside, I felt that I was seeing the real man for the first time. A hunter. Dangerous, rapacious, desperate. I wondered why I'd never noticed it before.

"Where is Bertie?" I demanded, jerking my arm away. He made a move to swipe at me but I blocked his arm and grabbed his wrist. "Watch yourself," was all I said as I flung it away from me. I wasn't going to let him think he could manhandle any woman anytime he wanted to.

"I'm over here, Ann." Bertie never called me Ann. I tried to appear calm, but inside me a murderous white heat was building.

Franklin laughed. "Thank you, Ms. Jones. Now shut up."

I turned to look into the gloom. The building was surprisingly large inside. Obviously used to paint several cars at once, large curtains of plastic hung from the ceiling that could be pulled to isolate a bay. It resembled a large, untidy hospital room for mechanical patients made of metal.

To my left was a large cage area where supplies were stored. The mesh doors were closed. An open padlock hung from the hasp. Bertie was inside. Martine Edwards stood on the outside, her back up against the mesh. Their faces were white, tense.

On the floor just in front of where they stood, a man was lying on his back. His right hand was thrown out from his body. The light gleamed on a chunky gold ring. It was Mr. Nugget, the thug from Ruby D's and the Parnelli's elevator. I looked back at Franklin, who just laughed.

"I was just getting ready to add to my collection, when that gentleman interrupted me." He dangled a key in my face. I realized that he had a gun in his other hand. A nasty, snub nosed, indecent lump of dull gray metal. I felt my skin shrink as if my body was trying to become a smaller target.

"Okay." I began to walk toward the cage. The floor was wet. I had been so consumed by my own anger and shock that I hadn't noticed the fumes. The smell of the lacquers and whatever you thinned them with was so strong it made me dizzy. Enough stuff had been splashed around to insure an intense fire. I turned. "You really are a crazy bastard after all," I said to his face. "You're screwed up, Damon, or Franklin, or whatever the hell your name is."

"Shut up and get over with the others," he said with quiet menace.

I mentally calculated the time I had left. "You need us, Franklin. You can make a deal with us," I said, trying to slow him down.

"What I don't need is advice from you, you bitch. Get over there with them now."

"What do you intend to do?" I slowly moved toward the cage. I had a pretty good idea, though. He was going to lock us in the cage and then set fire to the warehouse incinerating some loose ends. I had to keep him talking. "You won't get away. They know you killed Mona and Emma." It was a guess, but I really believed he had done it.

"How could I have killed anyone? I'm dead," he sneered. His eyes were too bright, too crazy. He really thought he had outsmarted everyone. He lowered the gun to point at my chest. I held my breath, my heart racing. Words failed me.

Suddenly from nowhere and everywhere at once came a tremendous swell of noise. No, it was music. It was Wagner's 'Ride of the Valkyries' at a deafening decibel level.

Franklin spun around momentarily turning his back on me. I sprinted to the cage grabbing Martine, pushing her." Get down! Get down!" I hissed.

Bertie kneeled on the other side of the wire door and opened it inward. She scrambled out with us. I put my arm around her, shielding her with my body as we shrank away across the floor. Out of the corner of my eye I could see Martine down, scrambling away on her hands and knees.

Franklin laughed, a hideous mad laugh. "Do you really think you can get away? I'm going to hunt each of you down and shoot you." He laughed again. "I'm going to start with you, Ms. Jones."

I guided Bertie around the edge of a set of vinyl curtains. They were smoky with the over spray of a thousand paint jobs. We crouched down. I could feel Bertie's heart racing as I held my arm around her.

Suddenly a shot rang out, then another. The curtain next to my head whiffed in the air. I thought we were hit for a minute. I turned back just in time to see Franklin sink to the floor, screaming. I had threatened to cut off his balls. Evidently, Martine had managed to shoot them off, or close to it. She was sprawled across Mr. Nugget, the hood with the big ring. She'd somehow managed to get her hands on his gun and had gotten off a shot.

"Are you all right?" I said rushing to her side.

"I think so." She pushed herself up onto her knees. The ring man moaned gently. I had thought he was dead.

"Throw the gun away," I said. She was wearing those rust colored gloves I'd noticed the other day. She gave me a look like 'are you crazy'?

"Trust me." She put the gun back on the floor a safe distance from the ring man.

I walked toward Franklin. He was writhing in pain clutching his groin and making a tremendous amount of noise. I gingerly pushed his gun out of range with my foot. The door opened and Chev stepped through.

"What's going on?" She ran to me.

"Great diversion," I said and hugged her shoulders.

"Thanks," she said as I knelt by Franklin. "We'd better get an ambulance over here."

"Just stay where you are, lady." A man stepped out of the shadows from behind one of the plastic curtains. It was the other hood, Mr. Nugget's friend. The thin guy with the gold neck chain and the skinny eyes. He was holding a gun on us. I didn't know hoods traveled in pairs like deer. I decided that I was in favor of stricter handgun legislation. Chev and I backed up. "You other ladies come out here now." Skinny eyes motioned to them with his free hand.

"Shoot them. Shoot the bitches," Franklin spat out. I looked at Chev. She caught my look and moved a little closer to me. Franklin let out another yowl and kicked at the man. Skinny eyes calmly turned, pointed his gun at Franklin, and shot him in the chest. Franklin shuddered, then lay perfectly still.

I looked at the thin man's eyes, no emotion there. "Get out here," he snapped again. Martine came up on my right. Bertie lagged back. Finally, she pushed between Chev and I. She was hunched over, her face pinched, holding her chest.

"God Bertie! What's wrong?" I tried to put my arm around her, but she shrugged me off, seemed to lose her balance and tottered toward the gunman.

"It's her heart!" I was losing it, my voice gaining a few octaves as I reached for her. Bertie faltered and began to turn back toward us. Then she snapped her arms out and a huge shower of grit and dirt hit skinny eyes in the face.

I pushed everybody I could reach out of the way, grabbing Bertie's sleeve and pulling her behind me. "Get down. Get away," I hissed.

The gunman sneezed and swore, rubbing his eyes. He was momentarily blinded. Enraged, he began firing.

"Run!" I screamed pushing towards the door.

Boom! Boom! Boom! There was a volley of shots and skinny eyes hit the floor. Policemen were pouring into the building. I recognized Harrison. He walked quickly over to us.

"It took you long enough," I fumed, "it's been at least twenty minutes since I called from the gas station."

"Sorry. The dispatcher had the address confused. Are you alright?"

"I think so." I did a visual head count. Everyone seemed okay. I guessed that none of the bullets had found their mark.

"Nice work." He nodded at Bertie.

"Thanks." She pulled at her shirt. More dirt fell to the floor. "Kitty litter," she said. "They use it to soak up the oil."

"Well, it was very effective. Why don't you ladies wait outside?" He motioned and a couple of younger looking cops came over. "Take the ladies outside and get statements from them."

The two young cops began to move us to the door. "That one over there is still alive." I motioned toward the older man with the nugget ring. "Or he was."

I followed them outside. Patrol cars filled up every available space in the parking lot. A female cop opened the back door of one of the cars and offered Martine a seat.

"Come on." Chev took Bertie's hand. She led us to the 57 Chevy and opened the door. We all three slid into the front seat.

Bertie's hands were shaking. I put my arm around her shoulders.

"You were great."

"He killed my dog," she said, a big shudder going through her. "I let him outside and when he didn't come back I went out to look for him. Chaddy ate some meat left in the yard by that evil man. He was collapsed on the grass. I tried to get him up but then the man grabbed me and I had to leave Chaddy." She choked back a sob. "He's killed my best friend."

"Almost." I stroked her arm. "He's at Dr. Peter's. She thinks he'll make it. We'll call when we get out of here."

"Call now." Chev opened the glove compartment. She took out a cellular phone. "The code's written here." She indicated the door of the glove compartment.

I dialed Dr. Peter's office. When she came on the line I lost my voice for a moment, then I asked about Chaddy.

"He's fine? Chaddy's fine!" I nodded handing the phone to Bertie who started crying. She was laughing by the time she switched the phone off.

"He's sleeping. The doctor said he was very gassy. An after effect of the tranquilizer that Franklin gave him"

"Did you tell her that that was his normal state?"

"Now, Stella." I hugged her. I couldn't image life without this crazy little woman or her big ugly dog.

CHAPTER FIFTY-THREE

The statement process was long and boring. I didn't mention Martine's gunplay. By the time we'd all given statements it was almost two o'clock in the morning. Harrison had been in and out. The ambulance had screamed away with Mr. Nugget a long time ago. They were just beginning to bring out the bodies of Franklin and the other thug.

We were all sitting in the 57 Chevy by the end of the interrogations. Martine sat in the back seat, quiet, remote, waiting. Harrison walked over. "How are you all holding up?" As he looked at each one of us he smiled. "Not that great, huh? Well, you can all go home, if I have any questions, I'll come by and see you." He helped us out of the car, one by one, like a doorman clearing a limo. He took special care handing Bertie out. He bent to her and whispered something. Her face beamed. Then he turned and walked away. I guessed Martine was in the clear.

"He's got my daughter," Martine said quietly behind me. "That's why I came here tonight. He said I had to come if I wanted to see Aurora again."

"She's probably alright. She was with him of her own free will. If she watches the news at all she'll hear about it."

"I want to tell her first."

Something in her voice caught me. "Tell her what? That Beau was her real father? That the monster she's going to hear about on the news was just her uncle?"

Martine only paused a second. "She doesn't know. I never wanted to tell her about our family sins. I was pregnant when Beau died. When Beau was killed, I didn't know how to go on. Damon was so kind to me, offered to marry me. He said he would protect me. I believed his motives were unselfish. I let him think the baby was his because I thought he'd be a better father."

"Until you began to suspect that he had killed his own brother to get you."

"His father was suspicious, too, although he tried to keep it from me. I finally came to that conclusion." She hunched her shoulders and I suddenly realized how fragile her emotions were.

"So he staged his own death in the boating accident. The dead man that washed up was probably the hit man he hired to kill Beau, to make it look like an accident and tie up his loose ends. It's his pattern." I jammed my hands in my pocket. I felt the envelope with Franklin's phone bill. Something nagged at me. I pulled it out and looked at it again. The B. B. and T. office had been the billing address, but some of the calling card charges had been to another number in Maryland. The telephone exchange had been listed as Kensington. I had it.

"I think I know where your daughter is. Come on, I'll show you." I took off at a run. Bertie and Chev followed me as we wound our way through the junkyard. We left in a caravan of cars. Bertie and I, then Chev, then Martine. We were very close. Kensington was only about ten miles away.

S. Alden Reilly

We zigged and zagged like a line of Rockettes through old parts of Kensington. Finally, I found the street, drove three blocks and parked in front of a small bungalow.

We all piled out. "Wait here." I walked toward the house. I ducked into the shrubbery and peeked in the window. There was a slender girl sitting on the sofa. Her hair was a mass of soft red curls. She was the image of Beau Edwards. She seemed to be alone. I walked back over to the group and touched Martine's arm. "Just go up and ring the bell. She seems fine."

We watched while Martine climbed to the porch. The light came on, the door opened, and the rest was hugs, tears, and kisses as she and Aurora embraced.

Martine motioned for all of us to come inside, a wide smile of relief on her face. If I had ever seen the girls together I would have figured this whole thing out a lot earlier. The family resemblance was so striking that I immediately thought of Cynthia Reeves.

"May I use the phone?" I asked Aurora.

"Of course." She directed me to the kitchen away from the hubbub of their voices. Layne answered the phone on the third ring just as I was beginning to get anxious.

"Layne are you and Cynthia alright?"

"Yes, we're fine. We went shopping today and then we caught a bite to eat."

Layne sounded a little down already, but I had to tell her. I couldn't wait for her to finally watch the evening news. "I have some news that's going to upset you. Franklin is dead, really dead this time."

For a moment she didn't say anything. "Good," she breathed into the phone.

"Can you get over here as soon as possible?" I gave her the address.

"I'll be there in five minutes."

Exactly five minutes later, she pulled up to the curb. Chev and I waited on the porch. "Isn't this the house from that first night?" she asked.

"It sure is. We were better investigators than we thought. Come on." I headed for the garage. Chev and Layne were right behind me. Bertie was taking care of Aurora and Martine, but she watched from the window as we crossed the yard.

I stopped at my car and got my crow bar. The garage was still locked. The big padlock on the double doors didn't look promising so I went to one of the papered up windows on the side. I pried with the crow bar at the bottom of the window. The lock was fastened, but the wood was so old and soft that it began to give way. Finally with a loud pop, the window raised up.

"Here, give me a boost," I called to Chev as I pushed the window the rest of the way up. Chev came and made a step with her hands for my foot. I jumped up and fell right through the window just catching myself before I hit the floor.

"Graceful to a fault, you are, Stella dear," I muttered under my breath. I fumbled for a light switch then noticed in the dim, filtered light from the street lamp a string hanging down from the ceiling. I pulled it and the bare bulb came to life. It threw off an intense light, probably a two hundred watter. I unlocked the small side door and let Chev and Layne in.

The garage was filthy. The light from the bare bulb glared off the yellowed newspaper that covered the windows. The walls were nothing more than the interior framing of the building. No finish work had been done. It was an odd garage. No tools, no nails, bolts, or screws, or odds and ends in little jars. Just a big, dirty, empty space.

"It doesn't look like anything's here," Layne said.

S. Alden Reilly

Chev smiled. "And with a padlock and chain that would choke a horse."

"He didn't like nosy neighbors?" Layne asked.

"True." I knelt to look at the dirty floor. "There are other explanations."

The floor was littered with newspaper, grit, and fluffy debris that looked like old insulation. I could see the marks of a large vehicle. 'Big Blue', if I wasn't mistaken from the wide spread of the tire impressions.

I got down on my hands and knees and started with the left front tire depression. I cleared an area with my hands. Nothing. I kept clearing the dirt away working to my right crossing over the other tire depression. A thin crack showed in the floor.

I wanted to yell 'Eureka!' or 'Hello!' in the best Sherlock tradition, but instead I just brushed the dirt away more furiously. I uncovered a gray metal rectangle.

"It's a safe," Chev said excitedly.

"Sort of a homemade, one I think." I looked around for a tool. My crowbar was too thick. Attempts to use my fingernails to pry it open were also unsuccessful. "Well, hello. Look at that." I'd just noticed something leaning against the wall, partially hidden by one of the studs. It was a big nail-like thing with a flattened end. I scrambled over to it, ripping a piece of newspaper off the window to grasp it with.

"What's the matter?" Chev asked.

"This is Mona's." I gingerly fit the blade to the edge of the metal lid. One little twist and the box opened. "Here, stick that back over there like we found it." I handed the tool to Layne careful to only touch the paper. "Franklin's prints are probably on it." I reached inside and pulled out a packet of papers wrapped in a plastic bag. "We've got it." I looked up at Layne and Chev. "Now we can finish it."

THE PHOENIX

CHAPTER FIFTY FOUR

By the time we got back to my house, I was exhausted but too keyed up to do anything about it, like sleep. Chev had insisted on coming with Bertie and me. Layne had gone home to be with Cynthia.

"I could use a glass of wine," I said, setting my purse on the kitchen counter.

"Me, too," Chev chimed in as I pulled a bottle of Merlot out of the wine rack in the pantry.

"That would be nice," Bertie said matter of factly.

I laughed out loud. "What? You don't drink."

"This is a special occasion. Now don't give me that look, Stella," Bertie scolded.

Chev carried three glasses over to the kitchen table. I followed her with the bottle and a bowl of chips and salsa. We sat down and Chev poured us each a glass of wine.

I must admit, I stared at Bertie, fascinated, as she took a sip. "What do you think?" I said, watching her face.

"Not bad. I like it better than the champagne we had in New York."

Chev snorted, "Stella, haven't you figured out that your aunt is a woman of the world yet?"

Bertie beamed. "Thank you, dear. Mildred insisted that we all have a toast when we went out to dinner after the helicopter ride." She raised her glass. "Here's to two other women of the world. Exceptional, worldly women at that."

We all touched glasses. The tinkling sound was like music. Bertie set her glass down and looked at both of us. "Now, tell me how you figured this out. I've got some of it but I don't quite understand the two birthday thing."

"Stella, look in my purse. The files are still in there from when we visited Harrison." Chev pointed at the counter.

I got up and pulled them from her briefcase-sized handbag. I opened the folder containing our photos and carried them over to the refrigerator. Right after Michael's death Arianne had spelled out 'Arianne, Zara, and Mom' with bright letter magnets on the front of the refrigerator. It took her three packages to get enough vowels. She had scattered the rest of the alphabet around the edges. I pulled a 'D' from the surplus.

"This is Damon Edwards." I fixed the picture with the magnet. "This is Franklin Brody, the real Franklin Brody." I fixed the picture of Emma and her brother with a F. "And this is Franklin Brody as we knew him when he was married to Layne." I fixed a recent picture of the silver haired bastard to the refrigerator with an X.

Bertie frowned. "So Damon took the real Franklin's birthday?"

"Yes, he had to when he assumed his identity. But he couldn't give up his astrological sign."

Chev laughed, "Once a Gemini. Always a Gemini."

Bertie shook her head. "Oh, I see, you realized that he lied about his birthday because Layne said he read the Gemini's daily horoscope."

I laughed out loud. Chev grinned and patted Bertie's arm. "We weren't quite that astute," I said. "We just kept digging until we figured out everyone's real birthday." I held my hand across the bottom of Damon's face covering his chin. "Look, who does this remind you of?"

Bertie's eyes got wide. "That's the man who tried to kill my Chaddy!"

"Elementary, my dear Watson." I said as I picked up my wineglass.

Chev hugged her herself like she felt a chill. "I feel sorry because of all the people he hurt. All the people he killed or had killed." Her chin came up and there was a fierce look in her eyes. "But I'm glad he's dead and I'm glad we had something to do with it." She looked at Bertie. "Do you think that makes me a terrible person?"

Bertie's eyes were gentle. "No, my dear. It just makes you human. Something I wonder if that evil man ever was." She pushed her glass to the middle of the table. "Here, please help me finish this." She hadn't had more than the sip for the toast. I hid a smile. So much for the driving-Bertie-to-drink fears I'd been having since we sat down.

Bertie got up from her chair. She went over to the refrigerator and pushed some letters together to spell 'Stella'. She moved the letters spelling 'Mom' to the general galaxy of the alphabet around the edge. "There, that's better," she grinned. Then she came over to us to say goodnight. "I'm so tired I've got to go to bed." A smile crossed her face. "Tomorrow's a big day. I pick Chaddy up from the vet. He's going to be glad to get home."

We stood up and each gave her a hug goodnight. I was glad she was going back to her routine. It would be a lot safer to have her out of what Chev and I had decided to do next.

S. Alden Reilly

CHAPTER FIFTY FIVE

I dressed carefully in black, all black. Black suit, black silk blouse, black hose, and black shoes. My shoes were new, but everything else I'd worn to Michael's funeral. It had rained that day and ruined my shoes. That's why I had new ones.

My hands shook a little as I adjusted my blouse. It wanted to bulge out at my waist. I was amazed that everything fit again, even though it was a little snug. I guess a steady diet of stress can really knock the weight off. I turned off the lights as I left the office. It was just after four in the afternoon and Chev had already gone. The place seemed particularly empty. I gave the black rooster lamp a pat on the tail feathers for luck. "This is for you, Michael," I said under my breath as I locked the office door.

I don't remember much about the drive to Ruby D's. It was like a dream. I just kept repeating my speech like a mantra until I pulled up outside. I was meeting Robert Parnelli to discuss blackmail.

I was about five minutes early, but it wasn't the right neighborhood to sit outside in the car. I walked inside and looked around. The place seemed deserted except for Tighe. He was polishing the old wood bar while he kept an eye on a boxing match on ESPN. It looked like a welterweight bout.

I headed for the booth in the back. Before I got there a voice said, "Hello, Ms. Jones. Won't you sit down?"

Robert Parnelli, still the banker in a navy blue suit, was already in the next to the last booth. I slid in opposite him.

"I'm glad you agreed to meet me, Mr. Parnelli." Tighe shuffled over about then. I saw the light of recognition in his eyes, but he said nothing. I ordered a wild turkey and water on the rocks. I waited until he'd brought it and shambled away before I continued. "You see, something has turned up that I wanted you to know about."

"Yes?" His small eyes were like two black marbles behind the thick glasses.

"I believe I've found the correspondence and contracts that Franklin Brody misplaced." I sipped the bourbon. Luckily, it was mostly water. Still, it burned down my throat like sweet smoke. I kept my eyes on Parnelli. He was interested, very interested, but he wasn't going to show it. I waited.

"I'm not sure I know what you're talking about."

I resisted the temptation to throw my drink back in one gulp. It would have been a mistake. Because I don't drink very often I'm a cheap drunk. Instead, I sipped a little more whiskey and made a motion as if I was getting ready to leave. "Sorry, I guess I've wasted your time, Mr. Parnelli."

"Wait." He was a little too anxious. He was losing his cool.

I sat back down. "Look, if you're interested, I can arrange to meet you."

"Well." He looked up at something behind me. Before I could turn to look, the large body of a man slid in next to me. Robert grinned a nasty little know-it-all grin.

"Leo, what do you think?"

Leo was the opposite of Robert. Robert was lean, all sharp angles. Leo was big, bulky with broad features. His eyes were the `same, though. Dead. Twenty-twenty vision, but dead.

"I was just explaining to your brother that I've found some papers. Of course, I'm sure you've already heard all this from the next booth."

Leo laughed. "So you didn't bring the papers with you?"

"No."

"Well, how do we know that you're not just making this up?"

"Believe me. I'm dead serious." I pulled a thinly folded paper from my purse. "Here's a sample. It's one of the altered inspection reports from the building on Fourteenth Street along with a statement from the inspector who altered it." Leo took it from my hand. "You can keep it. It's just a copy. I've got the originals in a safe place."

"I don't know what you're referring to," Robert said, looking at Leo.

"Fine." I was ready to move. "Excuse me."

Leo didn't budge. "Wait a minute." His gravely voice was low and menacing. "How do we know you're not wearing a wire?"

I gave him a haughty look. "The only wire I'm wearing is the under-wire in my bra."

Leo looked at Robert and started chuckling. It wasn't a happy sound. Robert sputtered.

"Now, Mrs. Jones."

"It's Ms. Jones."

"Oh. Sorry." He blinked. "I know that I can speak for my brother when I say that although we had no prior knowledge of these documents, if they belong to Parnelli Construction Co., the property should be returned."

"They're my property right now, but I'll consider returning them for a fee."

"What fee?"

"Five hundred thousand dollars."

"You're crazy!" Robert yelped.

I shook my head. "That's cheap. Especially if you weigh the cost of lawyers for the trial, the damage to your reputation, the scandal over the fourteenth street property, possible jail time . . ."

"Okay. I get the idea." Leo snarled.

"Ms. Jones, I'm afraid what you're asking is out of the question. There are laws against blackmail, you know." Robert said haughtily.

I took a quarter from my purse. "Here, call the police." I was losing it. I didn't like being bullied. They both just looked at me. I tossed the quarter on the table. "Look, you've got my price, you've seen a sample of the merchandise. Call me if you want to deal." I scrambled up onto the seat of the booth, stepped up on to the tabletop, hiked up my skirt and jumped down to the floor.

"Now Ms. Jones, why don't you sit back down?" Robert was on his feet. Leo just stared, then moved toward me. A tall, muscular man in a dark blue sweat outfit with the hood pulled up walked into the restaurant and up to the counter where Tighe was engrossed with a soccer match on the TV that hung from the ceiling. The man got his attention and ordered coffee.

Robert and Leo backed away and sat back down in the booth. Robert stirred his coffee, long cold by now.

I backed away from them. "I've got an appointment. Think it over. I'll call back here in an hour. If you want to deal, I can be back here with the papers in fifteen minutes." I turned and walked out, holding the door open for the jogger who followed me out.

S. Alden Reilly

The streets were fairly deserted. I got in my car, adjusted my blouse again and pulled away fast. I checked my rear-view mirror. A black car pulled out about a block behind me. I was being followed or, in detective parlance, tailed.

CHAPTER FIFTY SIX

I led the tail on an intricate pattern of city streets. He stayed with me. I pulled up outside Meyer's Hamburger Palace on Georgia Avenue and went inside. I ordered a big greasy Tucson burger smothered with Jack cheese and guacamole, curly fries and a large iced tea. I got my number and went to the pay phone by the exit door to call Chev.

"Hi," I said when she answered.

"Hello. What are you doing?"

"Plan 'A' is under way."

"Are you all right?"

"So far. I've got company."

"Oh? Where are you?"

"Meyer's, Georgia Avenue. I'm about to eat my month's quota of fat and cholesterol."

"Go for it. You might need the energy," Chev laughed.

"I intend to. I'll call you in an hour."

"Ten four." I hung up just as they called out my number. I picked up my order and ate by the window so I could watch my car. Just outside the restaurant's parking lot, at the curb, I could see the nose of a black car through the shrubs. It looked like my companion had decided to forego fat and cholesterol.

I called the Parnelli's back at the appointed hour. Tighe answered and for a moment I thought they'd wriggled off my hook. But then Robert got on the phone and I started reeling him in. "Have you decided?"

"My brother and I feel that we should examine your evidence."

"Great. Do you have the money?"

"Ah, yes. We'll have the funds you requested."

"Okay, I'll be over."

"Well, actually we'd prefer another meeting place."

"Such as?"

He named a spot near I-70 Where State road 97 intersects. It was a lonely, still largely rural area. "At six-thirty." It would be getting dark by then. They really thought I was a moron.

"Sure, that will be fine." I calculated that I had about an hour and a half before I needed to meet them, so I headed downtown to Union Station, found a parking place and went inside. My shadow squealed to a stop at the circle. It was too late; I'd already seen them.

I was in and out of Union Station in less than fifteen minutes. I came out carrying a small canvas duffel bag. I got back in my car and watched my tail get excited. I entered the stream of traffic from the station and headed west. The black sedan was maneuvering to get next to me. I kept to the right lane in case I needed to change direction quickly.

I glanced ahead. A moving van about two blocks up had double-parked. The doors were open, the blinkers flashing. I would be trapped if I got behind it. I tried to merge to the left. The black sedan hung there. It's windows were tinted such a dark color, I couldn't see in.

I decided to turn right at the next street. It was a one way going the wrong way. Too many cars to play 'Chicken'. I kept going. I was just about five car lengths from the moving van. It was now or never. I rolled down my window, grabbed the canvas bag, and flung it out the window. It hit the hood of the black car and bounced off. The black car hit the brakes so hard, I thought they would swerve into me. I pulled in front of them and hit the gas taking the next street east then rounding back until I was going west again.

The black car was long gone when I cut across M Street and turned north on Wisconsin Avenue. Traffic was terrible as usual, but there were plenty of people. The ride up Wisconsin was pretty good. Once I passed the Cathedral it got easier. I stopped near White Flint Mall and called Chev.

"What's up."

"It worked."

"I knew they'd go for it. What's next?"

"They want me to meet them at the intersection of 97 and 70 west."

"When?"

"Six-thirty."

"Okay. Are you ready?"

"As ready as I'll ever be." I said matter-of-factly. Actually, I was so keyed up I didn't think I'd sleep for a week. If I lived, that is.

"Why don't you have some coffee and calm down?"

"No time. I've got to get going."

"I'll meet you later." Chev paused. "Watch your ass."

"Right." It wasn't my ass I was worried about.

S. Alden Reilly

CHAPTER FIFTY SEVEN

The drive up 97 was really pretty. The sky was a deep purple, under-lit by the setting sun. The road rolled up and down the hills. A few trees already glowed red in the twilight. The rest had that old green look, the dusty green the leaves get when the color is on the verge of turning some incredible shade of gold or purple or red. Fall was just a frost away.

I pulled up in front of a combination general store and gas station. 'Irma's market' was hand painted on a sign over the door. The gas pumps looked like they were from 1910 with glass-domed tops borrowed from some turn of the century deep-sea diver.

I tugged my blouse down and went inside. The interior was dark with an incredible jumble of items offered. Evidently, you could pick up a little ammo, salt for your water softener, deli meats, and a variety of personal hygiene products in one visit.

I went to the ladies room, we won't go into those accommodations, which were from a bygone era much like the gas pumps outside, and came back out. I picked up a bottle of contact lens cleaner, the disinfectant kind. I also bought a few Mounds bars. If they could only make them with almonds. I prefer dark chocolate.

I paid the clerk, obviously not Irma. She was too young, too bland to own anything. I went back out to my car and poured the disinfectant into my imitation nine-millimeter automatic water pistol. I'm a crack shot and have been since appropriating it from one of my students years ago. I wear contacts and I can personally vouch for the fact that this stuff stings like Hell if you accidentally get it in your eyes.

I drove the rest of the way to the meeting place. It was a picnic spot near the exit onto Interstate 70. I didn't see any cars so I drove into the small car park area and got out, first pulling the hood release. I put the hood up and stood there with my water pistol on the air filter cover. The sky was turning a dark smoky color as the sun went down. I waited.

It didn't take long. A dark car with tinted windows pulled up, then another, and then another. The Parnellis must have a fleet of them. The cars hovered, their headlights pinpointing me. I ducked a little further behind my hood.

"Car trouble?" It was Robert. I pulled at the front of my blouse nervously.

"Yeah. Have you got the money?" I wondered if Leo was nearby. As if to answer my question, he stepped up behind Robert.

"Have you got our papers?" Leo said unpleasantly.

"Yes. I do."

He swung a canvas bag from behind his back and pulled a wad of newspapers from inside it. "Better not pull a funny stunt like this one again." He threw the bag on the ground.

"I don't like being pushed. I told you I'd swap the papers for five hundred thousand, and I intend to keep my word." I pulled a packet from behind my battery. I had wrapped the package in a heavy rubberized piece of canvas. I didn't want battery acid to destroy the evidence.

Leo made a motion to grab it, but I held it back motioning for my money. Robert handed me a small canvas satchel, which I opened. It contained bundles of real money, lots of bundles. I fanned a few to make sure they weren't doctored, ones in the middle or something. But they were good. Hundreds throughout.

I handed Robert my packet and rested my hand on the air filter cover while he examined it. I didn't really expect them to let me walk away with five hundred thousand dollars of their money. I was right.

Robert pulled a little nickel-plated revolver from the inside of his expensive cashmere overcoat. It was so small and pretty, it could almost be a toy. I doubted if Leo would be caught dead carrying such a feminine piece. "Really, Ms. Jones, such an amateur. I'll take my money back please."

"I see. You're going to renege on our agreement."

"Yes. It pains me to have to pay for my own property."

"Well, you shouldn't have been so careless in the first place." I toyed with the bag, holding it on top of the air filter housing.

"It was stolen," Robert snapped.

"By Jerry Derr?"

"Very clever. Yes. He picked them up one evening."

"After he pushed Deseeca's foreman down the elevator shaft? What did Jerry do, suddenly become entrepreneurial? He sold them to Franklin. Did you realize that? You actually thought Deseeca had them then Franklin started blackmailing you. Getting you to kill people for him?" Robert just looked at me. No expression on his face. "People like my husband."

"Your husband?" Robert was having trouble following the story.

"Michael Strayer. Medical Examiner for the western counties. Franklin had you kill him, didn't he?"

Robert had an ugly sneer on his face. "We never get directly involved in such matters."

"You just let Jerry Derr handle it. He killed Michael and Nikki Fortuna because they could expose Franklin. That was a part of the deal for getting your incriminating evidence back." He gave me a blank look. I pushed. "It was part of the deal, wasn't it?"

"So what if it was?" Robert sneered. He was losing his sense of humor.

"So how did you let a man like Brody double cross you? I wouldn't think one man could defy an operation like yours."

Robert laughed but there wasn't any humor in it. "He thought he was so smart. That he could lead us around by the nose. But we had tabs on him the whole time. We don't get crossed."

"Yeah, he ended up paying for it just like you're going to." Leo snarled.

Robert glared at me and snapped his gun hand up on a straight trajectory with my eyes. I didn't want to end up like Moe Green in the *Godfather* so I handed the bag over.

"Now walk out here away from the car," he demanded.

"I thought you didn't get directly involved."

"I'm making an exception."

I leaned forward on my car with two hands as if to steady myself. When I leaned back, I shot a stream of eye solution right across Robert's face. At first he had no reaction, but then he screamed, dropped the gun, and began wiping his eyes with his fists. I ducked down and scrambled to the opposite side of my car.

"Not so fast." Leo was waiting. His gun was big, black, and quite convincing. I stood up holding my water pistol. "Drop it." I did. Leo marched me out of the circle of light made by the car's headlights. I could feel the nose of the gun poke me in the ribs as we walked further off the road

into the trees.   I turned to the side slightly.   "Right there."
He raised his gun.   My flesh crawled.   I held my breath, my
heart pounding.

"Are you really going to kill me?"

"Shut up and turn around."   I slowly turned to face
him.

"Hold it right there."   A deep, calm voice said evenly.
It was Leo's turn to look uncomfortable.   The nose of a gun
was pressed against his head right behind his left ear.   "I said
hold it! Drop the gun!"   The voice said again.

Leo handed his gun, butt first, over his shoulder to
Harrison.   Harrison slipped it into the jacket pocket of his
dark blue jogging sweats.

Lights went up all around us, brilliant lights like the
ones at football games that gave off enough wattage for
surgery or TV coverage.   Out of the corner of my eye I could
see Leo's face.   He didn't look happy.

"Put down your guns."   Harrison commanded.   The
figure of a man moved out from behind the lights, then
another, and another, all with large guns pointed at Leo's
men. Now I could see lots of men.   Men in uniforms moving
in, closing the circle.

Leo flung his arms out.   "Hold up, boys. They've got
nothing."

"I wouldn't be so sure," Harrison growled.   "Come
on, Robert. Join the party."   Harrison motioned to his men
with a shrug of his shoulder.   They moved to surround the
Parnelli's men and disarm them.

Robert still leaned against the car rubbing his eyes.
He stumbled forward.   "The bitch shot my eyes with acid.   I
can't see," he whined.

"It's not acid," I said as Harrison's men cuffed Leo
and turned their attention to Robert.   "It's contact lens
disinfectant.   It'll stop burning in a little while."

THE PHOENIX

Harrison grinned at me. "Go get yourself unwired."

Both men's heads snapped up at that. Leo gave Robert a look that seemed to put his eye discomfort in perspective. He stopped rubbing them and meekly dropped his hands to be cuffed behind him.

The rest of the entourage was escorted away while I submitted to the technicians in a large blue van. I was standing in my bra with my skirt loosened when Harrison stuck his head inside the back door. He looked right at me. No shyness or apology in his eyes, just appraisal. "A friend of yours is here." He ducked back out as Chev walked up behind him. Harrison helped Chev climb into the trailer. When he turned away I thought I saw a smile on his face.

"Go ahead." The lab guy un-taped the last wire from my waist and handed me my blouse. A little late for my modesty. I should have sold tickets.

"Thank God." She exclaimed and climbed up to me. I grabbed her and we hugged fiercely for a few moments tears rolling down our faces.

"It's time to start living again," I whispered just before we stood back from each other.

"Let's go get a cup of coffee. My treat." Chev's face beamed.

"And French fries," I said, tucking in my blouse.

CHAPTER FIFTY EIGHT

The next couple of days were very strange. I was questioned by the FBI's organized crime task force several times, then by Harrison and his men. I know Layne had been in to see them and Chev, too. Even Bertie got her fifteen minutes of fame when she was called in to go over her statement about the night Damon was killed. She had her picture on Channel four news. I figured the gray panthers would be after her to join or become their spokesperson.

Chaddy took all the hubbub in stride. On his first visit after coming home from the vet's, he'd headed straight for his spot under the kitchen table with a half roll of Ritz crackers.

"Have you read this?" Bertie asked holding up the paper for me to see. We were sitting at the kitchen table having a Caesar salad and drinking ice tea. Chaddy was chasing slobbery crackers across the floor.

The Post had had a field day with the Parnellis and the Edwards family saga. Some investigative reporter uncovered the whole sordid side of the Mississippi Edwards'. It seemed that Jonathan Edwards made his money as a young man during prohibition. He'd had amassed a fortune and achieved respectability by the time he'd married. He had two sons, Damon and Beau. One son was all good deeds, honors and courage. The other manipulative, selfish and untrustworthy. You can guess which one Damon was.

The article, which went on for several pages inside the newspaper, detailed all the dirty secrets of both families with a blow by blow account of Damon's murder spree over the last twenty years and the Parnellis' mob connections.

The Parnellis' wounded thug Joey Withers, Mr. Nugget's real name, had decided to testify and enter the witness protection program. With his testimony and mine, backed up by the tape I'd worn over my navel, the Parnellis stood to do some real time. I was glad it was all out in the open, although it was painful to read the whole sad story again and again, to see the faces over and over on every TV newsmagazine show.

"He was such a sick man," Bertie said, shaking her head at me.

"You could say that again. Look how many lives he ruined, and for what?" I rubbed my arms shivering at the pure evil of it.

"What was he up to at the end?" She said, thinking out loud. "The newspapers don't explain that."

"Well, I have a theory." I picked up a cracker that was stuck to the floor and handed it to Chaddy. "I think he was about to assume a new identity."

"Whose?"

"Mona's brother." I leaned back in my chair with my hands crossed behind my head. "Did you notice the bruising around his eyes and the swelling in his jaw when he was pushing us around in that warehouse?"

"Yes, but I just thought he'd been in a fight with one of those hoody men."

I smiled at her characterization of the Parnellis' hit men. Being called 'hoody' in Bertie's day must have made one a social pariah.

"I think he had just had plastic surgery to look like Mona's brother who had conveniently died two years ago." Bertie just waited, an expectant look on her face. And something else, too: admiration and pride. Pride in me. It made me smile. I blushed with pleasure. "Although he didn't have anything to do with the death. Chev checked. The guy died of a heart attack. Franklin was going to take his identity and start over again. But this time the man's sister wouldn't go for it." I leaned forward resting my arms on the table. "Mona was furious when she realized what Franklin was up to. She idolized her dead brother. She even contacted Martine and Nikki to cause trouble for Franklin. They fought about it that last day and he killed her."

I rubbed my hand across the table as I thought about my theory of what happened. "When he killed Mona, he had to get rid of Emma. Emma knew too much and she would never keep silent about Mona's murder. She was tired of the 'horror' the 'evil' as she put it in her letter to Cynthia. She wouldn't be a party to another murder." I looked at Bertie. "To me, her death was the saddest. I think that Franklin really loved her in his own sick, twisted way. He strangled her while they were in an intimate embrace, the ultimate betrayal to a woman he'd already betrayed too many times."

"A real sick puppy," Bertie said, cutting to the heart of it as usual.

I thought about what that sickness had cost me, Chev, Layne, and all the other victims of Franklin's greed, his immorality, and his disregard for human life.

CHAPTER FIFTY NINE

I was on my way to the office. I had spent the entire morning, my last morning at Harding College, cleaning out my desk. I'd told the president, Sarah Mills, that I was making a life change, that I wouldn't be back. She'd been very understanding, although I don't think she believed me.

I pulled up outside the office. I opened my wallet and looked at my new PI license. I'd rubbed my finger over it inside my purse the whole time I'd been talking to Sarah. I knew I was ready for a new life.

There was a workman at the front door. He had a big canvas tarp spread over the entryway so I headed for the back door. Chev opened it, her smile wide and cherry pink to match the suit she had on.

"You look like Ann Strayer in that get up."

I looked down at my hunter green slacks and Black Watch plaid jacket. It was my college garb. I ran a thumb around the inside of my green turtleneck. It was itching me. I felt like I was choking. Maybe it was being in Ann's uniform again that seemed so confining. "Don't worry, I brought a change of clothes."

I fingered the strap of a small overnight bag on my shoulder. We were having guests. Chev had planned a small open house to thank some of the people who had helped us with our case. She had been very mysterious for the last few days. While I had been involved with severing my life with Harding College, she had been renovating.

Chev led me to one of the former bedrooms. It had very recently been stuffed with boxes, files, and odds and ends of furniture. "Do you like the new conference room?" Chev asked as I walked in. "I got permission from Troy to put all his stuff in one of those public storage places. I told him his mother needed the room."

The Fortuna agency had received an enormous check from the Edwards estate, a reward for clearing up several family mysteries and burying the skeletons. The room was painted white with micro mini blinds at the windows. The conference table, a small pine topped, white-legged refugee from a dining room was pushed up against the wall.

"It looks great," I said sincerely. It did look great. It also looked like home. It looked like where I belonged. My neck stopped itching.

Chev took my arm. "I want to show you something." She led me down the hall to Nikki's old office and opened the door. It was amazing. Everything was white: the walls, the new desk, the furniture. A new computer was set up on a rolling cart beside the desk. A beautiful amethyst vase held a dozen purple irises, the only other color in the room. The deep purple matched the upholstery on the chairs.

"It's yours. If you want it."

I stared. "I don't know what to say."

"Just say you'll be my partner."

I looked at everything and suddenly realized why I'd been so anxious for the past few days. I'd wanted to do this again, be on our next case, figure out the next puzzle.

"You've got it." I stuck out my hand and shook hers.

"Why don't you look around for a minute. I'll call you when the cake's ready." I smiled and walked around the desk. My desk. I liked the way it sounded. Chev looked at me. "And, change your clothes. Stella has some people to meet." She laughed as she pulled the door shut behind her.

I opened my bag and took out a black crew neck sweater, slim black slacks, and silver earrings. I piled the Ann clothes on top of my desk as I changed. It was cathartic to rid myself of my old identity. The artificial one I had been trapped inside of for so many years. I was musing on this when a knock on the door startled me. I ran my hand through my hair as I opened it. It was Tony Deseeca.

"Congratulations."

"For what?"

"For everything. Solving your case, being partners with Chev, you know."

"Well, thanks." I smiled. This man unnerved me. At first I thought it was his position, his impeccable suits, but he still made me feel backwards dressed in a hunter green turtleneck and khaki Dockers, in my own office.

"Like the flowers?" He said.

"They're beautiful."

"They're from me."

I pulled out the card. 'You're one hell of a woman, Stella Jones, Tony.' was written on it. There was a folded piece of paper, too. I opened it. A check for thirty thousand dollars was inside, made out to our firm. I heard a gasp and guessed it came from my mouth.

"Just a thank you for clearing my name." He chuckled a low deep chuckle. "And for getting two very unpleasant brothers off my back." He suddenly took my hand and held it to his lips. He kissed my knuckles like a courtly knight. It made my stomach jump. "I knew you were going to be important in my life the minute you walked into my office that first time. You were like an angel, all in white."

I flushed red to my spiky blonde roots. "An angel? I thought I looked like a battered ice cream vendor."

Tony laughed. It was a carefree hearty sound. "Why don't we go out to dinner one night next week?" he said. He pulled my hand to his chest moving me closer to his body. "I think it's time we got to know each other better."

I was completely mute. I couldn't breathe. I just looked at him like a deer in the headlights. Then I felt his arms around me. "Dinner would be nice," I said, stepping back a little.

He smiled and pulled me closer, then brushed my lips with his before he released me. "Okay. I'll call you in a few days." He turned and left.

CHAPTER SIXTY

My face burned with the blowtorch effect again. My heart was beating so fast that I felt lightheaded. I shut my eyes for a moment and leaned against the desk to regain my composure. When I opened them, Harrison was standing there looking at me. He must have come from work. He had on a black suit. It made his eyes look golden brown and emphasized the gray in his hair. His face had the usual deep lined expression, but the hint of a smile played across his lips.

"Actually, he seems like a pretty nice guy although I have to admit I had my doubts about him for awhile," Harrison said, shrugging in Tony's direction. "Here, you'd better have a drink of this," he said, handing me a red plastic cup with what tasted like ginger ale in it. I took a long sip as he sank the whole long length of him into one of the purple upholstered guest chairs facing my desk.

"Who do you think you are? My dad?" I said after I swallowed.

"No, but a little fatherly advice never hurt anyone." He watched me as I walked around to sit behind my desk.

"I'm not ready for a relationship," I said. I put my hands on my cheeks seeking to cool them to a reasonable temperature.

"Stella. Dating is just dating. You talk, you spend time together. You get to know someone. Relationships come later." His smile turned into a grimace. "Of course then the relationship goes sour, you tear each other apart, and you find yourself in Hell," he finished in a sardonic tone.

"Great," I said, smiling in spite of my embarrassment. "And you want me to go through that?"

He fingered the lapel of the suit he wore. He looked very distinguished and more handsome than ever. "I wouldn't wish this on anyone." The pain in his voice was so touching I immediately forgot my own awkward feelings.

"I'm sorry you're unhappy. Bertie told me a little about it." I extended my hand across the desk with my palm open. "Thank you for watching over us. Chev and me and Bertie. You saved our lives. I'll never forget that."

He looked slightly flustered as took my hand. He gave it a little squeeze then he changed the subject. "Well, what's next?"

I changed gears with him. "Another case."

He grinned. "You've already helped clear up five homicides for my department. I'm all for it." He stood, leaning his hands on my desk. "Good luck, I think you and Chev will be a success." Some of the warmth of the man came through. "I'll look forward to working with you again."

I looked at him and saw the smile fade out of his eyes as the world-weary expression returned. It touched my heart. I came around the desk, put my arms around him, and gave him a hug. "I hope you will remember you said that the next time I get in your way. I know we pushed you to your limit."

He hugged me back and for a moment his arms tightened. I felt his lips brush my hair. Then he let go of me. He looked down at the floor as if suddenly shy. "Hey, it's just part of my job, but the three of you are exceptional women." He looked into my eyes his own suddenly naked, honest. "I meant what I said."

For the second time in less than five minutes I could feel myself get pink. Tony laughed somewhere down the hall. It was time to rejoin the party. I walked with Harrison back to our new conference room. Chev was getting the cake ready. I walked up to her and handed her the check. She looked at me for a minute then glanced at the check. Her eyes got as big as two silver dollars.

"Wow!"

"'Wow' is an understatement."

"This will come in handy for the lean times."

"Hey, there aren't going to be any lean times. You know everyone will be beating down our doors to have their problems solved," I protested.

I could see 'you have a lot to learn' on the tip of her tongue, but she just snorted and turned back to the cake. "Okay, come on, Cynthia." She motioned to Cynthia to join us. "You light the candles." Chev handed her some matches. "We're celebrating. Layne's got a surprise."

"God. I hope she's not engaged," I muttered under my breath.

The conference room was full of people. There were balloons everywhere. Some big Mylar ones said 'congratulations' and 'best wishes'. The pine table was covered with a festive tablecloth and loaded with food, soft drinks, beer, and wine coolers. There was a big sheet cake with a cover over it.

Bertie, resplendent in a pale peach pantsuit, hovered with the plates and cups serving the pizza and drinks. She came over and gave me a kiss on the cheek. Then she took Harrison's arm and pulled him away to the table. She was taking her hostess duties very seriously. Pretty soon Harrison was sitting on a stool next to Bertie balancing a plate of pizza and a bottle of Corona with a lime wedge.

Layne looked elegant in a navy blue pantsuit. She was chatting with Cynthia and John. She and John were definitely an item now. He looked like a man who's seen heaven and knows he's got a place there. She looked vibrant, more alive than I had ever seen her.

David Ramsey and Tony Deseeca were chatting in a corner balancing plates of pizza. David was drinking a soda, but Tony had mug of beer in one hand.

Chev took my arm as I looked around the room. Other people milled about, people I had never met. Pretty soon Chev began the introductions. I met Jonathan, Chev's contact at MVA; Betty, her friend from vital statistics; Louise, her reference librarian friend and a host of policemen and policewomen. There was also a generous mixture of Chev's clients including Blanche Connor, the only client that kept the agency on a retainer.

I mingled, meeting and thanking the people that had helped Chev and I get the monkey off our backs. I always managed to veer off in plenty of time to avoid Tony. I didn't want to turn crimson again.

Chev poured us each a glass of champagne, the sweet bubbly kind I like. Then she tapped her glass with a long red fingernail until she got everyone's attention.

"We want to congratulate Layne Brody and Cynthia Reeves on their new venture." She looked at me. "Layne and Cynthia are going into partnership when Cynthia graduates." Our guests murmered their congratulations. "And Stella and I are going into partnership immediately. I think Layne intends to specialize in divorce, so there will be plenty of work for Stella and me." Everyone laughed. It gave me a warm feeling.

When Layne came over to congratulate us, Chev pulled an envelope from her pocket. "Here, this may help with the new law firm's expenses." Layne looked at her. "I found the money. The money that Franklin took from your accounts. He had it in a new account under a different name. I had the bank pull a statement for you."

"Charles Freeman?" Layne looked at the statement quizzically.

"Mona's brother," Chev said.

"Mona Freeman's brother had my money?"

I thought I had better step in or we might be there all night. "No, no, no. Franklin was going to become Charles Freeman. He had already set up a social security number and a bank account. Chev found it all for you. You'll just have to get Harrison's help with the paperwork to get your assets back. This is all part of the evidence."

"How did you guys figure this out?" Layne said, looking happily amazed.

"We're just damn good," Chev laughed. "Stella figured out what Franklin's new name was going to be and I started calling. Vin helped me get access to the FBI records of bank transactions of ten thousand dollars or more and I found the account in a Bank in southern Virginia. I asked Vin to order the statement. He's got the authority. And here it is," she grinned, "all of it."

I thought Layne was going to squeeze the life out of Chev in gratitude. I watched Cynthia. She seemed happier. Layne was happy, too. She was taking her role as Cynthia's stepmother very seriously. I knew she was pursuing Cynthia's inheritance with the Edwards estate. It seemed that the Edwards family was more than willing to cooperate. After all, Cynthia was Damon's only child. Aurora was Beau's child. Cynthia was entitled to a share of the estate in spite of her father's actions. She was an innocent victim just as the others were. Martine had flown home with Aurora, and we'd heard that all was well. Layne said that they were keeping in touch with Cynthia. She was a nice kid. I thought she'd make it all right.

CHAPTER SIXTY ONE

Chev and I were sitting with Bertie in the conference room. Everyone had gone and we had just finished cleaning up.

"That was a great party," Bertie said as she wrapped some leftover pizza in foil wrap and went to put it in the refrigerator. It could be lunch for us tomorrow. "I heard nothing but good things about you two. Layne kept going on about her money and the way you found it, Chev."

"It was nothing," Chev said as she picked up the cooler. She headed for the kitchen to dump the water.

"It was good deduction," I insisted as I followed her with the unused plates and napkins.

"Speaking of good deduction," Chev paused as we walked from the kitchen, "how did you come up with Charles Freeman in the first place?"

"Yes, tell me, Stella." Bertie said, beaming at both of us like we were her favorite children. "How did you know?"

I rubbed the conference table with a damp cloth. "I remembered the picture of Mona and her brother. They looked so close but Harrison mentioned that Mona had no 'next of kin' for the police to notify." I straightened up. "I began to wonder what happened to her brother and then I wondered if it had anything to do with her death."

"You were right about both things," Bertie said proudly. Chaddy quit snoring and cocked an open eye at us.

Chev joined us. She'd been cleaning the cooler in our little kitchenette, but had heard every word. "Yes, she was. Didn't I tell you that you were right for this job?"

I was placing the unopened soft drink cans back in the box. "Yes you did." I grinned at her. "And I'm glad you did. I love doing this."

"See," was all Bertie said.

"Hey, here's a mystery to figure out," Chev said with a chuckle. "What happened to Elliot?"

"Layne threatened to kill him." At their incredulous looks I snorted. "Just kidding, she said she gave him the 'it's not you, it's me speech'."

"And it worked?" Chev laughed.

"So far."

Chaddy got up and wagged his tail. Bertie gave him a hug. "I've got to go home and feed Chaddy," she said, catching a big drool that hung down from his lips with a napkin. "He can't just eat cookies. Come here, Cheverly." Chev smiled as Bertie enfolded her in her arms. "I can't tell you how glad I am that Stella found you. You are a treasure."

Chev's face turned pink. I thought I could see a tear in her eye. "Thank you, Bertie. I feel the same way about you and Stella. You're like family."

Bertie beamed then she turned to hug me. "I'm proud of you, baby. You're on your way."

It was my turn to choke up. "You were my example. I'll be lucky if I end up being half the woman you are." I said with all my heart. Bertie hugged me fiercely then she was gone in a flurry of shopping bags and Tupperware.

CHAPTER SIXTY TWO

When we came back into the conference room from seeing Bertie off, Chev smiled. "How about a toast?"

"Sure, why not?" I said, sitting at the little table again. Chev returned with a bottle of champagne and two crystal flutes. "Wow! We get to use the fancy stuff."

"Yeah, I saved something really special just for us. Peach champagne from France." She poured a glass for each of us. "Here's to us."

"Here's to us." We touched our flutes to each other's. I took a sip. It was smooth with a scent of peaches and flowers. Heavenly.

We sat for a while content just to sip our champagne in companionable silence. "I feel like I've been re-born," I said, breaking the silence. When Chev gave me a strange look I laughed. "No, not in a religious sense, I mean I feel like a new person with a new life."

"I know what you mean. I've been having some of the same feelings, but it's more like I've earned the permission to go on. To put the past behind me." She held up her hands. All the little rings were except one diamond band on the ring finger of her right hand.

"I took off all the rings. I never wore them when Nikki was alive. I just was punishing myself with the bad memories they represented. Trying to, trying to. . .I'm not sure what I was trying to do."

"Maybe trying to negate his memory. Because it hurt too much to think your marriage might have finally been working right at the end."

Chev looked down at her hands and rubbed the little indentations where the rings had been. She twisted the eternity ring on her right hand. "This is the ring Nikki gave me last Christmas. It was for our new start. Our new beginning."

"And you'll always have that," I said quietly.

Chev sighed. "I know. That's what I decided, too." She straightened her shoulders. "I've given myself permission to be happy again. To go on," she ended with a smile.

"Well, speaking of going on, Tony asked me out," I said, anxious to hear her reaction.

Chev chuckled. "I knew he wouldn't be able to resist you. You hit him pretty hard when he first met you." She patted my hand.

"You think I did? I would never have guessed," I said, smiling to myself.

"Stella, you've never been with anyone but Michael. It's going to be a whole new experience for you." She smiled gently. "You're going to make some mistakes, you're going to get hurt a few times, but you've got to get in the game."

"Ha! What about you? Why do I have to get into the game while you watch from the sidelines?"

Chev laughed. "Oh I wouldn't be so sure Ms. Smarty-pants. I'm going out with David Ramsey this Saturday for dinner." My mouth must have been wide open because Chev started giggling. "You should see your face."

I grinned. "Okay. I'm just going to have to get used to the fact that my partner is always one jump ahead of me."

Chev stood up and took my arm. "Come here, partner. I've got something else to show you. A small surprise."

"What? You've done enough already."

"Come on." She headed towards the front of the building.

I followed her into the reception room. The workman was long gone. I went over to the black rooster lamp. "This guy must never go," I said solemnly. Chev laughed. "I'm serious. He's lucky for me."

"Okay, whatever you say. You're a partner. You can have opinions."

"Well, thank you."

"So what's your opinion on this?" She opened the glass front door. The light from the porch illuminated 'Jones and Fortuna, Investigations' stenciled in beautiful gold letters on the glass. My eyes misted over.

"Looks good." I smiled.

"Looks damn good," Chev said.

The Phoenix by S. Alden Reilly is the first novel in the Stella Jones series. Stella Jones and Cheverly Fortuna will return in *The Cassandra* in 2002.

S. Alden Reilly lives and writes in Western Maryland with her English Bulldogs, Fanny Lucille, Ripley, and Bubbalicious.

Watch for Stella and Chev on their website at: www.stellaandchev.com. And S. Alden Reilly at www.saldenreilly.com